A
DEATH
IN SWEDEN

ALSO BY KEVIN WIGNALL

INDIVIDUAL WORKS

People Die

Among the Dead

Who is Conrad Hirst?

Hunter's Prayer

Dark Flag

SHORT STORIES

"The Window"

"Retrospective"

"A Death"

"Hal Checks Out"

A
DEATH
IN SWEDEN

KEVIN WIGNALL

THOMAS & MERCER

Text copyright © 2015 by Kevin Wignall

Published by Thomas & Mercer, Seattle

www.apub.com

ISBN-13: 9781503947870
ISBN-10: 1503947874

Cover design by bürosüd° München, www.buerosued.de

Printed in the United States of America

Prologue

Siri was all in black. She saw her reflection in the windows of Mr. Olofsson's car as she walked past and she liked the totality of it—black leather jacket, tight skirt, patterned black leggings, black knee socks, boots. It made her skin look even paler than it was, and her hair, casually spiked, was almost as translucent.

She'd thought about dyeing her hair black too, because blonde hair was all too common in northern Sweden, but keeping it blonde somehow reminded her that she wouldn't always be here. She'd escape to university first, then to the world beyond—London, Paris, New York, and who knew where else besides.

Pia was already at the bus stop and so was the older guy who always got on at their stop. Siri nodded to Pia as she got there and gave a half-smile but they didn't speak. Sometimes they did, today they didn't, not out of animosity, just a quiet understanding that there wasn't always a need.

The bus came, not the usual driver, but the same passengers. There were the two middle-aged women sitting at the front who talked continuously and got off at the next stop. There were the two boys from school—they usually nodded to Siri but never spoke. Pia knew them and always sat with them, sometimes laughing and joking. And that was it, at least for the next few stops.

Siri walked two-thirds of the way up the bus and sat down. She didn't walk all the way to the back because the older guy who got on with them always sat on the back seat, and stayed on after they got off for school. It was just one of those weird unwritten rules—they all sat in the same seats, every morning, no change of routine, not ever.

Siri put her earphones in and turned on her music, then closed her eyes against the bright September sunlight and relaxed with the smooth movement of the bus pulling away and gliding along the road towards another day.

A few minutes later she felt it slowing down, then stop, and she knew that the two women would be getting off—normally they'd chat with the driver for a few seconds, but perhaps not today if they didn't know him. They set off again, Siri's eyes still closed but glowing orange inside, the music cocooning her.

She felt the bus braking a couple of times more than it usually would have done, the driver slowing down at stops where the familiar driver would have sped past, knowing no one ever boarded there. They didn't stop though, and then the bus picked up a little speed on the open road.

She became lost in herself and her music, thoughts falling away. Once, briefly, she opened her eyes, saw Pia chatting enthusiastically with the two boys, saw the kaleidoscope of shadows and sunlight flickering along the road edge and among the trees. She shut it all out again and could almost have fallen asleep.

Then she opened her eyes a second time, because in some odd way she could feel that something was wrong, almost as if she was moving sideways rather than forwards. The bus was braking, but the movement seemed wrong somehow. The older guy appeared at her side, quite suddenly, making her jump a little. She thought he was walking down to the front of the bus.

She tried to look forward, to see what was happening, but the older guy stopped and turned abruptly and she realized now that his actions were urgent and directed at her. Before she could respond, he grabbed her, pulling her from her seat with frightening ease. She screamed, the sound of it muffled and contained inside her own head by the music from the earphones.

Briefly, she caught a glimpse of Pia and the two boys. They'd stopped talking, she thought, but none of them turned to see why she was screaming. One of the boys had his face pressed against the window. Siri didn't have time to think through what it meant because the man was pushing her further up the aisle, a sickening strength in him.

She fell backwards, crashing to the floor in slow motion and without any noticeable impact, as if she was falling against some opposing momentum, as if gravity had briefly failed. And then the man fell on top of her, and she could see him speaking to her, looking desperate and terrifying, but she couldn't hear him, only the music.

She felt a jolt, and suddenly he held himself tighter against her body, and she saw that his hands were gripping the underneath of the seats, pulling himself harder against her, the weight crushing, suffocating her. She screamed again, looked imploringly, but his own eyes were elsewhere, lost in the monumental effort of keeping her pinned down.

Another jolt, this one shuddering through her, and instantly the man was gone, his weight lifting so abruptly that for a moment she felt she, too, was flying, but she was still almost where he had thrown her. She felt the cold air, and turning, saw that the emergency door at the back of the bus had opened, and without knowing it, she scrambled up, to her knees, to her feet, leaping out onto the road and running maybe a dozen steps before the swiftness of her own escape finally caught up with her and she stumbled to the ground.

One of her earphones fell out, and hearing the world, the

desperate braking of a vehicle on the road, the blare of a horn, she yanked the other one free and turned to look behind her. Only now did she understand what had just happened, but it was almost impossible to believe it *could* have happened.

She was sitting in the middle of the road, looking at the wreckage of the bus she'd been traveling on and the timber truck with which it had collided. Cut trees were strewn along the Tarmac, and both vehicles were so mangled it was hard to see where one began and the other ended.

She heard someone running towards her, the driver of the vehicle she'd heard braking hard. He stopped, crouched down, put a hand on her shoulder. She didn't look at him but she could see in her peripheral vision that he was wearing a check shirt, work clothes.

"My God, are you okay?"

His voice was full of incredulity and horror. She nodded.

"There are other people."

He'd taken out his phone and held it to his ear, but said to her, "I don't think so. Stay here."

He got up and walked tentatively toward the wreckage, speaking into his phone, the words not quite audible though she guessed it was the police. And it wasn't the sight of the crushed and twisted metal that convinced her the man was right, but the disturbing stillness. No one else could have survived that accident.

She should not have survived it herself, and felt strangely lightheaded with the realization that she was unharmed, that she was sitting here alive in the middle of the road, and a man she had seen every day, but with whom she had never exchanged a single word, had undoubtedly saved her life.

4

Chapter One

Ramon Martinez had been living under an alias in this prosperous Madrid suburb for nearly two years now, and had probably reached the point of believing he'd never be found. Maybe it had gone beyond that, and he'd fooled himself into thinking they weren't even looking for him anymore.

But they *were* still looking for him, and after eighteen months of drawing a blank, they'd finally employed Dan Hendricks. In the end, that's how simple it had been—Ramon Martinez didn't know it, but his time was almost up.

Dan had spent the last two days watching him from the building across the street. He'd had a grandstand view into the Martinez family apartment, observing the man's day-to-day life with his wife, his young son and baby girl, the maid and the live-in nanny.

This morning, confident of their routine, Dan went one better and walked out of his own building just as Martinez set off to walk the boy the short distance to kindergarten. Dan fell in behind them as they strolled without haste in the autumnal sunshine.

The boy was maybe five or six, wearing a little rucksack, and he talked animatedly to his father as they walked along, his voice carrying on the still morning air. Martinez responded now and then in good humor, even showing contrition when his son chastised him for laughing at something that wasn't meant to be funny.

They turned right into a long quiet street and Dan dropped back a little, though he needn't have worried. Martinez was oblivious, as if the matters being explained by his son were the only things of importance in his world.

Briefly, longingly, Dan thought of his own son, but he packed the memory away quickly, determined not to let his concentration slip, determined not to see parallels or even similarities. Nothing was the same, and in truth, he could hardly compare his own life to that of Ramon Martinez.

But it seemed Martinez had found a real happiness here and Dan couldn't help but feel sorry for him, a little advance regret for what he was about to do to him and his family. And with that thought he stopped and turned, walking back again and waiting in the window until Martinez returned on his own twenty minutes later.

Dan had nothing more to do for now. He thought about heading back to the hotel but, instead, lowered himself into the fold-up sun lounger he'd positioned near the window and let his thoughts drift, soaking up the immediate silence, the indistinct sounds of traffic in the wider city somewhere beyond.

When his phone rang, he checked his watch, surprised to see that forty minutes had elapsed, time in which he'd thought of almost nothing. It was Hugo Beck, probably pretending to be interested in how things were going, but actually calling with a new job. Dan didn't mind that, and would rather keep busy than not.

He answered and Hugo said, "How's it going? Any problems?"

"None at all. Charlie and Benoit fly in this afternoon. We'll pick up the target in the morning."

"Great, great. They should have come to you a year ago. But you know . . ."

He fell into silence and Dan said, "What's the job, Hugo?"

"I'm not calling about a job. In fact, I'm not sure you should take anything else on for a little while." That was out of character enough to get Dan's attention, but before he could even ask what Hugo was talking about, he went on, "What do these names have in common—Mike Naismith, Paul Gardener, Rich Woodward, Karl Wittman?"

Dan had worked with them all, and considered a couple of them friends, including Mike Naismith who'd been killed a few weeks before in a hit-and-run in Baltimore, but he couldn't see any obvious link beyond that. Even so, he didn't like the sound of this. Hugo liked to talk in riddles at the best of times, but there was something in his tone now that suggested this was more serious than a guessing game.

"I don't know, Hugo, why don't you tell me?"

"How about the fact they're all dead?"

"What are you talking about?" Dan laughed a little, dismissively. Yes, people got killed in their line of work, but casualties had dropped off since the spikes of Iraq and Afghanistan. People got killed, but not in those numbers. And besides, he'd spoken to Karl a couple of weeks ago. "Hugo, Mike's dead, but the others—"

"I'm telling you they're all dead. Naismith you know about. Paul Gardener was killed last week—someone broke into his house in Durban, Paul disturbed them, got killed in the struggle. Rich Woodward was last week too—he was in Athens to meet a potential client, killed in a street robbery. So far, it's only coincidences, no?"

Uneasy, almost not wanting to hear it, Dan said, "What about Karl?"

"Exactly. Coincidences can take time to produce, but it looks like whoever it is, they're speeding things up. Karl was found day before yesterday on a building site in Munich. Executed, hands behind the back, shot in the head. The official story is a gangland feud, but . . ."

Dan didn't respond at first. He and Karl had talked after Mike's death. Karl had been pretty cut up about it, and it seemed unreal that he was dead too, that his grief had been wasted.

It was obvious that Hugo thought the deaths were linked, and it was hard not to share that view, so when Dan finally spoke, he said only, "Who do you think it is?"

"I don't know. Worst case? CIA—a cleanup operation."

"It's more than two years since any of us worked for them."

But they'd all done their fair share before that, carrying out the kind of work the agency couldn't or didn't want to do for itself. It had all dried up at around the same time that some of it had become public but, until now, Dan had never expected it to come back at them like this.

Hugo said, "What's two years to the CIA? But look, we don't know it is them. I'll see what I can find out and let you know."

"Okay, I'll call you tomorrow, once we're done." He thought about it, then added, "Who else could it be, if not Langley?"

"Dan, if those four deaths are connected . . . I don't think it could be anyone else."

"Okay. I'll speak to you tomorrow."

"Good. And good work on Martinez."

Dan ended the call and sat for a moment or two. In theory, his life had always had its risks, but this was the first time he could remember that there had seemed a tangible threat. If it turned out to be the CIA, and they were set on wiping out a lot of the people who'd contracted for them, he wasn't sure what he could do about it—he certainly doubted it would be enough to lie low in Thailand for a few months.

His instinct was still to fight, no matter who it was on the other side, and he had advantages—a few of these other guys had settled into some sort of domestic routine and that had probably made them easier to pick off. Dan knew he'd be harder to trace, and that for the time being, they probably wouldn't think to come looking for him here.

He glanced around the empty apartment, his brief moment of superiority crumbling with the reminder of the life he was actually living. The edge he had over the others was that he had nothing much to lose, and he wasn't sure how much of an edge that was or if it was worth the price he'd paid.

Dan stood and looked through the scope. Martinez was in the sitting room, talking to the nanny. She was young and attractive, and Dan watched, somehow dreading that Martinez might be about to disappoint him, showing himself up as less than the perfect family man he seemed. But the body language between the two was entirely platonic, and Dan smiled as Martinez nodded his assent to some request and they left the room in opposite directions.

Dan sat again, conscious of the irony of his situation since receiving that call from Hugo and how instantly things had changed. Time was almost up for Ramon Martinez, and Dan still felt a little regret that he was about to bring this family idyll to a close, but it seemed Dan's future was now no less certain. This was the only real difference between the two of them, an empty apartment, and another full of life.

Chapter Two

He went back to the hotel just after lunch to wait for Charlie and Benoit, but couldn't settle in his room. The news from Hugo had already started to work on him, putting him on edge, plying him with unanswerable questions—how would they come for him, would it be someone he knew, who could he trust?

So he moved down to the lobby and found a good spot to watch over the people coming and going. He couldn't imagine anyone knowing he was here, not yet, but it didn't hurt to be vigilant.

Just after three, a cab pulled up and Charlie got out, alone. He walked in, carrying an overnight bag, looking as if he'd been built on a larger scale than the people around him—he was too big to be inconspicuous and yet it was amazing how often his size was the only thing people remembered about him.

Charlie scanned the lobby as he walked, and when he spotted Dan he smiled and changed course.

They shook hands when he got there and sat down again as Dan said, "Where's Benoit?"

"Didn't show. And before you ask, I tried to call him—he's not picking up."

Dan didn't want to believe Benoit had been caught up in the same business, not least because it would mean it was already getting a little too close to home but, instinctively, he knew this wasn't good.

"You speak to Isabelle?"

Charlie seemed relaxed and said, "Yeah, she said he had to go away the day before yesterday, didn't say where. But he should've told me if he had another job. Will it be a problem?"

Dan shook his head as he said, "No, as it turns out, I wouldn't have needed him anyway, but . . ."

As if making the link at a subconscious level, Charlie interrupted, the tone of someone passing on news that didn't directly concern them, saying, "Did you know Paul Gardener's dead? Someone broke into his house."

"Yeah, I know." Something about Dan's tone snagged and Charlie looked at him askance. "I had a call from Hugo this morning. Rich Woodward's dead too, killed in a street robbery in Athens. And so is Karl . . ."

"Karl Wittman! I only spoke to him . . ." He ground to a halt, trying to remember when they'd last spoken.

"He's dead. They're all dead. Worse, Hugo thinks it's concerted, and he thinks it's intensifying. Karl was shot execution-style, left on a building site."

"Fuck." Charlie brought his hands up and cupped them over his mouth, the sound muffled as he repeated quietly, "Fuck, fuck, fuck." When he lowered his hands again he said, "Does he know who's behind it?"

"He said he'll make some inquiries. I'll call him tomorrow. But he does have a theory, and if these killings are as organized as they appear, I'm inclined to agree with him."

"Bastards." Dan didn't need to spell out who they thought it might be. He also knew what Charlie's next move would be, and he watched patiently as Charlie took his phone and tried to call Benoit again. He shook his head as he lowered it a few moments later and said, "Voicemail."

"He didn't speak to you before he disappeared? Nothing to suggest he was nervous?" All the while, as Dan spoke, Charlie was shaking his head, the concern growing greater. "Okay."

Charlie and Benoit had always been closer, even after Benoit had settled a year or so back, and he said now, "What will they do, Isabelle and the baby?"

Dan smiled and said, "Don't write him off yet. For all we know he could be lying drunk somewhere with his old Legion buddies." Charlie nodded, not really buying it. "Look, we'll find out more tomorrow. For now, we concentrate on getting this job finished."

Charlie nodded again, making an effort to focus on the task at hand, and said, "Envisage any problems?"

"I don't think so—finding him was the tough part. Why don't you check in and we'll take a walk over there."

Charlie smiled without much conviction and stood up, saying, "Give me ten minutes."

He was a little more than that, but it didn't matter, and only gave Dan more time to think about Benoit not showing. He didn't want to think the worst because he was a decent guy and had finally done what so many of them had failed to do and built himself a life, but Dan had a bad feeling they wouldn't be seeing him again.

The best-case scenario was that Benoit had been tipped off or that he'd read the runes better than the rest of them, that he'd gone into hiding on his own, protecting Isabelle and the kid by being away from them. More likely was that they'd picked him up and it was only a matter of time until the body surfaced.

Charlie had clearly been thinking about it too, because as they walked from the hotel together, he said, "I don't think Benoit's been caught up in this. He's too good to be taken down that easily, too smart."

Dan didn't want to point out the obvious. Karl Wittmann had been one of the best people he'd ever worked with—tough, resourceful, scarily efficient—so if they'd taken him down they could take any of them. In Dan's view it didn't matter how good a person was, no one could cover all the angles, so it was just a matter of taking them when they weren't looking, or when they were crossing the street with their mind on something else.

He didn't want Charlie to dwell on it, so he said, "If it's all about being smart you're in serious trouble."

Charlie laughed and threw a playful punch at his arm, still powerful enough to register and knock Dan slightly off his stride.

When they got to the apartment, Charlie looked through the scope and said, "Now that is one hell of a view. What a piece of luck finding this place."

"A small piece of luck. I pulled strings."

"I bet you did," Charlie said without taking his eyes away. He seemed to have temporarily forgotten the other business, and Benoit's disappearance, and he smiled as he said, "Wow. His wife is *very* attractive."

"Dark hair?"

"That's her."

"Actually, that's the nanny. His wife's blonde."

"Okay, so the nanny is very attractive. Even better."

Dan checked the time and glanced down to the street now. Sure enough, there they were just coming around the corner.

"Here's Martinez walking back with the boy."

Charlie reluctantly pulled away from watching the nanny and looked down to see Martinez strolling amiably along the street, chatting with the boy who seemed to be explaining something about his day, some description that involved lots of arm movements.

It was such an inconspicuous sight, one probably seen in neighborhoods the world over, but Charlie watched their progress as if looking at something extraordinary, and finally said, "It's amazing." He turned to Dan. "No bodyguards at all?"

"Not that I've seen. Makes sense in a way—bodyguards would only make people suspicious, maybe question who he really is. His real security was that no one knew he was here."

"You did."

"Yeah, well, no one can disappear completely."

Charlie nodded and said, "How do you wanna take him?"

"We'll do it in the morning." He pointed along the street. "He turns right up there, into a long street, very quiet. We'll be able to park up, take him on the school run."

"On the way back?"

"No, on the way there. I don't think he's armed but, whether he is or not, he'll be more compliant if his kid's with him."

He looked back to the street, though Martinez and the boy had already disappeared into their building. They both looked across then, Dan picking up the binoculars, and waited until the two of them emerged into their apartment, a flurry of domestic activity engulfing them.

Almost to himself, Charlie said, "He's had a good setup here." Implicit in that was the acknowledgement that it was about to come to an end, that regrettably, they were about to end it. "I could live like that. Couldn't you? You know, don't you ever wish you'd settled, had kids?"

He realized immediately what he'd said and stood back from the scope, turning to Dan with a look of horror.

Dan lowered the binoculars and smiled as he said, "Don't."

"Dan, I'm sorry, I didn't mean . . ."

"I know what you meant, don't worry about it. It was a long time ago."

Charlie shook his head, clearly still angry at himself for that careless comment. The irony was, it was referred to so rarely, Dan was so reluctant to discuss or even acknowledge the wound he'd carried around these last seven years, that Charlie's momentary lapse was hardly surprising.

"I'm still sorry. I know you don't like to talk about it, but I . . . I don't know."

"You got that right." He laughed a little, trying to show Charlie it really didn't matter, then said, "So let's concentrate on getting this guy back to Venezuela, then we'll see what we can do about our own futures."

Charlie nodded and they both turned and looked across the street, at the Martinez household as it eased into the evening ahead of them. Ramon Martinez would have absolutely no idea that this was his last night of freedom, that everything would change tomorrow.

Maybe Charlie was thinking along the same lines as he watched, because he said, "You think we're in trouble?"

Dan smiled. It was a question he'd asked Dan many times over the years, and he always seemed reassured by Dan's stock response, "Nothing we can't handle." Dan hadn't always been as certain as he'd sounded, but it had always ended up being true.

"Nothing we can't handle," he said again now, and even without looking he knew Charlie was smiling too.

Chapter Three

It was another fine morning, the promise of heat later, and Dan and Charlie were parked part of the way along the side street, just around the block from the Martinez family's apartment building.

Charlie was in the driver's seat, and Dan had a city map opened out on the dash. They were facing away, but with the mirrors arranged to give them both a good view of the street behind them.

Dan spotted them first as they came around the corner, Martinez and his boy. They had that same relaxed attitude about them, as if nothing could possibly go wrong on this sunny autumnal morning, in this particular neighborhood.

"I see them," said Charlie, responding to the subliminal change in Dan's body language. He studied them in the mirror and added, "I'm glad it's just a pickup."

Dan nodded in agreement, although this was more typical of their work anyway—they picked them up, usually so that other people could kill them at leisure.

He slipped the gun under the map and waited. Martinez had become so comfortable living here that he didn't seem to notice the car, and didn't look uneasy even as Dan opened the door and stepped out.

Martinez saw the map and started to preempt him in Spanish, but fell silent in response to something he saw in Dan's expression.

Dan glanced at the boy, then said, "Let's not make this any more difficult than it needs to be, Mr. Martinez. Just get in the car."

Martinez nodded. He was calm, but he'd probably inferred that any difficulty would involve his son in this, and he was clearly desperate to stop that from happening. He turned to the boy now and spoke rapid reassurance, and Dan picked up enough to know that he was explaining that he had to go with these men, that the boy was to go home.

Martinez climbed into the back seat of the car, but the boy stared at him, bewildered, and said, "Papa?"

The word sent a chill down Dan's spine, memory spilling in on the back of it, but Martinez called back with cheery reassurance to the boy. Dan climbed in beside him and closed the door, and Charlie started the engine. He didn't pull away though, and glanced at Dan in the rearview.

Dan looked out of the window. The boy was still standing there, confused rather than upset, but looking completely lost.

"Charlie, he's right around the corner from his building—he'll head back once we pull away."

Charlie turned and said, "You can't just leave him there." Dan looked askance at him, an answer in itself, but Charlie persisted, saying, "Dan, he's a little kid. Anything could happen to him."

He wasn't sure what his life had come to that Charlie Hamsun was now his conscience, but he shook his head and said, "Okay, watch Martinez and I'll be back in a minute." He turned to Martinez and said, "If you try anything while I'm gone I'll kill you and your family."

He handed his gun to Charlie, opened the door and climbed out. The boy immediately stepped back in fear but, once again, his father's voice came cheerily, telling him to go with the man.

Dan started along the street and the boy fell in with him and put his hand in Dan's. The touch of his warm little hand sent a jolt through him. Maybe it was because of what Charlie had said the day before, or because of the boy using that word, *papa*. Maybe it had just been playing on his mind since following them the previous morning.

He was younger than Dan's boy would have been, maybe only five or six but, whether or not, the memory was as raw as ever. And just as raw, his anger with himself for feeling like this, certain in some way that he had not earned it. He pushed the thoughts away, smothered them, and thought only of the job, the here and now.

The boy let go of his hand as they reached the building, perhaps feeling he was on familiar ground again. And he pressed the buttons in the elevator and knocked on his own apartment door when they got there.

Dan rang the bell too, out of the kid's reach, and was about to walk away, but the door opened instantly and the nanny was standing there looking at them. She said something to the boy, confused and surprised, then looked up at Dan and said something else—again, he knew enough to know that she was asking what was going on.

Their eyes met, and he wasn't sure whether she knew the truth of her employer's identity, or if it was something about Dan that told her all she needed to know. Either way, she said no more, but kept her big dark eyes fixed on him as she shepherded the boy back inside, edged backwards herself, and closed the door.

Dan headed down the stairs and back around the corner. As he climbed into the car, Charlie handed his gun back, but Dan was aware of Martinez looking at him expectantly.

Dan turned and said, "He's fine. I left him with the nanny."

"Thank you. He's not streetwise." He looked mournful and resigned as the car pulled away, and a few minutes elapsed before he said, "Are you CIA? Or working for the CIA?"

Dan looked at him and said, "No, Mr. Martinez, you're going home."

"I see. The government or . . ."

"The government."

He looked surprised, and perhaps relieved. It seemed that, out of the three possible scenarios for what had just happened to him, the CIA was the worst, private concerns second, and the Venezuelan government the most preferable. Dan wasn't sure why that might be and didn't really care—he was just being paid for tracking the man down and handing him over.

The airfield was quite a way out of town and Martinez seemed happy to sit in silence, staring out of the window at a city that had been home but that he would probably never see again. Dan thought of the way he'd looked walking with his son and imagined he was thinking of that too, of the years that he would lose with his family. It was too bad.

When they arrived, Dan left Charlie with the car and walked Martinez into the small office. The three Venezuelan intelligence officers had been sitting drinking coffee, but all stood when they came in and seemed to treat Martinez with a degree of respect. Dan guessed the man had been right to see this as the most favorable option, no matter what happened from here on in.

Martinez turned and offered his hand to Dan, saying, "Thank you, Mr . . .?"

Dan shook his hand, but said, "Dan. You don't need to know my other name."

"I thank you anyway, for making sure my son got home, and for not making it . . . difficult." He looked curious then, and said, "How did you find me?"

"You left a trail, everyone does, very faint in your case, but still there. I just followed it."

Martinez nodded understanding, and said, "So that makes me wonder if your other name is Hendricks."

"Like I said, you don't need to know who I am. I didn't do this. Have a safe journey."

As he came back through the office door, he could see Charlie was out of the car and on the phone. He strolled over, enjoying the warmth on his skin now that the job was done, but then he saw Charlie's face fall, saw him lean back against the car, almost as if he needed it for support. This could only be about Benoit, and Dan knew it had to be the worst possible news.

Charlie hung up as Dan reached him and looked ashen as he shook his head and said, "They found Benoit in the trunk of his car at the airport, bullet in the head."

The news created a strange disconnect, between what Dan thought he ought to be feeling and what he actually felt. Benoit had been a good friend, perhaps as good a friend as Karl, more so than Mike Naismith, but he hadn't seen him much in the last year and couldn't quite find the right emotional response.

Charlie looked as if he'd been physically weakened by the news, his huge shoulders slumped, his face leeched of color. They'd been closer, of course, spending a lot of time with each other even after Benoit had become a family man.

"Was that Isabelle on the phone?"

It took a moment for the question to register, and he said, "Her mother. Isabelle's sedated." Charlie looked at his phone, as if it might provide some answers or guidance, then said, "This wasn't meant to happen."

Dan said, "Turn your phone off." Charlie did as he said, automatically, but he looked cut up, his mind elsewhere. "I know you're upset, Charlie, but we're as dead as he is unless we move fast."

Charlie nodded, zoning in again as he said, "Okay, what do we do?"

Dan smiled, acknowledging that Charlie was back with him, focused. And they would need to remain focused now, vigilant, ready for the assault that would certainly come.

"You drive. We make straight for the airport. I'll call Hugo on the way and just hope he's turned something up."

Behind them, the engines of the private jet fired up and they both looked beyond the building to where it sat on the apron. Dan thought of Martinez, how hollowed out the guy had to be feeling at being taken away from his family, the future uncertain. Perhaps, but as Charlie had said, he'd had it pretty good there for a while.

As soon as they were driving, Dan put in the call and when Hugo answered, he said, "Tell me you've found something, because I just heard Benoit Claudel took one in the head."

"I heard about that too, and it doesn't surprise me. Things are moving fast." There was a pause, and then he went on, "It's the worst-case scenario. Seems they're purging people who worked the dark side for them, and they're serious, which I guess you knew already."

"Okay." As Dan replied, he was making a series of calculations, how long could they survive in this kind of environment, what would it take, where would be the best place to disappear?

Then Hugo shut off those thoughts when he said, "There is something else. I had a call from Patrick White. He wants to set up a meet with you."

Dan felt a spike of adrenalin, sensing the promise but also the dangers implicit in that information. Patrick White was the man who'd brought them so much of the work for which Dan and his associates now seemed to be paying such a heavy price. So maybe the meet was a setup, a way of adding Dan to the list, but that didn't seem like Patrick's style, somehow, and that in turn held out the possibility he was being offered a way out.

"Did he leave a number?"

"Yes, he did."

"Okay, patch it through to me and I'll see what he wants."

"I'll do that." There was the briefest of pauses before Hugo said, "Is Charlie with you?"

"Of course."

"Am I on speaker?"

"No."

A few seconds elapsed this time, long enough that Dan began to wonder if he'd lost the connection, but then Hugo said, "I'm hearing chatter. They checked your place in Paris two days ago but, of course, they have no idea where you are. So they did Benoit while they were in the city. They're heading out to Charlie's place next, maybe as early as tonight."

That would make sense in a way. Charlie had a place about halfway between Annecy and Bonneville, a reasonable next stop for them after Paris.

"How sure are you?"

"Pretty sure. And look, Dan, you know I like Charlie, but you have to concentrate on you. Let Charlie take the heat, and use that head start to get your ass out of Europe."

Dan smiled, admiring something about Hugo's ruthless streak. Dan made him a lot of money and it was that income stream that really concerned him.

"I hear you, Hugo, and thanks. I'll be going offline for a few days, but patch that number, and anything else you can find out."

He ended the call and switched off his phone. They drove in silence for a little while.

It was Charlie who broke it, finally saying, "Langley?"

"Yeah."

"Hugo suggests sacrificing me?"

"Yeah."

Dan laughed, and then so did Charlie and said, "That bastard! I'll teach him a lesson one day."

Dan nodded, not even bothering to defend Hugo's character, then said, "He thinks the team that killed Benoit are on the way to your place, probably tonight."

Charlie looked across at him, saying, "But I'm not there."

"No. But we will be by tonight. Let's find out what these guys are up to." Charlie smiled at the prospect of some payback, but Dan pointed ahead, reminding him to keep his eyes on the road, then added, "And Patrick White wants to meet me."

Charlie risked another sideways glance, and said, "A setup?"

"Could be. I guess I'll know when I see him. But we'll see what we can find out tonight first."

"Yeah!" Charlie hit the horn triumphantly, immediately getting a reply from some other random car. "Fuck, yeah!"

He laughed, and Dan laughed too, though he suspected they both knew that it was little more than bravado, that there was a limit to what they could achieve on their own. And Dan couldn't help but wonder if they'd already made a wrong move, because, right now, he suspected, they both should have been on that plane to Venezuela.

Chapter Four

Charlie's place was a big modern take on an alpine-style chalet, set in its own clearing out in the woods. It was designed as a place to escape from the world, but with the kind of security and sightlines he'd need if the world came calling.

It was already getting dark by the time they arrived, and they spent the first hour checking the place over. Charlie set up his systems and brought some weaponry out of his secure room, including a sniper rifle, which seemed unnecessary somehow, and only served to remind them of the friends they'd already lost—both Benoit and Karl had been handy snipers, but it had never been a strong suit for Dan or Charlie.

Charlie cooked then, while Dan did a quick tour of the property, not entirely trusting the technology. He walked out past the utility room onto the wide verandah that surrounded the main floor. He stopped once he was outside, taking in the dark and the crisp mountain air, such a shock after the warmth of Madrid that it gave him an instant hit, clearing his head.

Slowly, he walked around the house, listening, looking out at the darkness of the woods. And when he reached the front, he looked down at the steps which led up from the meadow below.

True, any assailant would have to cross the open ground of the meadow, but it was all too inviting for an attack.

He turned and leaned against the rail, looking in through the full-length windows, beyond the open sitting area to where Charlie was busying himself in the kitchen. It was all about the technology because, without it, Dan wasn't sure he would have chosen this as a defensive stronghold.

They took their time over dinner, and it was already getting late by the time they'd finished eating. They stayed at the table and Charlie opened a second bottle of wine, both of them now suspecting that Hugo had been wrong on one point, that it wouldn't be tonight after all.

No longer thinking of its security, Dan leaned back in his chair and said, "It's a nice place you've got here."

"It's not bad, is it?" Charlie looked around as if taking it in himself, then said, "Of course, I kind of hoped when I bought it that I might find someone to share it with."

Dan said, "Charlie, I'm flattered, but . . ."

Charlie laughed, and said, "I'm serious. I think of Benoit and I'm kind of glad I haven't found anyone, but if we get out from under this I wanna make some changes, settle down, maybe even get married."

For all their years living on the edge, often reckless and carefree in the ways that mattered, he'd always known Charlie had this side to him, the desire for the simple domestic life. Maybe they all had it, but Charlie, in his core, was meant to be sitting at this table with a large and chaotic family around him. Perhaps he'd be that person one day, but not just yet, and not for a while to come.

"We've done okay, Charlie. We've had fun being single. You've got this place, I've got my place in Italy, the apartment in Paris."

"But we're not living, not the way we should." He sipped his wine and said, "You remember Darija?"

Dan nodded. The previous summer they'd spent a couple of months on the Dalmatian Coast, between jobs. Charlie had picked up with a Croatian, a dark-haired beauty, but he'd never mentioned her since.

"I've been thinking a lot about her lately. We were really good together, you know?"

"So why didn't you stay in touch?"

He shrugged.

"I don't know. But once this is done I might see if I can track her down." He waited a second and said, "What about you?"

There was no equivalent of Darija waiting in the wings for Dan, nobody he would want to reconnect with. Even if there had been, he wasn't certain he would want to inflict the baggage of his life on another person. Besides, he didn't have much confidence that this would ever be done—even if they found a way out now, there were no guarantees it wouldn't happen all over again in the future.

"I'm okay—I don't mind being single. But if you don't find Darija, I know someone who can track her down for you."

Charlie smiled and said, "I wanna find her, not kidnap her."

He poured more wine into their glasses, and they talked on for another hour before a short alarm beeped on the other side of the room.

Charlie stopped mid-sentence, then looked pleased with himself as he said, "That alarm's attached to one of the motion sensors I've got out in the woods around the house."

"Could it be a deer?"

"Not unless it's a mutant. That alarm doesn't sound if it picks up movement—it sounds if someone deactivates it or cuts the wires."

He pushed himself up and Dan followed him across to a laptop he'd set up. Charlie played with the keyboard, then studied the screen closely as almost identically indistinct pictures appeared one after the other.

"Thermographic cameras. You have these at your place in Italy?"

Dan shook his head slowly and said, "I never thought anyone was trying to kill me before."

"Dan, you of all people should know, in our line of work someone always wants to kill you." He stopped and pointed at the screen, which now had two illuminated shapes in the middle of it. "There they are, two of them, probably scoping the place out, deciding how to play it."

"Sure there are just two?"

Charlie flicked through the other images again before landing once more on the two intruders. If there were just two of them it probably wouldn't be a problem. Trouble was, just as Dan had mistrusted the technology earlier, so he now mistrusted what he could see in front of him. It looked too easy and, in his experience, that meant they were missing something.

Chapter Five

The two shapes didn't move for quite a while, and after standing staring at the screen for a few minutes, Charlie said, "Wonder what they're waiting for. Backup, maybe? Or maybe they're just waiting to see if I respond to the motion sensor?"

"Could just be a surveillance team." Dan didn't believe that for a second, and didn't like the lack of movement.

"The rifle's got a night sight—I could take a shot at them." He studied the screen again, though, and said, "Trouble is, they're in an awkward position. I'd have to go out onto the decking and then I'm exposed to them."

He meant the verandah surrounding the floor they were on, and Charlie was right, it would leave him vulnerable to return fire, but Dan felt the need to point out the other obvious flaw.

"If Benoit or Karl were still with us, maybe, but neither of us were ever really sniper material."

"I've been practicing. I'm pretty good nowadays."

"I'll take your word for it, but we want one of them alive anyway."

"True."

They stared again, the shapes of the two men bristling with movement, so that it took a second for Dan and Charlie to notice when they finally stood and started to move forward.

Charlie pointed towards the large windows and said, "They're heading for the stairs that lead up onto the decking at the front."

"Good. They think you're alone, so you stay in here, make them think you're an easy target. I'll go out onto the decking at the back and come around on them."

Charlie nodded and said, "You want some night vision?"

"I don't think so. But if something goes wrong, let me know, preferably by shooting someone."

Dan walked through the utility room again, taking the same route as before, walking slowly to the corner of the building where he stood and listened. He could hear an owl or some other night bird deep in the woods, the soft drone of a passenger plane high above, nothing else.

He didn't really expect to hear a footstep on the wooden stairs—he didn't think they'd be that complacent—but he listened all the same, for anything, for even the sense of movement, knowing that no one could be completely silent.

When he did pick something up, it was probably little more than the friction of fabric on fabric as they climbed the stairs. Dan wouldn't be visible to them when they reached the top, nor would he be able to see them without looking around the corner, but they'd come close to where he was standing.

As a result, Dan could almost hear the breathing as one of them crossed from the top of the stairs to the wall around the corner from him. Just one, he was certain of that, and hoped only that the other was still at the foot of the stairs and not circling behind.

He knew exactly what this first guy was doing, though. He could imagine him sliding along the wall to the side of the windows, taking one fleeting look in, then another. Dan heard him edge away from the window again, back along the wall to the corner.

The guy whispered into a radio, "He's on his own. We stick with the original plan."

Dan wasn't sure if he heard an even fainter reply in the earpiece or if he was just imagining it. The guy started moving again, back toward the window, and Dan stepped around the corner, seamless and silent, and took in the guy standing there.

He was in black combats, and somehow, even from behind in the limited light, there was something familiar about him, the loose-limbed build, the head that seemed too small for his frame.

In one smooth movement, he lifted his arm and pushed the end of the silencer into the base of the guy's skull.

The guy tensed into stillness.

"Not quite alone. Drop the gun."

He dropped the gun onto the decking with a clatter. Dan kicked it clear, and he was sure now that he could hear a desperate whisper in the guy's earpiece, his partner no doubt wondering what was going on. The stairs were only just in Dan's peripheral vision, so he shifted slightly, pushing the guy away from the wall.

"This won't change anything. Your time's up."

Dan lowered the gun and shot him in the back of the knee. Even with the silencer, the shot seemed to crack the night open. The guy screamed as he fell and swore incoherently as he rolled onto his back, reaching down, trying to assess the damage.

And Dan saw now who it was, Jack Carlton, a guy he knew, who'd been in Paris years ago and had then moved to Madrid of all places. He didn't know where he was based now.

Dan was waiting for the other guy to come up the stairs, but then the window slid open and Charlie burst out carrying the sniper rifle and said, "Yellow bastard." He ran to the far end of the verandah and crouched down, resting the rifle on the top of the balustrade. There was a moment's pause, Dan only vaguely aware of Carlton trying to control his breathing, and then Charlie fired.

Another moment passed, Dan and Jack Carlton equally expectant. Charlie stood and came back over.

"He got away, but I think I hit him, in the leg."

"Think or know?"

Charlie shrugged and said, "He went down. Maybe he dived. I think I hit him."

Then Charlie raised the gun again, urgent, leveling it at Dan. Neither had time to speak, but Dan understood instantly, and with time slowing down around his thoughts, he knew he'd been right, that there couldn't have been just two of them—they'd been waiting for someone else to get into position.

Dan dropped like a deadweight even as Charlie was still trying to level the rifle. A shot, muffled but percussive, tore through the air, then another as Charlie fired. As Dan hit the floor, he rolled onto his back and caught sight of the shadowy figure who'd appeared in the same spot that Dan had used. Dan aimed, fired, and the figure staggered backwards and collapsed.

Dan fired another shot even as the body fell, then turned urgently, but Jack was lying almost motionless, and when Dan jumped up he saw that Charlie had the sniper rifle pointed at the prone man.

Dan moved over and checked the third guy was dead—the first shot had done it, hitting him in the neck, the second one not clearly visible, but perhaps lodged in his body armor. He didn't look familiar.

As Dan walked back, Charlie said, "Have you got him covered?"

"Yeah."

"Good, 'cause I'm hit." He put the sniper rifle on the floor and held up his left hand which was slick with blood.

"Is it bad?"

He wiggled his fingers, grimacing the whole time, and said, "Motherfucker. Who was it?"

"I didn't recognize him—no one I ever worked with." He pointed then and said, "Do me a favor, Charlie, check the screen in there, make sure there's no one else around."

Charlie nodded, looked down at his hand, as if he couldn't quite believe he'd taken a hit, and walked inside. He was lucky that's all it had amounted to, but Dan was even luckier, because that bullet had been meant for Dan's back and only Charlie's response had given him the edge.

He looked down at Jack now and said, "Jack."

Grudgingly, Jack said, "Dan. Didn't think you'd be here."

"Clearly."

"The guy you just killed is Rob Foster."

"He was pretty good. New in?"

"Moved over from Military Intelligence two years ago."

Charlie came back out and said, "I don't see any more of them, and the guy I hit is long gone." He looked down. "Jack."

"Charlie."

Dan said, "Okay, Jack, let's make this easy. Who's running this, where are you working out of, what's the game plan?"

Jack tried to smile, though his face seemed reluctant to comply, and he said, "If you're asking you probably know already, but I'll tell you one thing, this isn't some faction or rogue office—it goes to the top. Like I said, nothing against you guys personally, but your time's up."

Charlie was studying his hand which still looked worryingly sleek with blood, turning it one way and the other, but he looked to Jack now and said, "It's Patrick White, isn't it?"

Jack looked curious in response and said, "So you don't know? Then you're in even bigger trouble than you realize."

Dan stood on his leg, immediately above the wound, pressing it into the decking. Jack gritted his teeth through a scream.

Dan took his foot off then and said, "This isn't what I do, Jack, you know that, but I need to know. About Patrick, and about who's running this."

"Patrick White's finished, gone. This is Brabham's operation, so there's no favors left for you to call in."

Charlie said, "Bill Brabham?"

"Bill Brabham," said Jack.

"Why? What's the objective?"

Jack looked at Dan, but his mind seemed to leap through a few steps, seeing where this was going, what his chances were, and he simply shook his head and said, "You just don't get it, do you, Dan? We're housekeeping, and whatever happens here tonight, you're both dead. At least Claudel had the grace to take it like a man."

If he'd been trying to goad them, it had worked, because Charlie looked dangerously intrigued now as he said, "You killed Benoit?"

"I liked Benoit, but you know how it is. People like you, you've become a liability . . ." He gritted his teeth together and breathed hard as a jolt of pain ran through him. His teeth were still slightly clenched when he said, "You're both dead. I killed Benoit Claudel, I killed Karl Wittmann. And you can kill me if you like, but there'll be another me, and another, and another . . ."

Charlie looked at Dan, asking him the question, and it was little more than a courtesy because it was likely to happen anyway. Even so, Dan nodded his assent and held out the gun. Charlie took the gun in his good hand and pointed it at Jack's face. Jack closed his eyes and Charlie pulled the trigger.

He looked at the mess of Jack Carlton's face for a moment or two, then looked up at Dan and said, "This decking's ruined—it'll have to be replaced."

Dan smiled and said, "Let's get that hand cleaned up, then we both need to get out of here."

They moved inside but before they got to the bathroom, Charlie said, "If Patrick White's finished, why does he want to meet?"

"Let's find out." Dan turned on his phone and called the number Hugo had patched through to him. As soon as Patrick answered, he said, "It's Dan. I'm told you want to speak to me."

"Good to hear your voice, Dan. Can we meet?" Quickly, he added, "It's about a job, one that might help you to . . . escape the current situation and, before you ask, I'm not with my old employers anymore."

So Carlton had been telling the truth.

"How many people do you need?"

"Just you." He seemed to understand the question then, and said, "If you have a friend, I would suggest he goes on vacation for a few weeks. By then we might have cleared things up."

"Okay, when and where?"

"Tomorrow? Usual time. Somewhere with nice waitresses." Dan smiled—he was talking about the Café Florence, a place they'd met a few times in years past, and where Dan had complained jokingly about the lack of attractive waitresses.

"See you there."

He ended the call, and said to Charlie, "Come on, I'll talk while I'm working on your hand. We haven't got time to sit around."

He relayed the details of the call as he washed Charlie's hand and then Charlie said, "So? You think he's up to something?"

He could tell Charlie didn't want to believe it, and nor did Dan, because they'd always trusted Patrick in the past and if he was playing them now, he'd probably been playing them all along.

"I really don't think so. I could be wrong, but I never thought he was the type. Then there's what Jack said. Who's Bill Brabham?"

"I knew him when I was starting out, Paris station chief for years. He had a really attractive daughter, only sixteen or so at the time, and a son who was only a few years younger than me. Harry—he was a decent kid."

"And Brabham himself?"

"I didn't deal with him enough to have an . . . Ow, goddamn it!"

Dan had put pressure on the hand and knew now that one of the bones was badly splintered.

"You'll have to have someone look at this."

Charlie nodded and said, "I know a guy in Innsbruck can see to it."

"Toto or whatever his name is?"

"Tito," said Charlie, laughing.

"I never liked him, never trusted him."

"He's okay. I'll get him to fix this, then I'll disappear somewhere."

"Good. Until the dust settles, so don't do anything stupid." Charlie smiled, one eyebrow raised. "What?"

"I'm taking a vacation. You're the one who's meeting up with the guy who got us into this mess."

He had a point, but the truth was, Dan would rather be doing something dangerous than nothing at all. He'd spent the last ten years tracking people down, and it just wasn't in his DNA to sit on a beach somewhere while other people tried to do the same to him.

Chapter Six

Café Florence was decent enough, but it wasn't the picturesque kind of place that attracted tourists—it was geared more towards locals. The street, too, was bustling, but not so crowded that Dan couldn't make an assessment as he approached—if Brabham or Patrick White or anyone else had people in the area, they were either really good or Dan was slipping.

He walked in and immediately spotted Patrick sitting at the table he always chose, in the far back corner. He looked no different, smartly dressed, short grey hair neatly side-parted, like an upmarket lawyer or old-school banker.

Patrick smiled as he saw Dan and gestured to the guy behind the bar. He had coffee and cognac in front of him and was asking for the same for Dan.

Dan checked out the other people in there as he walked through, then nodded to Patrick, who reached up and shook his hand, saying, "I knew you'd come. I banked on it."

Dan kept hold of his hand for a second and said, "I hope that's all you banked on, Patrick, because if anyone follows me out of here, it'll get messy."

Patrick looked a little hurt, encouraging in itself, and said, "Give me some credit, Dan. No matter what, I would never set you up—you have my word on that."

Dan nodded, wanting to believe in him and in his own judgment. He let go of his hand and sat down opposite, unable to resist another quick glance back out to the front of the café and the street beyond.

"So what are you doing here, Patrick? I heard you were finished."

"Finished is putting it a bit strong, but I'm not a company man if that's what you mean, not anymore." So it was true.

Patrick reached into his jacket and put a card on the table. "I'm heading up a newly established office at the ODNI. Can't go into too much detail but my team's charged with tackling some of the more . . . troubling elements that have grown up within the CIA and other agencies in the last few decades."

Dan noticed a waiter heading over so he picked up the card and slipped it into his pocket. They watched in silence as the waiter put down Dan's drinks. Then Patrick raised his cognac.

"To old times?"

Dan nodded, giving him that, and said "To old times." They touched glasses and drank. Dan held the cognac in his mouth for a few seconds, the flavor and fire vying with each other, then swallowed it and said, "So you're poacher turned gamekeeper?"

"Actually, that's what I'm hoping you might become. By the way, did you pick up Ramon Martinez?"

"Never heard of him." He waited a beat. "Unless you're talking about the former Venezuelan Defense Minister—he was called Martinez, wasn't he?"

Patrick smiled and said, "I guessed it was you. As it happens, he was a good man, not that we cared either way once he went into hiding. Still, on balance, shame you had to find him."

Dan saw a flashback of Martinez strolling along the street with his son, laughing and talking about the things that mattered in the boy's world. And he couldn't help but remember the child holding his own hand, the soft pad of his footsteps next to him as he'd taken him home.

But still he said, "If you'd paid me not to find him, I wouldn't have found him. I'm a business, not a charity."

"Which, of course, is why I'm here. I need help, specialist help, and even before the recent . . . Well, what I mean is I know commissions from the CIA dried up with the Arab Spring."

"I'm not sure how much help I could be. It seems I'm on a list, and I'm guessing I'm pretty well near the top by now." Patrick nodded, his expression grim, as if the current situation grieved him. "What's going on, Patrick? What happened?"

"WikiLeaks happened. Edward Snowden happened. The paradigm shifted. The reason they used you—*I* used you—in the past is the very reason they want to shut you down now—deniability."

"They're taking down everyone who worked on the dark side? That's a lot of people."

"Not everyone, but a lot. In my view, it's insane, but I know all too well how things like this happen—call it a concerted attempt to future-proof what's left of the agency's reputation."

Dan nodded, sipped at his coffee, and said, "Makes sense."

Patrick laughed in response, saying, "That's it? No moral outrage?"

Dan shrugged.

"I'd probably do the same if I were them. Doesn't mean I'll let them do it, but I think I lost any right to moral outrage a long time ago." Patrick looked ready to object, but Dan said, "Patrick, you paid me to track people down and make them disappear, either to a country and facility of your choice or off the face of the earth."

"Yes, dangerous people, people who'd done despicable things."

"Maybe, but that description applies to us too—if it didn't they wouldn't need to silence us now." Patrick leaned back in his chair, conceding the point. "So, you said you need my help."

"I'm hoping we can help each other."

He took a newspaper from his overcoat and opened it out. It was an old *International Herald Tribune*, a few weeks old. Patrick turned the pages and folded it, placing the paper in front of Dan.

It was a story he vaguely remembered seeing himself, a story of unusual heroism. The two pictures said it all really. One showed the mangled wreckage of a bus and a timber truck in northern Sweden, barely recognizable as the vehicles they'd once been. The other showed the face of a pretty teenager, a girl who, almost miraculously, had been saved by a fellow passenger and had walked out of that wreckage unscathed.

Chapter Seven

Having brought the story to Dan's attention, Patrick seemed to ignore it now and said, "The operation that's targeting you is being run out of an office in Berlin. Not an office I was ever familiar with. It seems autonomous; we're struggling to get information on them and even people I used to count as friends are being evasive about its activities. What I do know is that it's headed up by someone called Bill Brabham."

"Yeah, that much I already know."

Patrick looked puzzled, perhaps impressed, but continued, "He was the Paris station chief for years. I never liked him, always thought he was a bad apple."

"I'm guessing other people don't share your view."

"Not the right people." Dan understood the implication—Brabham was clearly well connected. "I want to put a stop to what Brabham's doing, and the ODNI sees it as a priority to rein in this kind of program, but it isn't easy. That's where I'm hoping you might come in, and this . . ." He tapped his hand on the newspaper story. "This could be the way to get at them. You might have seen it in the news a couple of weeks back. A bus crashed into a timber truck in northern Sweden—both drivers were killed, and four passengers on the bus, including three school kids."

"Yeah, I remember it. The girl in the picture survived, saved by one of the other passengers."

"That's right, a guy in his late forties or early fifties. He was killed, of course, and he was carrying ID marking him as a French national, Jacques Fillon. Trouble is, there's no such person. He's been living in a house in the woods up there for the last twelve years, but no one knows who he is. Apparently he spoke pretty good Swedish, but the guy in the local store said that when he first arrived he spoke English with an American accent."

"Doesn't mean he was an American. Nothing in the house to suggest his true identity?"

"Nothing—he was living a pretty simple life."

Dan thought about it, then said, "Okay, you've got me—a guy who might or might not be an American, who's now dead, has been living under an assumed name in the middle of nowhere for twelve years, and you want me to find out who he was. Why? How does this connect to Bill Brabham? More importantly, how does it get Bill Brabham and his team off my back?"

Patrick finished his coffee in a single gulp, and said, "Bear with me." He seemed to be relishing this now, as if he didn't enjoy his new role in the ODNI as much as he'd hoped he would, and this was reminding him of more interesting times. "Both the CIA and FBI were sent pictures of the guy and all the markers. The FBI ran it but didn't come up with anything. The CIA said the same, but then one of their guys flew up there and took a look around the house. And this place isn't easy to get to—it's up north of Råneå. What really piqued our interest is that the guy who went up there wasn't based in Stockholm . . ."

"Let me guess, he was one of Bill Brabham's men."

"Exactly. We've been hitting a brick wall ever since, but we're pretty certain Bill Brabham knows exactly who Jacques Fillon was. So I want you to find out the same, and find out why Brabham's so keen to keep the information under wraps."

"You had access to the same prints, the same profile?"

Patrick nodded but said, "And drew a blank. All the systems we could access suggest the guy never existed."

Somebody came into the café, a guy in his thirties, but he immediately started laughing and joking in French with a couple of the regulars and Dan relaxed.

"So you're hoping I find out something that'll undermine Brabham. Two questions. Firstly, why don't you look into it yourself? You must have resources."

"The same reason I used you in the past—deniability. As I suggested earlier, Brabham has a lot of support, and the ODNI needs to build its case in the dark if we've any hope of shutting him down. The other thing is that I do have resources, but not the kind I need for this. Finance, not a problem, great legal minds, not a problem, researchers, you name it. But someone like you?"

"Okay." Dan looked back down at the newspaper story. It was intriguing, who the guy was, why he'd gone up there, what he'd been running from, but intrigue on its own wasn't enough, and nor was the money, not in the current climate. "Second question. Give me a good reason why I should do this. I could just go after Brabham myself."

"You could. It wouldn't be easy, but you'd stand a chance, I guess. Trouble is, you know the reality—working on your own, you might cut a head off the Hydra but it'll grow back. If we work together we go for the heart."

"Nice analogy."

Patrick smiled, and waited a moment before saying, "So you'll do it?"

It was an easy choice, because Dan would rather be doing any-thing than sitting around trying to work out who was coming for him and how. But there was something interesting here, and he believed Patrick's assessment—if Brabham was hiding something, they could disrupt his operation by uncovering his secret, even if they didn't manage to shut it down.

Of course, that would only apply if they succeeded. And even then, in the meantime, it could well lead to Dan attracting more fire. Whatever the arguments, Patrick had come to him for a reason, and he guessed his chances of survival might be marginally higher working for the ODNI than out on his own.

Perhaps, ultimately, it came down to whether or not he could trust Patrick, and even a short time in his company had been enough to convince him that his instincts had been right. Whether this job would save him was another matter, but apart from Charlie, Dan suspected Patrick White might be the only person in the world he could trust to help him right now.

"Okay, I'll do it."

"I knew I could count on you, Dan."

"Well, I'm still alive."

"It's a start." He reached into his pocket and placed a USB stick and a British passport on the table. "All the background we have is on there. UK passport in the name of David Porter. Your contact in the Swedish Security Service will probably need to know who you are, but we'll use the alias for most of the others."

"What if the Swedes share the information with Langley, let them know what you're up to?"

"They won't. I still have some influence. I assume you'll want to go up to Fillon's place to begin with, see where the trail starts, and I can arrange for your baggage to bypass Security for that trip, but thereafter it might be better if you make your own arrangements."

"I always have in the past."

"The CIA wasn't trying to kill you in the past."

Dan nodded, put the passport and USB stick in his pocket, and drank the rest of the cognac. He wasn't entirely sure what he'd just agreed to, and wasn't really sure what he'd expected out of this meeting anyway. He certainly hadn't expected a trip to northern Sweden but, on the positive side, he doubted Brabham would ever think of looking for him there either.

Chapter Eight

Dan was met off the plane at Arlanda by a guy called Henrik Andresen from the Swedish Security Service. He was in his forties, looked older, and came across like a slightly rumpled high school teacher.

He addressed Dan as Mr. Porter, then as David. They bypassed Security, headed to a small spare office which had the feel of an interview room, and Andresen brought him coffee and pastries.

They stayed there for just under an hour, Andresen talking primarily about the weather and how much colder Dan might expect to find it up in the north. At no point did he refer to the job or Dan's position.

When his next flight was ready, Andresen carried out the same courtesies in reverse. Then, with some relief on Dan's part, he said goodbye to him, explaining that another colleague would meet him in the north.

Dan sat by the window for the hour or so of the internal flight and, as he looked down at the seemingly endless landscape of lakes and forests, he could understand more than ever why someone would choose rural Sweden for a hideout. If it hadn't been for the accident, he doubted anyone would have ever found Jacques Fillon.

Maybe that's what it would take to secure his own future too, if Patrick's plan didn't work. He imagined himself falling off the grid the way Fillon had, but wasn't sure he had it in him. True, he'd stayed out of reach one way or another for most of his adult life, but he'd also stayed on the move, and was less confident that he'd ever be able to settle permanently into some rural idyll.

Of course, he didn't know what Fillon had been running from, or what kind of person he'd been. Maybe he'd been one of life's natural loners, maybe he'd been a keen hunter or birdwatcher, or had possessed some other interest to explain the move. Or maybe he'd just been afraid enough to put up with it.

There was a woman waiting for Dan as he left the plane. She was in casual clothes, pretty and fair, a sporty leanness about her, almost too Scandinavian. He'd hoped she was there to meet him as soon as he'd spotted her, and it felt like a lucky break when she met his gaze and smiled, saying, "Welcome to Luleå, Mr. Hendricks."

She knew his name, which felt like it mattered somehow, and he stepped aside from the other exiting passengers and said, "Thanks, and call me Dan."

She shook his hand, saying, "Inger Bengtsson, from the Security Service. I know Patrick White quite well. Please, follow me."

They started walking. She had the sing-song voice that he was used to from Swedes speaking English, but also a brusque matter-of-fact quality that he liked.

"Are you based here, Inger?"

"No, I flew up from Stockholm, on an earlier flight."

"I thought you had an office in Umeå, covering the north."

"We do." She smiled, making clear she didn't see a need to explain herself. He liked her more for that.

Once outside, she pointed to a uniformed policeman standing next to a patrol car and as they reached him, she said, "This is Per Forsberg, from the local police—he drove down to collect us. This is Dan."

Dan couldn't help smiling to himself as he shook hands with the policeman, because she'd introduced him as Dan, not David Porter. That's what he got for relying on Patrick White to arrange his alias.

Per put Dan's case in the car next to Inger's and they drove out of the airport.

Dan and Inger were sitting in the back and as he looked out of the window he said, "Is it far?"

"I think about forty-five minutes, maybe a little more—I've never been there before now." He began to wonder if her brusqueness might not be as friendly as he'd first imagined, fearing perhaps that she and her colleagues even resented whatever pressure Patrick had brought to bear in order to have them babysit Dan on this trip. But she gave a smile now and said, "What about you? I guess you must have been to Sweden before, but have you ever been this far north?"

"Actually, this is my first time in Sweden."

He studied her reaction, trying to judge whether or not she knew he was lying, but she only smiled warmly and said, "It's your loss."

"I'm sure. And I should have come here before. I think my dad's great-grandfather was Swedish."

"I didn't know that. Your dad's American?"

"Was."

"Of course, sorry. And you're a dual national, US and UK."

"You've done your homework."

She wasn't interested in playing games, though, and seemed genuinely curious as she said, "Which do you feel most, American or English?"

"Oh, equal parts of neither. I've never really lived in either country for very long, spent my childhood in Bermuda, Switzerland, Hong Kong, attended international schools. I don't belong anywhere in particular."

She nodded, looking intrigued by his description, then said, "Maybe this man we're going to investigate, maybe he was the same. It seems he lived here a long time and no one missed him. Even now, no one wants to claim him."

Dan hadn't thought of that. The guy's body was lying in a morgue, probably destined for a final resting place even more unmarked and unloved than his own would be one day.

But now Per tuned into the conversation, looking in the rear-view as he said, "The people from the village want to bury him, if no one else claims the body. He saved that girl's life."

Dan nodded, once again reassessing their comparative places in the world. Whatever Jacques Fillon's life had been like, he'd at least ended it with something good, a selfless act of heroism. From the report he'd read, the guy might have saved himself if he'd invested the same amount of effort, the same swift response. But he'd reached out to the nearest person and saved her instead.

They drove through Råneå, a pretty little town lined with birch trees that caught the sunlight and gave the place a feel of spring rather than October.

"What a beautiful place." Even as he said it though, he could imagine how younger people dreamed only of leaving it, and how easily he would go insane there, his own nomadic history leaving him incapable of ever being part of this kind of community.

As if hearing his thoughts, Inger said, "Yes, it's quiet. There are no suitable hotels here and the village has nothing, but someone has provided us with a guest cabin they use in the summer for tourists. It should be fine for a couple of days and we can walk from there to the victim's house, so we don't need Per the whole time."

Dan nodded, his mind jumping forward, imagining a couple of days in a cabin with Inger. Briefly, those thoughts were fanciful, noticing her slender frame and small breasts beneath her lambswool sweater, a ballet dancer's physique.

It was fleeting, before the more practical reality hit home. It was possible they would be there for a couple of nights and he couldn't imagine there would be much in the way of entertainment. He was used to shacking up in all kinds of places but rubbing along with another person was a different story. She seemed pleasant enough, but he could easily imagine them running out of things to say within an hour or so.

There was no doubting she was attractive. But even on the outside chance that she'd be interested, he had to concentrate his attentions on Jacques Fillon, on who he was and why he'd run all the way up here, on the reasons Brabham and his people had shown an interest.

In one way or another, Dan had bought into Patrick's argument, that the truths buried in Fillon's past might just provide the bargaining power to guarantee his own security. So that was the key, to focus on that. And besides, two days together in a cabin might be his idea of a fantasy scenario, but he somehow doubted that it would be Inger's.

Chapter Nine

They drove directly to the dead man's place. He'd been living the simple life, that had been the consensus, but it was an attractive red timber house in a private wooded setting, a separate garage, the whole place freshly painted and well maintained.

It wasn't set out with the same attention to sightlines and security that Charlie's place boasted, but then Fillon had been able to rely on something else. No one had known he was here, and here was a long way from almost anywhere else.

Per let them in and they walked from room to room around the house. It was clean and simply furnished, almost as if a magazine editor had wanted to create a classic Scandinavian interior. None of the rooms had a TV or computer. One room was lined with bookcases that were full, but there were no books lying around anywhere, no magazines or papers.

The kitchen was well stocked, but again, it was all tidy, hardly the stereotypical bachelor place. Both Dan's place in Italy and the apartment in Paris probably looked more lived in than this, and that was saying something because he seemed to spend hardly any time in either.

Dan turned to Per, who'd walked into the kitchen after him, and said, "Did he have a cleaner?"

"A woman from the village came in once a week. We spoke to her, but she said there was never much cleaning to do. She said he liked to talk, maybe just to practice his Swedish. He wanted to be fluent."

"And she knew him as Jacques Fillon?"

"Jack. People called him Jack." He turned to Inger and added, "Nobody knew he was French."

She nodded, and said, "We still don't."

Dan sat against the kitchen table, looking around the room, thinking over the house they'd just toured, trying to imagine himself inside the mind of the man who'd lived here. Even harder, he was trying to imagine himself living here, in this space, the hours of each new day yawning in front of him.

"What did he do here? How did he fill his days, his evenings, the winter nights? He's been living up here for over ten years, but he doesn't have a TV, doesn't have a computer."

"He has a lot of books," suggested Inger.

"True, yet no book by his bedside, none left by a favorite chair." He looked at Per and said, "Have you found out any more about where he went on the bus every day?"

"Nobody knows. And it's only because of Siri and the regular driver that we know he took the bus every day. We can't even find anyone who saw him on the bus coming home."

Inger said, "Siri was the girl he saved."

Dan nodded.

"What did he do?" This time the question was to himself, but Per looked on expectantly. Dan was trying to think of all the things that were missing, then said, "You searched the place, right, looking for another ID?"

"Yes, we searched, but as you can see, we put everything back where it was. There was no other ID, no passport."

"Were there any guns?"

"No." He laughed and said, "Not everyone up here's a hunter."

Dan smiled in response, but his thoughts were snagging all over the place. He noticed Inger didn't smile, that she'd understood his question perfectly. It was all about the kind of scenario that might have brought Fillon up here. In one way or another, he had to have been on the run, and very few people on the run would ever get comfortable enough to be completely without a weapon. So where were they?

It was just one of the many things he couldn't make sense of, and he still had a dozen unformed questions circling, none of which Per would have an answer for.

Inger ended the confusion anyway by stepping in and saying, "Okay, I think, Per, if you take us to our accommodation now, we can walk back here on our own later."

"Sure, but you can call me any time you need a ride." He looked a little bashful, and Dan guessed he'd already taken a shine to Inger.

She smiled in response, but not in a way that suggested she'd be returning the sentiment. Briefly, Dan sympathized with her—she had the sort of easy-going beauty that meant she probably spent a good part of her daily life dealing with the fanciful thoughts of male colleagues. He laughed to himself, then, not sure why he thought he was any different.

They left and Per locked the door and handed the key to Inger, but then looked at Dan, struck by a sudden thought.

"You asked what he did all the time. The postman, he didn't come very often, just bills, you know, things like that, but he said normally Jack was in the garage."

Dan looked across at the garage. It was open at the front and a pretty new-looking SUV was poking out.

"I can't imagine that car needing much work."

Per smiled and said, "I said exactly the same thing, but the garage is bigger than it looks from here. There's a big old motorbike behind there, a real old wreck—he was always working on it, that's what the postman said."

"Okay, thanks." For want of something else to say, he added, "I'll take a look at it later."

What he was actually thinking as they climbed into the car and drove back onto the road was that this had been a half-life lived here, a half-life curtailed by that bus crash.

Yes, the man who hadn't been Jacques Fillon had come here for a reason, escaped for a reason, was a person of interest to the CIA for any number of reasons, but this, the last twelve years, had not been a life. It had probably been as depressingly dull and limited as it looked on the surface.

The man had lived with barely any human interaction, no apparent connection with the outside world, and his days had been spent visiting a nearby town or tinkering with an old wreck of a bike. Dan didn't want that to be the sum of it, but he knew all too well that it most likely was.

It disappointed him somehow, and also made him see that the coming weeks were more all or nothing than he'd first envisaged. They either freed themselves completely from the threat, or this was the best they could ever hope for.

Charlie had been the one talking about needing to get a life, and for the first time, Dan understood that siren call, because he knew that this, the existence carved out by the man who wasn't Jacques Fillon, would never be enough. He wasn't sure what he wanted exactly, but he knew it was the opposite of this.

Chapter Ten

They didn't drive far along the road before turning off again into the same woods and along a narrow track to another house, bigger than the one they'd just been to. Per was about to continue beyond it on the track, but a lean grey-haired man came out onto the steps and waved them down.

They stopped and got out of the car and Per introduced them to Mr. Eklund, the owner of the cabin where they'd be staying. He said hello to Dan and welcomed him but didn't seem confident speaking English and reverted into Swedish for an extended but friendly negotiation with Inger.

They left him with smiles then and drove another hundred yards to the cabin, which was in the same style but pretty much hidden from the main house.

As they were getting out of the car again, Inger said, "They've stocked up some essentials for us. Mr. and Mrs. Eklund wanted to know if we'd like to join them for dinner tonight or if we'd prefer them to bring dinner to us, if we have a lot of work to do."

"What did you tell them?" He was hoping it was the latter, even though he doubted they'd have much work to do, doubting even that this visit would yield any serious clues as to who Jacques Fillon had been.

"I said we'd have a lot of work, and it would be better if they could bring dinner to us. I wouldn't have said that, but I got the feeling it was what he wanted. I think they're quite private people."

"Yes," said Per. "Private. We talked to them about Jack, but they'd spoken to him only very few times."

He smiled then as he gestured towards the door, as if to show Dan that they weren't unfriendly people up there, even those who liked to keep to themselves.

The cabin was a perfect summer retreat, a couple of bedrooms, a bathroom, a kitchen and a large room that served as a sitting and dining room. There were landscape paintings on the walls of the main room, and more in the bedrooms, all apparently by the same amateurish hand, probably one of the Eklunds.

There was no nonsense about choosing a room. Inger dropped a laptop bag on the dining table and took her small case into the nearest room, leaving it at the foot of the bed before going into the kitchen. Dan took his case into the other room, looked through the window into the woods, then came back into the main room.

Per was standing waiting for instructions.

Dan said, "Can I get you a coffee, Per?"

"No, thanks, I think maybe I should . . ."

Inger appeared in the kitchen doorway and said, "I think we're okay now, unless you want the coffee."

He looked as if he wanted to change his mind, but said, "I should be going, but call if you need me, and maybe I'll drop by in the morning."

Inger thanked him warmly, slipping into Swedish.

Dan said, "Yeah, thanks for everything, Per. See you tomorrow."

Inger walked back out with him, leaving the door open. They stood chatting by the car then for a few minutes, their voices low. Inger's back was to the door but Dan could see Per's face which looked grave with whatever he was being told.

His own responses were short, his expression compliant. On one occasion he responded to what Inger was telling him by glancing back toward the cabin, a look that was hard to decipher, one of intrigue or concern. He noticed Dan standing there and looked away again quickly.

Were they talking about him? Was Inger explaining exactly who Dan was and how he made his living? The worst-case scenario was that Inger had flown up from Stockholm as much to investigate Dan as to find out about Jacques Fillon. He didn't think Patrick would have knowingly put him in that situation, but the fact was, Dan *had* been to Sweden before and it was quite probable that the Swedes didn't like what he'd been doing there.

A moment later Per got into the car and drove off and Inger came back, closing the door behind her. She walked into the kitchen without saying anything. He could hear the small domestic noises of spoons and cups being moved about, the only sounds now that Per's car had faded back into the woods. The aroma of coffee drifted out.

Dan didn't move, an unexpected inertia rendering him immobile, perhaps because of finding himself embedded in this depth of peace when, in truth, his life was in turmoil. He stood in the middle of that big room, acutely aware of the hollowness in the air, of the underlying silence, of time paused.

For some reason it made him think of Ramon Martinez again, of him ambling along that sunny Spanish street with his boy. That in turn made him think of his own son, but that was where the daydream broke down. And Martinez now knew what Dan had known for years, that it could all be snatched away in a moment.

The sudden appearance of Inger in the doorway brought him back slowly, and he smiled at her as if from a long way away. She was carrying a tray with coffee pot and mugs, but hesitated when she saw him.

"I'm sorry, are you tired? I guess you've had a long journey."

"No, I'm fine, a little out of it, that's all."

"You prefer to get some sleep?"

"No, seriously, I'm good." He moved over to the sitting area and she followed, putting the tray on the coffee table. They sat down opposite each other and she leaned forward and poured the coffee as he said, "The last few weeks have been pretty hectic, the last few days particularly so. Being here is just a bit of a . . . well, it's a bit like an out-of-body experience."

She laughed a little and handed him his coffee, saying, "Sugar, cream?"

"No, this is fine, thanks."

"You were hectic on a job?"

He studied her face. Did she not know what had been happening? She knew about his background, he was now certain of that, but it was quite possible the other intelligence agencies hadn't fully caught up with what had been going on these last few weeks or months.

"Yeah, I was on a job, but . . . there are other things too." He paused, and said, "Just how much do you know about me, Inger?"

She put her own coffee mug down and said, "I know you were in MI6 for a few years. I was curious about that, why you applied there and not CIA."

"SIS approached me, that's the only reason. I'm not the applying kind."

"So why did you leave?"

"Well, I guess for me the key things were the money, the glamor, the excitement, and once I realized there wasn't any, I got out."

She laughed again, but said, "So you went to Blackwater . . ." The laughter had seemed genuine, and the curiosity personal as much as professional, as if she'd read his file and was trying to see how it fit with the person in front of her.

"And others, but for some years I've worked for myself. And I'm sure you know that for most of that time I contracted primarily for the CIA."

"Yet now you're working against them?"

"I work for whoever's paying."

He noticed a hardness creep into her expression in response to that—so she didn't like the mercenary aspect of his career. She picked up her coffee and sipped at it, looking down to her cup rather than meeting his gaze. He'd met a lot of people over the years who disapproved of the way he earned a living and it had never much mattered to him in the past—he wasn't sure why it bothered him with Inger, but he wanted her to at least see the full picture before judging him.

"Inger, you may not know about this yet, but a CIA office in Berlin is overseeing the liquidation of a lot of the specialists who've worked for them this last decade. I've lost five friends recently, nearly lost another a few days back. They want me dead too. So yes, I am now working against the CIA."

She finally looked up at him again, but didn't give away how much of that had been news to her. Her thoughts appeared to snag, though, and she said, "The guy who came to look at Jacques Fillon's house, *he* came from Berlin."

"From the same office. That's why I'm here. Patrick White ran people like me before his move to the ODNI. He doesn't like what's happening, doesn't like this Berlin outfit or the person running it. He's hoping Jacques Fillon's story might be the material he needs to undermine them. That's why I'm here. I need to find out who he was, why he disappeared and what, if anything, he had on these people."

She nodded and said, "Thank you for being candid."

He smiled, touched in some way by the odd choice of words, then said, "How about you being straight with me?" She looked confused. "First off, are you keeping the CIA informed about this?"

"Not as far as I know. The order to offer every assistance to Patrick White came from very high up." He didn't respond. "There was something else?"

"Yeah, I was wondering why they sent someone from head office, instead of from Umeå. And I was thinking that you knew I was lying when I said I'd never been to Sweden before. And then I was thinking I'm maybe not the only one with a mixed motive for being here."

She stared at him for a few seconds before finally saying, "It's a priority for us to identify Jacques Fillon, and the involvement of the ODNI is quite unusual." He didn't acknowledge the point, just stared back, and eventually she said, "You're right. Or partly right. I assume you've been to Sweden before because we believe you're responsible for the disappearance of Ahmad Habibi a few years ago. And Jacques Fillon is the reason I'm here, but it's a bonus if I come away from this with information about Habibi."

Dan nodded subliminally, not sure how safe it was to admit to anything. She said they wanted information, but he had no way of knowing what the Swedes would do with it. Would they come after him if he admitted to it, would Patrick's influence be enough to keep him in the clear?

His tone measured, he said, "I was under the impression Habibi disappeared on a visit to Paris, so surely not a Swedish problem?"

"He was a Swedish national."

"On paper. This was a Swedish national who planned the fire-bombing of Jewish centers, who was planning a string of car bombs, all for the country that gave him refuge. Don't get me wrong, I'm not taking a moral position but, secretly, your government must be a little bit happy he disappeared."

"That's not really the issue." She looked perplexed for a moment, then said, "Look, we don't intend to pursue you or make it a public matter if that's what you're worried about. We simply want to know what happened to him; if he's still alive and, if so, where."

Dan thought back to the hours he'd spent with Ahmad Habibi. A lot of the time he'd been calm and they'd talked about the state of affairs in the Middle East and elsewhere, about politics and history and religion. He'd had periods, though, coming on in waves, of getting emotional, even hysterical, pleading and crying, usually in the name of his children. It was amazing how many of the people he'd taken had pleaded on behalf of their children, usually men who'd shown a completely callous disregard for the children of others.

"I'm not admitting anything. In every sense, the disappearance of Ahmad Habibi was nothing to do with me. But I'll tell you what I know to be true. The original plan was to take him in Stockholm. When he flew to France it was decided that would be easier. So he was picked up in Paris. He was flown from a private airstrip to a military airfield in Romania. From there he was taken to . . . a facility, to be interrogated. My understanding is he died of a heart attack on the second day."

"What happened to the body?"

"Probably cremated," said Dan, shrugging. "They did an autopsy, because having someone die like that isn't what they want to happen, and it turned out he had a weak valve or something, that he would have dropped dead one day soon anyway."

"Did you torture him?" It seemed to matter to her, and oddly he took some encouragement from that—an indication, perhaps, that she liked him?

"Interrogation isn't my thing. And remember, I'm not admitting to involvement in any of this, but if I had been involved, my job would have ended when he was handed over to the facility."

She sighed, and looked slightly thrown that he'd been so forthcoming, but said, "Thank you."

He nodded, not entirely sure what he was being thanked for, or what this did to the dynamic between them. He was at least under the impression that she believed him, and she seemed more relaxed as a result, perhaps not yet seeing him entirely as a fellow traveler, but perhaps accepting that they *were* on the same side.

He tested the water by saying, "The guy who came here from Berlin, do you know how long he spent at the house?"

"Yes, Per went with him. He said maybe only forty minutes, quite a quick inspection, and he didn't take anything away with him."

"A long way to come for that." He looked out of the window, trying to work out how many hours of daylight they had left. "We should get back over there, I suppose."

She didn't answer at first, but after a couple of beats, she said, "You don't think we'll find anything, do you?"

"Yeah, I do. It may not be what we're looking for, but we'll find something. No one can disappear completely."

She smiled and said, "He did a pretty good job."

And Dan had to concede that. It had been his mantra; no one could disappear completely, but the man who was not Jacques Fillon had done a pretty good job of it.

Chapter Eleven

Approaching through the woods, little more than a five-minute walk, the deserted property looked even more forlorn. Apart from being in good order, it was as if it had been empty for years, not just a couple of weeks. It somehow looked both aesthetically perfect and yet totally devoid of personality. Even their little cabin seemed to have more to say for itself than this house.

They stopped at the top of the wooden steps and turned to look out at the small clearing in which the house was set, the woods beyond already gathering up the darkness of the evening ahead. The stillness had an intensity about it that was unsettling, as if it was unsustainable, as if something dramatic or violent would surely have to happen here before long.

"I guess he didn't get lonely," said Inger as she looked up at the bleached-out blue of the sky.

"I hope not," said Dan, knowing he'd go insane himself living in a place like this, no matter how strong the motive for running away from everyone.

Inger opened the door and they stepped into the even more profound silence of the house. Dan looked around, then opened a door down into the cellar.

"Okay, I guess we need to do our own search. How about I start in the cellar, you start upstairs, meet back on this floor?"

"It's a good idea."

He looked into the room that doubled as a library and said, "You think Per and his colleagues looked through all of those books?"

"I guarantee it. They should have looked inside any paintings as well, but it doesn't hurt for us to look again." Dan nodded and she said, "We're looking for a passport, right?"

"That would be a break. Let's just hope he hasn't left it in a safe-deposit box somewhere."

He smiled and set off down the steps into the cellar, but it only reinforced his existing conclusions—that this house had not been lived in, not in the way normal people lived. There was no junk, nothing that had once been useful or cherished but had now been discarded into storage limbo.

The cellar had been kept clean and tidy, but there was hardly anything in there. He moved around the walls, checking high or low for hollows or suggestions that there might be a hidden room or even a cubbyhole, but there was nothing. Once he'd finished, he stood looking at the half-lit gloom that surrounded him—it made him want to visit the morgue, just to see proof that there really had been a man calling himself Jacques Fillon.

He could hear the faint and indistinct sounds of Inger going through the upstairs rooms, and that spurred him on. He left the cellar and went into the room with the books. Before starting his search, he took in the room, imagining the places he might think of hiding something.

But as he stood there, he sensed a shadow or a change in the light beyond the window, and a second later a girl appeared, looking in. She was dressed in black, but was startlingly pale and blonde—spiked hair, leather jacket.

Dan felt himself jump slightly, but that was as nothing compared to her reaction on seeing him. She almost fell backwards, and was immediately on the move, turning, disappearing again.

"No, wait!"

The house was so desolate that any clue to its former inhabitant seemed worth holding onto, even if it was just a local kid being nosy. He ran back out into the hall, out of the front door. The girl was already walking quickly away, not running, but determined.

"Please, wait a minute!"

Dan heard a window open above him and then Inger's voice calling out in Swedish, loud, authoritative, but not unfriendly. Whatever she'd said, it did the trick. The girl stopped and turned, then took a few steps back towards them, looking up at Inger and asking something.

Inger replied and the girl laughed, embarrassed, but she was walking towards the house now. The window shut again above and Dan could hear Inger crossing the floor and out onto the landing.

At the same time, the girl's gaze came back to him and once she was closer, she said, "Sorry, you scared me."

"Then I'm sorry. I didn't mean to."

"There was no car, so I thought no one was here." Her tone amused him, the perhaps unintentional suggestion that he was somehow at fault for not having a car, as if he'd deliberately set out to trick her.

"We're staying just through the woods there, with the Eklunds, so we walked." She nodded. Closer now, he could see traces of acne through the chalky-white concealer on her cheeks, but also that she would be a real beauty in time, the mixture of paleness and bone structure giving her an otherworldly quality. Inger came through the door behind him and he said, "I'm Dan, this is Inger."

Inger spoke in Swedish again and the girl responded, then said, "I'm Siri."

Dan made the connection easily, trying to remember now if the girl in front of him resembled the picture he'd seen in the paper, but Inger explained anyway, saying, "Siri is the girl he saved."

"Yeah, I know. Do you mind if we ask you a few questions, Siri?"

"No."

Quickly, Inger said, "We can come to your home sometime if it's better. Maybe it is better, for your grandparents to be there."

She smiled, old enough to find it funny that an adult might need to chaperone her in such situations.

"It's okay, but I can't tell much. The police spoke to me too."

"I should show you this." Inger showed Siri her ID. "You want to sit inside?"

The girl looked beyond Dan and Inger, into the house, a mixture of unease and anticipation playing out across her features. Still distracted, she nodded, and all three of them walked in and sat in the room with the books. Siri looked around, taking in the shelves.

Dan said, "Why did you come here today?"

Her gaze came back to him and she said, "I was curious. It's the first time I've been. I nearly came before but the police were here."

He could understand her being intrigued, not only because the guy had saved her life but because the rumor had surely spread locally; that he wasn't who he'd claimed to be all these years. Her survival had been miraculous and now, inadvertently, she was part of a mystery—what teenager wouldn't be curious about the man at the center of it?

Inger said, "You never spoke to the man who lived here?" Siri shook her head, as if baffled that Inger should even ask the question. "In the weeks since the accident, have you remembered any of the things he said to you when he pulled you from your seat?"

She shook her head again, but said, "I didn't forget. I wasn't hurt at all in the accident, not even a scratch. But my music—I couldn't hear him."

"You saw him every school day on the bus. You never saw him other times?"

Once more, Siri simply shook her head, nonplussed.

"Did he ever speak to you, say hello, smile? Did you ever notice him looking at you?"

Siri frowned, as if slightly freaked out by the implication. Dan understood Inger's line of thought completely though, because there was something undeniably captivating about the girl's appearance, and he could easily imagine a lonely middle-aged man becoming slightly fixated with her. Was that why he'd saved her?

The girl, in her own way, answered both Inger's question and Dan's unspoken one when she said, "I don't think he ever noticed me. We all sat in the same places every day. He saved me because I was closest. He couldn't reach the others, but I think if someone else was closer he would have saved them. I think that's just the kind of person he was. I was lucky."

Dan smiled, once again thinking how only someone so young could be so blasé about the fickle intricacies of fate. In the years to come, he was sure, the memories of that day would develop their own gravitational pull. Whether she knew it or not, surviving that accident, surviving it in that way, would become one of the defining moments of her life.

Inger said, "I know you answered this before, but you never saw him on the bus coming home?" Siri shook her head. "I thought so. And there's nothing else you've thought of or remembered?"

Siri looked blank for a moment, then said, "People are saying he might have been a criminal, because he was hiding."

"And what do you think?"

"I think he was a spy. Isn't that why you're here?"

Inger smiled, acknowledging the point. Dan smiled too. Did she want to have been rescued by a former spy rather than by a former criminal? Having known plenty of both, Dan wasn't sure which of them he'd bank on to save him in a crisis.

He also liked to think he would have acted the same way as Fillon if he'd been on that bus, but he had a nagging doubt that it wouldn't have been so. It just wasn't in his nature, to choose death, and he wasn't sure it ever would be, no matter how noble the motive.

"I still take the bus," Siri said now, unprompted. "But it's strange because it's just me. Even the two women who used to get off at the next stop, they don't come anymore, so for the first twenty minutes, it's just me on my own."

Dan looked at her. That had to be tough, twenty minutes each morning, alone with the thoughts and memories of that day, seeing the empty seats where the same people had always sat, people who were now gone.

Inger said, "Were they your friends?"

Siri shook her head, saying, "I was friends with Pia when we were little, but we drifted apart. I didn't really know the two boys." She looked around the room, as if taking in the book spines. "I thought a couple of times, if he'd survived, would I have visited him in the hospital, or maybe he would've become a friend of my family. You think that's weird?"

Inger said, "Not at all. I think I would be the same."

Siri shrugged, and said, "It's just strange, because until I saw the picture, I could hardly remember what he looked like, but now I'm curious and it's too late."

She looked at the bookshelves again, perhaps wondering what they might tell her about the man who'd saved her life. It was understandable that she was curious, and that she thought his books and this house might yield clues but, in truth, Dan suspected they'd tell her no more than she already knew—there was nothing of Jacques Fillon here.

Chapter Twelve

They said goodbye to Siri, then resumed their search. Inger went back upstairs, but joined him again after a little while and the two of them went methodically through the bookshelves, talking sporadically, their backs to each other.

Dan said, "Siri seemed to be handling things pretty well."

"Incredibly so." He was aware of her turning, and also turned to look across at her. She smiled a little as she said, "She reminds me of the way I was at that age."

Dan smiled and said, "I don't see you all in black, somehow, not even as a teenager."

She shook her head, dismissing that, saying, "I mean, that wanting to escape. I'm sure that's even part of her curiosity about Fillon."

He thought back to the way Inger had mentioned the quietness of Råneå and wondered if she'd been speaking from experience.

"Did you grow up somewhere like this?"

"Not quite. A small town, yes, but maybe only an hour from Stockholm. It was great actually, but you know, when you're young . . . Didn't you want to escape?"

"Kind of, but the opposite way. I always wished I'd grown up in one place, knowing the same kids all the way from kindergarten.

That's being a teenager, I guess, always wanting what you haven't got." She nodded, but with a look that suggested he'd just given her a glimpse into who he was. She turned back to the shelves then and so did Dan. "You mentioned her grandparents?"

"She's an orphan. I think her parents died when she was still very small. So she lives with her grandparents."

"Jesus. They probably want to wrap her in cotton wool after this."

She didn't respond and they worked on, but then she said, "Is your mother still alive?"

"Yeah, but I don't see her as much as I'd like. She lives in Bermuda. My sister lives there too, with her terrible husband and three kids. So they're all busy—they get along okay without me."

"Why is her husband terrible?"

"Oh, I didn't mean it like that. He's a good husband and father, good son-in-law too. I just don't like him very much. I think it's mutual."

"You're just not compatible?"

"That's it."

"And he's a good father, husband, son-in-law . . .?"

He laughed, liking the fact that she was comfortable enough to tease him, then said, "What about you, your parents still alive?"

"Of course. And I also have one sister, but I like her husband and children."

"Point taken." He'd reached the end of his shelf, and said, "I'm done."

"Me too, very soon."

He turned, looking out of the window. Beyond the reflection from the lights it already looked dark outside. He looked at Inger then, the snug beige jeans, the equally fitted sweater, the gentle flexing of her body as she reached up for a book, inspected it, put it back, took another, repeated the process.

She finished and turned, and when she realized he'd been watching her she raised her eyebrows and said, "If you spent more time with your mother she'd tell you it's rude to stare."

He smiled and said, "I wasn't staring, I was watching, and I didn't mean anything by it. I'm sorry."

She nodded, a truce, but looked around the room with a sigh and said, "What next? We must be missing something."

"I noticed a small cabin at the back."

"It's a sauna, I think."

"Okay, so I guess if he used it, not the best environment for hiding anything, but we'll take a look in there, check the garage."

"Good, but in the morning, I think. The Eklunds should be bringing dinner soon." Dan nodded but didn't move, and then Inger said, "Can I ask you something?" He looked expectantly. "I was thinking about the kind of person he must have been, and you told me people are trying to kill you now, that they've killed people you know, so I wonder, could you live like this, the way Jacques Fillon did? Could you disappear?"

"I've been asking myself the same question since I got here. I'm one of life's optimists, so I still believe I'll find a way out of this current situation, quite possibly with this guy's help."

"But if you don't?"

"Yeah, I guess I could disappear. It's what I've done my whole life, but I always disappear *to* somewhere, you know, I keep moving. What this guy had here, no, I don't think so."

"Nor me. I like all of this." She gestured toward the room, as if summing up the whole property. "But to leave everyone behind, no connections, I couldn't do that."

It summed up the difference between them, between Dan and most people. The difficulty of Fillon's life in Dan's mind was the boredom, the lack of color, the claustrophobia, whereas for Inger it was the thought of leaving behind friends and family.

It reminded him of the conversation with Charlie. What were they doing with their lives, what did they even hope to do with them? At least Charlie was fixed on the idea of getting back with Darija, as fanciful as that dream might prove to be.

Dan had nothing to aim for, only a continuation of the transient lifestyle he should have grown out of ten years ago. It wasn't enough, he knew that, but at least it meant he had nothing to lose, that he would never lose anything ever again.

"I guess we can't say what we'd do, not until we know his reason for coming up here. Maybe the guy was a natural loner, or maybe he just didn't have much choice."

She nodded, looked around the room one more time and said, "We should go."

They walked back in total silence, only the rough sound of their footfalls and the distant indistinct sounds of birds. Insects hovered around them as they walked too, probably the last of the year, before the cold encroached and added a new layer of peace to these woods.

They got back just as Mr. Eklund reached the cabin carrying a large tray. He was elderly, but Dan could see now that he was strong, that he'd labored in his life, either for his work or in the everyday chores of living out here, and he carried the tray effortlessly.

He left them alone to eat and they got beers from the fridge. It was meatballs in a sauce and some sort of dumplings, which amused Inger in some way, though she seemed to enjoy it.

And they talked casually enough, about the small town south of Stockholm where she'd grown up, about the global village in which he'd lived his formative years. They talked more about family, too. And elliptically, they talked about their work.

They washed up afterwards, stacking the plates and cutlery back on the tray, and then sat with another couple of beers in the lounge area. He'd been unsure how he'd get on with her, but now that he was with her it felt as though they'd been around each other a long time; a sense of familiarity that was out of step with the few hours they'd spent together.

He felt comfortable with her, even though he sensed she still had reservations about him, about his work and his past. Then he made a mistake. She swigged from her beer and hiccupped, then looked in danger of having a full-on attack, but held her breath until it had passed, and it was such an insignificant thing, but she looked so beautiful as she sat there, patient, her lips pressed together in concentration.

Before he realized what he was saying, the words had come out, "Do you have a boyfriend?"

She let the breath go, the resultant sigh like a response in itself, as if asking why he had to go and ruin things.

She looked at him for a moment or two, apparently unsure whether to even answer him or not, then she said, "I don't think it's any of your business, but I'm gay."

He tried not to let his reaction show in his expression, not only the disappointment but the fact he would have put money against her being a lesbian. Even now that she'd told him he probably would have bet against it, though that was probably just a mixture of wishful thinking and him knowing nothing.

He smiled, and said, "Girlfriend?"

"That's also none of your business." She gave way a little, though, and said, "I'm single right now."

"I didn't mean to pry. And I wasn't coming on to you." She raised her eyebrows. "Seriously. Look, I'll admit, I find you very attractive—who wouldn't?—and I was curious, that's all, but I still wasn't coming on to you."

"I believe you," she said, though clearly she didn't. "And it doesn't matter anyway, now that you know."

"Yeah, I guess it makes life easier anyway."

"Oh, we're here to work. I think maybe I could have resisted jumping into bed with you even if I was straight." Her delivery was deadpan, but she smiled, giving away that she was teasing him, and said, "And what about you, Dan, does your lifestyle allow you a girlfriend?"

"Never for very long. Sometimes I wish it weren't so, but that's how it is."

She seemed to take in what he'd said, and for a moment she looked on the verge of saying something in response, but then she changed her mind and said, "I have some work to do, on my laptop, but I think first I'll make some coffee. You want some?"

Her tone was friendly, but business-like, and he knew she'd changed course in some way.

He checked the time, and said, "Actually, I'm pretty wrecked. I think I might turn in early. And we've got a big day tomorrow."

She looked puzzled and said, "A big day how?"

"A big day because if we don't find any leads, I have to move on. I'm not just doing this for me. I have a friend, the guy they tried to kill the other night, and I may be safe up here for the time being, but I can't be sure he's safe wherever he is."

She looked shocked by the reminder that this was about a lot more for Dan than the identity of Jacques Fillon. And he'd needed that reminder himself. Even after a few hours, he could imagine being seduced by the peace of this place, one day slipping unnoticed into three or four. But all the time, even as he'd searched shelves of books or toyed with the now unattainable Inger Bengtsson, they were looking for him, and for Charlie, relentlessly narrowing the field, and unless something changed, they'd keep looking till they'd closed them down for good.

Chapter Thirteen

Whether it was the air or the quiet, or just a low-level exhaustion that had crept up on him these past weeks, he slept deep and sound, more soundly than he had in years.

When he woke it was because of a dream that tipped over into reality—his son was there in the room with him, shaking him awake, "Papa, Papa", and in his dream state he didn't see at first that it was Martinez's son, not his own. And as his consciousness took hold he was weighed down all over again by the sadness of remembering.

He shook himself out of it and jumped out of bed. It was after nine and Inger was out, her bedroom door open, bed made. He showered, dressed, made himself some breakfast. She still wasn't back by the time he'd finished, so he walked through the woods to Fillon's house, thinking she might be there.

The guy in Stockholm had told him how much colder it would be up here, how dull at this time of year, but once again, there was a clear blue sky overhead, and a gentle warmth, albeit paper-thin.

Even before he stepped into the little clearing, he knew Inger wasn't there. There was just something about the house that spoke of its emptiness. But there was nothing much to do until she got there, so he sat at the top of the wooden steps and waited, enjoying the peace and the feeling of time slipping away from him.

Within a few minutes, he was so embedded within the calm of the place that he almost didn't want her to come, just wanted to sit there feeling the sun's steady progress. Perhaps that was how easily it took hold, the ease with solitude that had surely governed Jacques Fillon's existence.

Dan had been there twenty minutes or so before he heard a car and stirred himself, almost as if coming out of a shallow sleep. It approached along the road, then turned and drove more deliberately, somewhere off in the woods. It took Dan a little while to work out that it had driven up to their cabin.

He heard two car doors open, then the cabin door, the sounds travelling cleanly on the faultless acoustics of this northern air. He couldn't help but imagine two of Brabham's men, a scenario in which Inger had tipped them off, unlikely as it already seemed.

But he smiled then as he heard Per and Inger talking, their voices unmistakable. Their conversation sounded like a short negotiation and Inger seemed to give way before the two car doors shut again and the car pulled away.

Inger had no doubt wanted to walk through the woods to Fillon's place, and Per had insisted on driving her, because Dan listened now as the car made its way slowly out onto the road, a short stretch at normal speed, then the same slower crawl to the clearing where he was waiting for them. Inger had probably been right, and would have been quicker walking.

She waved at him from quite a distance, then again as they got out of the car. Dan stayed where he was, sitting on the steps, while they all said hello to each other. Perhaps she hadn't tipped off Brabham, but he was still curious about where she'd been and why she was acting so nervously.

As if answering his unspoken question, but a little too eagerly, she said, "I had some things I needed to do, so I called Per. You were still sleeping."

He nodded, noncommittal, and said, "I slept really well." He looked at Per and added, "You have good air up here."

Per looked uncertain how to respond and said, "It's the only air I know."

"Then you'll have to take my word for it." He looked back to Inger. She seemed to be waiting for him to follow up on her excuse, asking what it was she'd been checking, but he said only, "Ready to get to work?"

"Sure." She turned to Per, saying, "Thanks for the ride."

"Anytime," he said, and took that as his cue. They said goodbye to him and watched as he got in the car and drove off, Inger standing, Dan still on the step.

Once the car had disappeared from view, she turned to look at him, and Dan stared back for a second before he said, "Can I trust you, Inger?"

"Of course."

"No, I mean, can I really trust you? I know you have your own agenda here, and that's fine, and I don't mind you going off with Per to do whatever it was you needed to do. I just need to know that I can trust you, that your agenda doesn't involve helping other people to bring me down."

She threw her hands up, as if to ask how she could answer that in any way that would convince him, but then said, "You can trust me as much as I can trust you. That's all I have."

He smiled and stood up, and involuntarily she took a step back before making an effort to look more relaxed. He hated that she was uneasy around him, perhaps even afraid, particularly when he had more to fear from her than she did from him. And ironically, her noncommittal reply had eased his mind more than any earnest assurances would have done.

"That's okay then. I didn't mean to put you on the spot, but you can understand me being a little touchy."

"I should have left a note. It wasn't anything that concerned you." She looked around then and he could see she desperately wanted to draw a line under it. She clearly made an effort to sound breezy and positive as she said, "So, should we check the sauna first?"

He nodded and gestured for her to lead the way, but stopped almost immediately, not looking at the sauna ahead of them, but at the back of the house. He'd been tired the day before, but he still should have spotted it, and the guy who'd come up from Berlin *really* should have noticed.

"He has a satellite dish."

She turned, looking at Dan first, then at the dish which was no ordinary domestic installation, but high-spec.

"Most people have . . ." She stopped, the significance of it hitting home, and then she said, "But why would he need one?"

"Exactly. No TV, no computer."

"There must be a hidden room, in the cellar, maybe . . ."

"Or in the garage. Remember what Per said—when the postman came he was usually working in the garage."

They started walking towards the garage, and now that they'd seen the dish, Dan was seeing the whole place differently, more critically.

He pointed and said, "Why did he take the bus every day when he's got a pretty new SUV sitting there?"

She looked, the nose of the vehicle poking out of the garage, but said, "Who knows? Maybe he just liked taking the bus. Maybe he went for a drink each day and didn't want to drive." But they'd reached the garage now and she pointed to the ground in front of it, a couple of deep, hard-baked ruts, the evidence of rainy days past.

"That's interesting, though, like he's had it parked part of the way out a lot of the time."

They both crouched down together, and looked under the truck. There was something there. At first it just appeared as if a rectangle had been carefully etched onto the smooth surface of the garage floor and it took Dan a second or two to realize what he was staring at; the flush lip of a concealed trapdoor.

Inger said, "Could it be a pit, for working underneath the car?"

He could tell in the tone of her voice that she didn't believe that. This had to be it—the satellite dish, the whole careful anonymity of the place, there had to be more and this had to be it, the truth of Fillon's identity. And, crucially, they'd found it first.

Dan stood again and said, "I'll look in the cab for the keys—we need to move this thing."

"No, I saw the keys on a hook, in the kitchen." She was already walking, but turned, clearly excited by the discovery, and said, "Maybe that's why he didn't take the jeep to town, because he didn't want to leave the door exposed."

Dan nodded and walked into the garage, looking at the old wreck of a bike that filled the floor space behind the SUV. It was a Harley, but ancient and in pieces, with various tools surrounding it on the floor, as if Fillon had just been disturbed in the middle of a major job.

And in truth, Dan doubted that Fillon had ever really worked on the bike at all. It was obvious when he considered how scrupulously tidy the house was, that this was just for show, the appearance of a time-consuming pastime, the perfect explanation for always being out here if anyone called.

He was still looking at it when he heard Inger's footsteps padding lightly but swiftly across the grass. She held the keys up to show him, then jumped in the cab and pulled forward. The vehicle had spent so much time in those well-worn ruts over the years that he saw the front of it sink down as the wheels found their second home.

He released the handle and pulled up the hatch as Inger got out of the SUV and came back to join him. He saw concrete in the dark below, and for a moment he was disappointed, fearing she'd been right after all about the work pit. But then he noticed it was a set of steep concrete steps, and he couldn't help but smile to himself, triumphant, as lights came on automatically, inviting them underground.

"Now *that* is quite something."

Inger seemed equally impressed, but said, "Maybe it was already here when he bought the place, you know, like a nuclear shelter."

"Maybe." Maybe. But Fillon had been making use of it, for whatever it was that had occupied him all these years, for whatever it was that had spooked Brabham enough to send someone up here from Berlin. It was all here, beneath this garage and this carefully crafted mundanity.

He started down the steps, one flight to a small landing, then another flight in the opposite direction, a metal handrail the whole way down. The depth suggested Inger might have been right about the pre-existing fallout shelter, likewise the heavy metal door they were faced with at the bottom.

She was close behind him and said now, "That's a relief—I was thinking he might have a keypad or something."

The door had a simple, if heavy-duty, handle, but Dan said, "I think you're right about the nuclear shelter—I guess being able to lock it from the inside is the important thing. Besides, look at the way it's hidden. He didn't need security."

Dan lowered the handle and pushed the door open. The lights in the room beyond flickered into life and they stepped inside. Whatever it had been in its former life, it was set out now like a busy office, probably not unlike the one Inger was used to working in.

There was a desk with a computer on it, paperwork, filing cabinets, corkboards around the room, all of them full of papers and photographs, news stories, notes. It was an astonishing thing to see, because Jacques Fillon might have been living in obscurity for the last twelve years, but he'd also been working on something for all that time.

And the nature of the scene in front of them was unmistakable. Fillon's real consuming passion all these years had not been a motorbike, and he hadn't spent his evenings reading from his library of books. This was clearly an investigation in front of them, and even at first glance, Dan instinctively knew what he was looking at—it looked like Fillon had spent these last twelve years investigating a crime.

Chapter Fourteen

"He did this," said Inger, standing in awe. Dan looked at her, and she met his eye and said, "You asked yesterday, what did he do? Well, here's your answer. He did this."

Dan nodded, taking in the room which looked like a nerve center for half a dozen operatives. Yet everything, every printout, the corkboards bursting with information, the filing cabinets that he suspected were all full, all of it was the work of one man's diligence, one man's obsession.

Inger went to the desk, where she sat down and started to work through the drawers. Dan walked over to one of the corkboards. Even at first glance, he could see that the board related to Bill Brabham, a picture of the guy in the middle of it, though he wasn't someone Dan recognized.

The next three boards were dedicated to Brabham's children. One son, Harry, was a South Carolina congressman, the other, George, was co-founder of an Internet company in Silicon Valley. The daughter, Natasha, was an attorney in DC.

Charlie had known these kids when they were young, but Dan doubted he'd have been able to shed much more light on them—their trajectories seemed all too typical for the offspring of the

Washington elite. The fact that Fillon had dedicated boards to them just seemed to underline the totality of his obsession with Brabham.

"Now I know why Bill Brabham sent someone up here, because our friend Jacques Fillon seems to have had a real problem with the guy."

"John Redford."

"Sorry?" He turned to look at her, and saw that she was holding up an American passport.

"Jacques Fillon was John Redford. Is the name familiar?"

Dan shook his head but walked over and looked at the passport. It had expired, naturally, and the picture was fifteen years younger and a whole lot more alive than the mug-shot he'd seen of Fillon's corpse. Redford's corpse. But given the nature of passport photographs, the guy looking out at him was barely less mysterious than he'd been in death.

The Redford of the passport was just an anonymous-looking guy in his late thirties, almost the same age as Dan was now, brown hair, nondescript features. Neither his face nor his name struck a chord, but that was hardly surprising given how long this guy had been out of circulation.

"I wonder if he was Jack Redford. Per said everyone called him Jack." For some reason, that brought an unwelcome flashback of Jack Carlton in the moments before he'd died on Charlie's deck, triggering a slight but nagging regret, though in truth he could only regret the details because none of them, not even Jack, would have expected any other outcome.

"So, he's Jack Redford. It would be better if you check with Patrick White than if I send it through my office."

"You think someone could tip off the CIA?"

She was quick to say, "No, but we don't know who Redford was, any more than we knew who Fillon was, and we don't know what he did, so it's possible anything I do will trigger an alarm."

"I'll speak to him later. First, I want to work out what this guy's been doing here." He handed the passport back, but she put it on the desk and stood, joining him in looking over the boards.

Some of them seemed random and unconnected except in tangential ways. One was covered by a map of Paris and clippings about the murder of a student. Another dealt with various stories of alleged corruption or suspicious trading, surrounding defense contracts, oil licenses, and intriguingly, Internet stocks.

A third board seemed to deal exclusively with people who'd been murdered or who'd disappeared for perceived political purposes. Dan felt his thoughts jar when he noticed the disappearance of Ahmad Habibi listed among them. It was quite possible that Brabham had pulled the strings on the Habibi job without Dan knowing about it, because he had no doubt Brabham was the thread linking all these stories.

There was only one serious problem. Dan could see what had happened here. Jack Redford had been involved with Brabham in some way, had known of his guilt in some activity or other, a knowledge dangerous enough to send him up here, but looking at these boards, it seemed Redford had become obsessed with Brabham's entire family, as if he'd wanted to find dirt on all of them, destroy all of them.

The worst-case scenario for Patrick White, and definitely for Dan, was that Redford had lost his grip on reality, his obsession tipping over into insanity during all these years of self-imposed solitary confinement.

Inger had moved on, and he heard her opening the drawers in a couple of the filing cabinets.

"Dan, there's enough material here to . . . I mean, tens of thousands of pages, and that's without searching the computer. This is ten years' work, far too much for you and me to sift through. And we have no way of knowing what's important."

That was true enough. Dan imagined Jack Redford looking at this room and knowing exactly what it all meant, the pattern that linked it all together. But he'd never imagined anyone else looking at it, so there was no key, there were no instructions, because Redford hadn't needed them.

Dan went back to the picture of Bill Brabham, the same smart corporate blandness of so many CIA station chiefs, the same glassy-eyed half smile. Redford had known something damning about Bill Brabham, but he'd never had the proof and had spent the last decade trying to find that proof or some other way of bringing him down.

"Do you think this is a new board he was starting?"

Dan turned and looked over to where Inger was standing. It was a corkboard on the other side of the room, but with just one large photograph in the middle of it. He walked over. It was a print of something like a yearbook photo, though it looked as though Redford had printed it himself on photographic paper.

The subject was a girl or young woman, dark-haired, pretty, a partially formed smile that gave her an air of timidity. It was frustrating, because Inger could be right, this might have been a new board, representing a new lead, but they had no way of knowing who she was or how she fitted in to the rest of it.

Dan shook his head, the sense of bafflement even greater than before they'd known who Fillon really was.

He looked around now and said, "Why don't you see what's behind the other doors and I'll take a look at his computer?"

"How will you know the password?"

He looked at it and said, "I doubt he used one, for the same reason the door wasn't locked."

"Maybe you're right." She hesitated a moment and said, "It's strange to think, he imagined he'd be back here later that day, that he'd pick up where he left off. Though I guess that's true for all of the ones who died on the bus."

He nodded, conscious that a handful of the people he knew had also set out one day or other in the last few months and never returned. It could equally happen to him one day soon, and it was perhaps even more poignant that Dan would leave no great half-finished project.

She walked along to one of the additional doors at the far end of the room and Dan booted up the computer. As he'd suspected, there was no password, and he brought up Redford's Internet history easily enough.

That was where he encountered his first surprise. Redford had been on a Baltimore news website looking at a story that covered Mike Naismith's hit-and-run death.

That was the only one of the recent deaths to occur before the bus crash, but it could only have been a few days before. It was astonishing that Redford could have made the link so quickly, because Dan guessed the only reason he would have been interested in Mike Naismith's death was if he'd believed there was a connection with Bill Brabham.

Was someone tipping him off? That was one possibility, that he'd still had contacts, still had a steady drip-feed of information from his former life. Dan doubted it though, doubted that someone so determined to disappear would have left a thread running through the maze. More plausible somehow, was the prospect that Redford had simply been good at this, the top of his game, master of all this information.

Inger came back out of the door, making for the other that faced it, but said, "Kitchen, bathroom, two small rooms with bunks, but the bedrooms are unused. This place is pretty big." She opened the other door and stepped inside, and Dan heard her say, "Wow."

He pushed away from the desk, realizing as he did that Redford hadn't quite been the master of all this information, in that he clearly hadn't yet found the thing he'd needed to bring Brabham down. That was key, because there was a good chance it was the same thing Dan needed to safeguard his own future.

When he stepped into the room, Inger was still standing motionless, just looking out at the stacks of shelves. It was bigger than the main room, "the office" as Dan already thought of it, and had probably been designed as the storage room for the people hiding out down here.

Redford had also used it as a storage room, but for someone looking at starting Armageddon rather than surviving it. There was a lot of weaponry in there, of almost every conceivable type, including some heavy-duty explosives. But there was also an incredible amount of electronic equipment, from small components right up to pieces of machinery that Dan couldn't even begin to identify.

Dan said, "I don't know what he was planning, but it would have been something to behold."

Inger still hadn't moved, but said now, "How did he get hold of all this stuff without anyone noticing? How did he get it here?"

The logistics of it weren't so hard to imagine. It was an enormous amount of kit, but he could have easily brought it in little by little over a couple of months and no one would have thought anything of it, even if there'd been anyone to see him unloading his SUV.

More interesting was what the sophistication of both the weaponry and the electronics said about Redford. They'd suspected it already, of course, not least because of the interest shown by Brabham's people, but this was certainly a more definitive declaration of that truth.

"He was one of us," said Dan. "This guy was clearly one hell of a specialist. He knew how to get hold of stuff, knew what he needed, was able to do it all without ever once appearing on the radar."

The day before, Dan had imagined this guy leading his half-life up here, traveling by bus and tinkering with his old motorbike, and he'd felt a mixture of fear and contempt at the thought of such an existence. Now, without knowing much more about him, he couldn't help but admire him and wish he'd had the chance to meet him.

Again, he thought about what might have happened had the man who wasn't Jacques Fillon not died on that bus. What endgame had he been working towards, how much of the equipment in front of them was part of it?

And at another level, thinking of the picture of Bill Brabham pinned to that board out there, Dan wondered how much of Redford's plan he could resurrect himself, and what his chances might be of seeing it through. Dan and Jack Redford had never known each other, but fate had put them on converging paths and, even without knowing the history of it, Dan knew that he had no choice but to make this his investigation now.

Chapter Fifteen

They spent the rest of the morning down in the shelter. Dan went through Redford's recent Internet history in more detail and searched the computer for other files that might have been hidden away on it—though Redford seemed to have been quite old school in that respect, and had apparently printed most of the stuff that had interested him.

That accounted for the filing cabinets. Inger started on them, working methodically through the drawers, and then Dan joined in too, though in truth, neither of them were entirely sure what they were looking for. Perhaps, if they were lucky, they would find something that at least pointed to the keystone, to the thing that lay at the center of all this endeavor.

They walked back to the cabin for lunch, and as they sat eating, Inger said, "How long will you stay?"

It was a complex question. As she'd already pointed out, there was too much material for them to go through in its entirety—Dan simply didn't have that much time. But he had to go through enough of it to provide him with a next step. And he didn't want to walk away from Redford's archive and then find it out of reach.

"Can we keep this between us?" She shrugged casually, but he sensed she'd misunderstood, and he added, "I mean, the shelter, the office, maybe even Redford's identity—does anyone else need to know about it for the time being?"

"Oh, I see." She thought about it, and finally said, "I think I would have to tell one other person, my superior, but I'm pretty sure he'd be okay about keeping it quiet. He's one of the reasons we're helping—he and Patrick White are old friends. I think we might have to reveal Jack's true identity, but we don't have to talk about the shelter."

"Good. And thanks."

"Why do you want it so?"

"Because of what you said. We won't have time to go through it all, but it's possible I'll need to come back, if the trail runs cold, or . . . I don't know." She nodded, acknowledging the level of doubt that surrounded everything in his life right now. "So to answer your question, another stint this afternoon, again in the morning, and maybe fly out of Luleå late tomorrow afternoon."

"Oh." She was surprised, but perhaps also disappointed. If he hadn't known about her sexuality he'd have taken encouragement from that, which in his present state of mind seemed like just another example of how skewed his life had become. As it was, any disappointment was probably based on the fact that she simply enjoyed his company, and as a result he felt oddly touched by it.

"There's nothing else you need to see up here?"

Dan shook his head and said, "Every single aspect of Jacques Fillon's existence is under that garage. Everything else is just window dressing, a distraction. The house, the area, even the accident—they tell us nothing about him. He could have been living on the moon, because his entire life is down in that shelter."

"Jack Redford." He looked at her, questioning. "You called him Jacques Fillon."

"Of course." He swigged from his beer. "I've been thinking about it too. I've got a clean cell to call Patrick, but I'll ask him to meet me in Stockholm the day after tomorrow. I'd prefer to give him most of this in person."

"You mean so that you can see his face, and how he reacts?" She clearly sensed that he didn't entirely trust Patrick, that he probably didn't entirely trust anyone.

Dan smiled, admitting there was some truth in that, and said, "He'll stay at the Grand so I'll need to be staying somewhere nearby but not obvious."

She nodded, thinking it over, then said, "Actually, there's quite a cool hotel on Skeppsholmen."

"That's good—it's been a while since I've been with the cool crowd."

She laughed but said, "No, it's the location. You know if you walk past the Grand, across the bridge, that's Skeppsholmen, so it's kind of close and out of the city at the same time, quiet."

"Okay, yeah, I know where you mean. That could be good."

"So you have been to Stockholm before?"

She was a master of deadpan delivery.

He smiled and said, "We should get back to work."

The afternoon continued in the same vein, without either of them finding anything that promised to narrow their search or provide leads. It also didn't help that Redford had obviously been a linguist. There were sheets in French, German, Spanish. Dan spoke a very little German, better French, and Inger spoke some German, but neither of them were really fluent enough to look through documents at speed.

Late in the afternoon, Dan booted up the computer again and used it to search for information on some of the stories pinned to the corkboards. He didn't bother looking for material on Harry Brabham because he knew he'd be swamped by all the public domain information surrounding a congressman, but he searched on the other two children, and on the allegations of fraud and favors, seeing if he could find a link between them.

Finally, he looked at the Paris murder. Most of the news stories pinned around the map of Paris were in French, but he was able to pull out the victim's name, Sabine Merel, and a date. He typed it in and hit Search and scanned the results. The third story he clicked on had a picture of the girl who'd been murdered and, as soon as it popped onto the screen, Dan felt his heart kick up a gear. Could this be it, the key to everything Redford had done here?

"Inger, you might want to take a look at this."

"What is it?" She was looking over, her fingers holding her place in the filing drawer she was working through.

"The murder in Paris that's on that board over there, I've just searched on it and found a picture of the victim."

She was reluctant to lose her place among the documents, so she pulled one proud of the others to mark her progress, and then came over saying, "What about it . . . oh."

"Yeah, oh." They both looked beyond the computer to the corkboard with the single photograph on it. It was the same girl, Sabine Merel.

Chapter Sixteen

Inger was quick to make one connection that Dan hadn't yet seen. She walked over to the board and said, "It wasn't new, and I don't think he planned to fill it. You're sitting there at the computer, you look up, and what do you see? This picture." She tapped the board. "He had it here as a reminder, I think, you know, always reminding himself what this was really about."

Dan knew she was right, knew it instinctively.

"So we have two questions. What did Sabine Merel mean to Jack Redford? And in what way did he believe Brabham might be responsible for her murder?"

"Could she have been Jack's girlfriend? Or daughter maybe."

Dan grabbed Redford's passport off the desk, checked the dates in the article.

"She was nineteen when she was murdered, he would've been thirty-seven. I guess it's possible she could have been his girlfriend, but it's a big gap, particularly when she's so young."

"But probably too small a gap for him to be her father. She could be the daughter of a friend."

"Maybe. But that brings us on to the other question. I don't know much about Brabham, so I don't know if he's the kind of guy who picks up young girls and murders them for kicks . . ."

He noticed Inger looking over his shoulder, and he knew she was looking at the picture of Brabham on his own corkboard.

He continued, saying, "It's more likely she was collateral damage in some way, that Redford took exception to it . . ."

"No, it's bigger." He looked at her questioningly. "Dan, think of the fact that he disappeared, that he spent all those years putting all of this together, that he built the stockpile in there. In some way, it has to be bigger. You don't do all of that because you take exception, you do it because you care deeply, or because you have no choice."

"You're right. But we have something to go on. We find out everything we can about Sabine Merel and her connections, how she died, where, whether anyone was ever caught or suspected. We find out who Jack Redford was, by which I mean, what he did, what his job was and how that brought him into contact with Sabine and conflict with Brabham."

She nodded this time and said, "He and Brabham must have known each other for sure, and Brabham must have had a strong reason for sending someone up here to look around Redford's house."

"We might find out more about Sabine here, and I want to see if any of the rest of this leads back to her. Patrick should be able to tell us more about Redford."

"You hope."

"It depends if he was a company man, or known to them. Looking at his stockpile, I just have the feeling we're dealing with someone who worked the dark side, and if he did that any time in the last twenty years, Patrick White will know who he is."

She turned and looked at the picture of Sabine again. Inger was standing in profile to him as a result, a beautiful sight that somehow caused him another little pang of longing, even in the midst of the low-level adrenalin rush he felt now that they'd made a breakthrough. He found himself transfixed, the strand of blonde hair loose behind her ear, the unpierced lobe, the smooth skin of her neck.

Inger stared at the photograph for a few seconds, and finally said, "Whatever he did, he was quite a selfless man, wasn't he?"

"How do you mean?"

"Well, we don't know his connection to this girl, but whatever it was, he still dedicated a big part of his life to seeking some kind of justice for her."

"You don't know that's what he was looking for."

"No, but it seems likely, in one form or another. And then his last act, saving the person nearest to him. I've seen people in situations like that, perhaps you have too, and they don't think they'll be the hero, but they can't stop themselves when the moment comes."

"I'll give you that, his last act was selfless. And maybe this was too." He smiled. "I'm sorry to say I'm not quite as noble. I'm only looking at saving me."

She smiled and said, "Maybe your moment just hasn't come yet."

Maybe. He liked to think it might be true but, as things stood, his record didn't look good—he'd delivered plenty of pain in his life, but had never yet saved anyone, not even those who'd mattered most.

Chapter Seventeen

Sabine Merel had been an art student in Paris, studying sculpture, sharing a small apartment with a couple of other girls. She'd been working late in the studio at the art college one night in May, but had arranged to meet her friends later at a party. They'd thought little of it when she'd failed to show up.

The next morning, her body had been found in the alley at the back of a restaurant. She'd been punched hard in the face, then strangled with her own scarf some short time later. She'd been robbed, and her clothes, casual clothes for the studio, had been left in disarray, top pulled up, jeans and underwear pulled down, but there had been no evidence of a sexual assault beyond that.

The police had subsequently suggested that both the robbery and the interference with Sabine's clothing might have been post-mortem attempts to suggest a false motive, and they'd speculated that Sabine had more likely been killed by someone known to her.

A student who'd also been in the studio that night had been questioned but then released without charge. A brief media storm had followed because the male student was of Algerian origin and, given the strength of his alibi, the police had faced accusations of racism.

There had been no other suspects in the murder of Sabine Merel and no one had ever been charged with the crime. It seemed that in the fourteen years since, no further leads had ever arisen, and the death of this young art student had been quietly forgotten, probably by everyone except her own family and friends and, of course, Jack Redford.

It had taken Dan the last hour of the afternoon to piece together that much, working through the French in the articles Redford had saved. In one sense it was nothing new or surprising to him. He'd known, seen, and sometimes even brought about, too many unjustified deaths to be much moved by the story of another.

Yet it *had* moved him in some way, his mood sinking as the hour had ground on, perhaps because of the gradual drip-feed of information, bringing the girl back to life, even though he knew it was an illusion and that nothing would undo what had been done to her all those years before. He doubted anything would stir within him the indignation Redford had clearly felt, but he felt sad all the same, and mystified by that sadness, for a woman he'd never known, who'd been dead a long time.

As they walked back through the twilight, a darkness that seemed to rise up from the woodland floor rather than descend from above, he summarized what he'd learned for Inger's benefit. She walked ahead of him in complete silence, though he could tell she was listening intently.

It was a simple story, yet harrowing for all that, and he felt his energy sapping away just in the telling of it, the all-too-familiar tale of a young woman with a promising future snuffed out for no reason at all.

He finished just before they got to the cabin and at the door Inger turned and shook her head and he noticed that a tear had worked its way free and glistened on her cheek. In some way he was both pleased and sorry that it had upset her.

He reached up without thinking and wiped the tear away, then immediately took a step backwards. "Sorry, I . . ."

She ignored the apology and said, "She would have been a year older than me, but I don't know why I find it so sad. Maybe just the thought of her being in the studio, you know, working towards something, creating, and then that. It's so cruel, unbearably so."

He wasn't sure what to say, but didn't need to say anything, because they both turned in response to an indistinct sound and saw Mr. Eklund walking along the track, carrying the dinner tray with his effortless and loose-limbed gait.

Inger said something under her breath in Swedish, something affectionate, brought on by the sight of the old man. And Dan understood the sentiment even if he hadn't understood or even heard the words properly, because it was reassuring after a day like they'd had, to be reminded that there were good things in the world, and good people, simple food cooked well, strangers sharing their kindness indiscriminately. Dan had been outside that virtuous circle himself for most of his adult life, but he was grateful to be inside it now.

It was only when they were sitting down over their meal that Inger went back to the story of Sabine Merel, though she'd put the poignancy of her death to one side and was business-like again, focusing on the case.

"Did you read anything at all that might have suggested a link with Brabham?"

"Nothing. She was from . . ." He struggled to remember the name of her home town. "Limoges, I think. I don't know what her parents did, but I couldn't see any suggestion that they moved in the kind of circles where they might have encountered the CIA's Paris station chief."

"So what will you do?"

"There has to be a connection. I'll find out if Patrick can tell me anything about Redford, and if Sabine Merel's murder means anything to him. Then I guess I need to do what both the Paris police and Jack Redford failed to do; find out who killed her and why."

He laughed at the enormity of it, the suggestion that he could find truths in a couple of weeks that had eluded even Jack Redford in all his years of searching.

She laughed too, and said, "How much time did you say you had?"

He nodded, accepting the point, but said, "Look, first off, Redford undoubtedly knew more than he had up on those boards—he knew there was a link and was just looking for a way of proving it. Second, he was in hiding, and that limited what he could do."

"You're kind of in hiding too."

"True, but I haven't quite become Jacques Fillon yet. So I visit her parents, I visit the friends she lived with, the Algerian, anyone else I can find. Remember, I don't have to prove anything, I don't have to make it stand up in court, I just need to find the trail that leads back to Brabham, and I need to keep moving while I do it."

"And if you fail? You must have some other option for escaping this . . . all these killings."

All these killings. Just as with the murder of Sabine Merel, the mention of the killings did nothing to evoke the reality of what had happened to those people. But unlike Sabine, Dan and his colleagues had at least lived in that world and had done their own share of killing. It gave them choices, albeit limited.

"There are always options, but none as good as this, and the odds are no better either." She took in what he said, and swigged at her beer, then Dan said, "So what about you? I guess this is essentially case closed for you? You found out about Habibi, you found out who Jacques Fillon was."

"Habibi wasn't important—we just wanted to know what happened to him."

"And the rest?"

"I'm not sure. Our interest was more than the identity of Jacques Fillon, and given what we found . . . I don't know. I'll have to speak to my superior. Maybe I'm done after tomorrow."

Dan nodded and said, "Well, it's only been a couple of days, but I've enjoyed working with you."

"Me too. It wasn't . . ." She stopped herself. He raised his eyebrows, a little mock curiosity, and she said, "As you know already, I read a little about you before coming up here, and yes, it's only been a couple of days, but you weren't how I expected."

Teasing, he said, "In a good way?"

She smiled, saying, "In a good way."

She didn't need to spell it out. Dan knew how he read on paper, and she probably hadn't seen the half of it. He'd spent years working the edge, no rules of engagement, a ruthless focus on getting the job done, no matter what the cost. The only distinction between him and the monsters he'd taken down was the legitimacy of being paid by the winning side.

Or at least, he'd been part of the winning side back then—he had no idea which side he was on now. And he wouldn't discover the answer to that question until he got back out into the world, to see how far Jack Redford would take him, and how much protection his secret afforded.

Chapter Eighteen

Per drove them to Luleå the following afternoon and they flew back to Stockholm. Patrick wasn't flying in until early the following morning, so Dan thought Inger might suggest getting together for dinner, but instead she gave him the address of a café and suggested meeting the following afternoon to brief each other on developments.

So he spent the night alone in the hotel on Skeppsholmen, almost as quiet and removed from the world as the cabin they'd been sharing the last few days. The hotel itself wasn't one he'd have chosen if it hadn't been for the location, so he went to bed early and spent an hour listening to the wind blowing the leaves from the trees, and the faint sounds of the very few cars that came onto the island.

He woke once in the night, knocked into high alert by a noise nearby, probably only a door closing in the corridor. He could still hear the breeze working through the branches outside, but nothing else of the city beyond. And as he lay, slowly yielding to sleep again, he thought of Inger, somewhere else in the city, sleeping in her own bed, a million miles away from him.

The next day was clear and sunny but there was a stiff breeze now, chopping up the water in the harbor, a cold bite to it. Seeing the island in the daylight, he realized he'd been here before. The hotel and the few other buildings had been part of some historic garrison, so the whole island had that leafy campus quality he'd often seen in military installations. Most of those leaves now lay thick on the ground and more skittered and whipped through the air on the wind.

He crossed over to the mainland and left a message for Patrick White in the reception at the Grand Hotel, telling him simply to cross the bridge to Skeppsholmen at eleven. The location was perfect in that sense, in that it allowed him to make sure Patrick was on his own and not being followed.

He went back, spent an hour in the modern art museum, then got into position with a decent view over the long bridge to the island. Despite the cold there were a fair number of people strolling across it, but he saw Patrick from some distance away.

Once Dan had spotted him, he let him go again, focusing instead on all the other people on the bridge. He wasn't expecting to see someone tailing Patrick in an obvious way, and he knew that the overweight guy leaning looking out over the water was just as likely to be part of a surveillance operation as anyone else.

But these guys usually gave themselves away in some other fashion, in much the same way that actors always seemed to find it impossible to play "real" people. There were tells, things that Dan could spot, sometimes without even being able to define it. So he was fairly confident, so far at least, that no one was following Patrick White.

Once he'd crossed the bridge, Patrick kept walking casually, as if he were heading somewhere specific but at no great speed. Dan shadowed him for a little while longer and finally caught up with him.

Patrick didn't turn at the sound of approaching footsteps, but just before Dan reached him, he said, "It's a little brisk, this morning, isn't it?"

"Brisk? I suppose so."

As Dan drew level, Patrick said, "Charlie killed Jack Carlton and Rob Foster, wounded Alex Robinson."

"I don't know Robinson." He didn't want to know him, either, figuring he was the coward who'd made a run for it. And he had to hand it to Charlie, he'd been insistent that he'd hit him and it turned out he had.

"I don't know him well, but he seems to be marked for greatness." He was certainly marked for survival, which Dan guessed was half the battle. After a pause, Patrick said, "He said Charlie had other people at his place, that he and the others were ambushed."

Dan gave Patrick a look, as if to ask if he was really that gullible, and said, "I liked Jack Carlton, I like him even more now that he's not trying to kill me, so I don't want you to infer that he or Foster fell short in any way that night, but there was no ambush and there was only one other person. Robinson wouldn't have known that because he abandoned his team without even trying to help. If he hadn't, they'd have had the edge on us because Foster came close on his own. Charlie took a bullet."

"Serious?"

"Messed his hand up, but probably not too bad. I hope not, anyway, because the bullet was meant for me."

Patrick nodded and said, "You might have told me all this at Café Florence."

"I might."

"Yes, I understand why you didn't. But either way, Brabham's used Robinson's report as justification for upping the game."

"I'm sure he has." There was nothing more to add. From the point of view of Dan and Charlie, it couldn't get much higher than having targets on their backs. He pointed ahead, and said, "Let's turn here. We'll take a ferry ride."

"You seem to know the place pretty well."

"Yeah, I spent a couple of weeks here some years back, researching a job for you—which my local escort asked me about, by the way."

"Did she? You tell her what happened?"

"Of course."

"She take it alright?"

"I think so." Patrick nodded and they walked in silence for a few paces before Dan said, "Who was Jack Redford?"

"Redford?" He sounded surprised, not as if he didn't recognize the name but as if he was struggling to work out the connection, perhaps thinking it related in some way to the Habibi case. "Redford. Where to begin? I never met him, very few people did, but he did a lot of work for us, a long time back. Ex-Special Forces, but he became a phenomenal one-man tiger team, usually testing the security of our own facilities, which is why very few people ever got to meet him. Sometimes he'd do other kinds of work . . ." He laughed. "Essentially stealing things for us from places we couldn't get to, breaking into secure facilities to plant surveillance equipment, that kind of thing. He was something else. One of a kind."

They'd reached the landing point and a little white ferry was slowly working its way across the harbor towards them. Dan looked around as they stood there, but there was no one else about.

"What happened to him?"

"Dead. He had a place in Paris. About fifteen years ago he went missing, and maybe two weeks later they found his body floating in the Seine."

"Murdered?"

"There were all kinds of rumors at the time. One was that he'd been asked to infiltrate the DGSE headquarters in Paris for us, that he'd been caught, that the French killed him. The French denied there'd been a break-in, understandably, and if we sanctioned an operation like that, I never met anyone who knew about it. I was in Moscow at the time."

"And Bill Brabham was in Paris."

Patrick looked at him in response, intrigued, but neither of them said any more for the time being because the ferry was maneuvering into position. Once they were on the deck and it pulled away again, Patrick looked at Dan, his expression alone inviting him to explain.

Dan nodded, looking out across the harbor as he said, "I don't know whose body they fished out of the Seine, but it wasn't Jack Redford's and someone must have known that." As an aside he added, "What happened to the body?"

Patrick shrugged and said, "He didn't have any family. I don't know what they did with it."

"Just as well. Because the real Jack Redford changed his name to Jacques Fillon and moved to northern Sweden, where a few weeks ago he died in a bus crash."

For a good few seconds, Patrick stared at him in complete silence, the ferry rocking over the choppy water, the wind buffeting them. But although Patrick wasn't speaking, he was obviously thinking, and the pieces were falling together quickly.

"So the DGSE story could be true, or at least, he did some kind of job for Brabham, realized he was in danger. That's why Brabham sent someone up there."

"I don't know if he was working for Brabham or if Brabham was the subject. But we discovered that Redford's been working for the last twelve years to find evidence that would bring down Brabham, and his family. It seems he believed Bill was responsible for something, and I'm guessing he was right—the guy who went up there obviously went to see if there was any evidence."

"But there wasn't?"

"No. What we did get were some leads. It might help if you can get me some of the details for the people on this list."

He handed a piece of paper over which Patrick studied before putting it in his inside pocket, quickly pulling his overcoat back around him.

"The parents of a Sabine Merel in Limoges. Brabham's home and office. It all seems very eclectic."

"It is, and I don't even know how much of it'll be useful. See, around the same time that Redford went missing, an art student living in Paris was murdered. Her name was Sabine Merel, and we're working on the assumption that Redford believed Bill Brabham to be responsible for her death."

Patrick nodded, deep in thought, assimilating everything he'd heard. What was most striking to Dan, though, was his response to hearing what should have been an outlandish suggestion, that the CIA's Paris station chief might have been involved in the murder of an innocent nineteen-year-old student. Patrick knew Bill Brabham, had known him for years, and he hadn't objected to the theory. Far from it—he hadn't even seemed surprised.

Chapter Nineteen

By the time the ferry was heading back to Skeppsholmen, Dan could feel the cold getting through to his bones and Patrick was stamping about and bracing himself in a good-natured way, as if the cold were something that had to be endured for sport.

They were still some way off the island when Dan thought he spotted a guy in a padded jacket and a beanie hat, watching them from the path that ran around the shore. It could have just been someone watching the ferry, but something about him had caught Dan's attention.

And at the same time, as if being aware that he'd been spotted himself, the guy turned and walked away. Somehow, the speed with which he disappeared from view also suggested more intent than Dan might have expected from a sightseer. Patrick didn't appear to have noticed anything, though that didn't mean he hadn't.

As the ferry made its final approach, Patrick said, "So what's next?"

"Help out with some of those details if you can. And if there's anyone from the DGSE who you think might be able to help . . ."

Patrick frowned, but said, "There might be one person from around that time. He's a former Legionnaire, so I might be able to use Benoit Claudel's murder to make him play ball."

"Good," said Dan, liking the way he was thinking. "I aim to prove a link, and if I can get evidence, all the better. You staying in Europe for the time being?"

"I'll be around." He thought for a second and said, "How did you get along with Inger Bengtsson?"

"Okay. She's smart, focused. Apart from the fact I'm not her type, what's not to like?"

Patrick laughed, but then looked distracted for a moment before saying, "So you wouldn't mind her remaining involved in some way?" Dan looked askance, wanting to know what this was about. "The complexities of alliances and old friends, favors. The Swedes feel they have a stake in this. I can't really deny them that—they've been very helpful—but if you can live with Inger being your point of contact . . ."

Dan found himself oddly attracted to the idea, certainly more than the guy who'd met him at Arlanda, whose name he'd already forgotten, but he was acutely conscious that there was a lot more going on here than a benign investigation into the obsessions of Jack Redford.

"I could live with her being involved but, Patrick, this isn't a collegiate thing, it's not collaborative. I have things to do and my own timetable to work to, and if I think at any point I'm heading over to the dark side, I won't want to be around anyone legitimate."

"I should hope not. The aim is to build bridges, not cause diplomatic incidents." The ferry jolted as they docked with a churning of water. They stepped ashore and Patrick said, "The guy watching the ferry from the shore, I presume you saw him."

"One of yours?" Patrick shook his head and Dan said, "I'll be fine. You walk on ahead—let's find out who he's following."

Patrick shook Dan's hand and walked off along the path. Dan held back for thirty seconds, then set off after him. They'd only walked a couple of hundred yards when Patrick stopped, seemed to admire a building off to his right, and sauntered towards it, into a more quiet area of an already quiet island.

Dan slowed a little more and immediately saw why Patrick had taken the diversion. The guy who'd watched them from the shore ran across the leaf-strewn road, as if he feared losing his target. So he was there for Patrick, and Patrick had headed into the quieter corners specifically to draw him out.

Dan picked up his own pace now. He looked around, making sure there was no one else on the street, no one watching him. He took his gun and attached the silencer, turned one corner just as the guy disappeared ahead of him, turned the second just as he was leveling his own gun at Patrick's back. Patrick was either oblivious as to how imminent the danger was or had an absurd amount of faith in Dan's abilities.

All the same, Dan didn't wait. He fired, hitting the guy in the back of the right shoulder. The guy grunted with the impact, span and fell, his gun clattering to the floor. Patrick turned, as if surprised by the noise more than anything. And even down and hurt, the guy scrabbled to get hold of his gun again.

To his own astonishment, Dan recognized him, and wasn't sure how he hadn't identified him earlier.

"Matty?" All familiarity aside, Dan kept the gun on him. Matty froze, then glanced up at Dan with a look of awkward despair. As if suddenly too hot, he pulled the beanie hat off, his fair hair left tousled and unkempt.

Patrick was back with them now and appeared genuinely hurt as he looked down at the prone man and said, "Mattias?"

Matty shook his head, pushing himself up and back against the wall nearest him. He looked embarrassed, shamed even, and above all, resigned to what would happen now.

Patrick bent down and picked up Matty's gun, looking at it with a keen professional eye. He still looked shocked and upset, maybe with good reason, given the amount of work he'd given Mattias Hellström over the years.

Dan looked around, making sure no one had been attracted by the shot, which already silenced, had probably been distorted further in the windy conditions. He looked at Matty then.

"You weren't following me?"

"I didn't even realize it was you on the ferry. I was sent after Patrick." He glanced up at Patrick and said, "Sorry."

"Bill Brabham?"

"I didn't like it, but I know what's going on and, you know, he made clear how much safer it was to be on the inside. I didn't allow for Dan."

"Jesus, Matty, he was spinning you a line. You kill Patrick, I guarantee you're dead in a week. Brabham's getting rid of all of us. There is no inside, not anymore." He heard someone laugh somewhere nearby, perhaps from inside one of the buildings. He looked at Matty then—the dark quilted jacket was covering up the injury pretty well. "We've got to get you off the street."

"You're not gonna kill me?" Dan felt a brief surge of anger, for all the jobs they'd worked together in the past, scrapes they'd been in, trusting each other completely. He stepped forward and cracked Matty on the head with his gun. "Ow. Fuck!"

"I should kill you for what you just did. Patrick should kill you."

Matty looked back to Patrick, and said, "I'm sorry, man."

"So am I, Mattias. It'll be a long time before I can trust you again after this."

Dan pulled him up to his feet, and said, "You owe me for this, Matty. Can you walk?" He nodded. "Get patched up, get off the grid." He looked at Patrick too, as if to reinforce that the latter advice probably applied equally to him now.

It was Patrick who answered, saying, "Dan, you go on your way. I'll call us a cab—he can't go to a regular hospital."

Matty, looking groggy now, said, "I can go to . . ."

"No," said Patrick, cutting him off. "Not this time. Don't worry, I'll take care of it."

And with that, Patrick handed the gun back to him. Matty looked at it sitting there in his hand, its return somehow encapsulating the scope of his betrayal, and he started to sob then, quietly, as Dan turned and walked away.

Chapter Twenty

Later that afternoon Dan had a cab take him to the address Inger had given him for the café. He'd already received a couple of messages from Patrick and had decided to fly out the next day, to Paris, then on to Limoges by train. The fact that Brabham was now trying to shut down Patrick as well as his former operatives suggested none of them had time to waste.

The café was in a part of the city he wasn't familiar with, and he wondered if it was near her office or where she lived. Inger was already there when he arrived, sitting at a table in the corner. He joined her, they exchanged a formal kiss and she ordered coffee.

While they waited for it to arrive, she said, "Patrick told me about Jack Redford. It's incredible."

"I guess it is," said Dan, even though he didn't think the new revelations were any more incredible than what they'd discovered for themselves.

"I have something for you too." She reached down into her bag and took out an envelope, saying as she placed it on the table, "That's the man who came from Berlin to look around Redford's house."

Dan picked up the envelope and pulled the picture out enough to look at it—a capture from a security camera at the airport by the look of it. It was a guy of around thirty, but nobody he recognized.

"Do you have a name?"

"Alex Robertson."

"Robertson or Robinson?"

"Sorry, you're right, Alex Robinson. You've heard of him?"

Dan nodded and looked at the picture more closely. He wished he could take something from it, but he was just an average-looking guy in a suit, almost suspiciously clean-cut—he probably got mistaken for a Mormon missionary.

Dan slipped the picture back into the envelope and said, "I understand you're staying involved with this in some way."

"Especially now." She looked around the coffee shop, a few of the other tables occupied, and said, "I hope you don't mind me accompanying you tomorrow. More as an observer, though we feel it does involve us, particularly after what happened on Skeppsholmen."

Dan smiled. So Brabham's attempt to have Patrick killed in Stockholm was being seen by the Swedish Security Service as a legitimate reason for their involvement. He couldn't blame them for that, and it hardly mattered that it had probably all resulted from Redford sticking a pin in the map—if he'd hit upon some other wilderness Dan would probably be having this conversation with an officer from another country's intelligence service.

"What makes you think I'm going anywhere tomorrow?"

"It's too late today and, as beautiful as my city is, I don't think you want to stay any longer. I'm guessing Paris?"

"Flying to Paris, then the train to Limoges."

"Oh." She clearly understood what that meant, that he intended to speak with Sabine's parents first. She almost seemed to have second thoughts, as if imagining how charged that meeting might be.

"Changed your mind?"

"No, but . . ." She hesitated, then said, "I think you'd call it in at the deep end."

He nodded, and they stopped talking for a moment because the coffee arrived.

Once they were left alone again, she said, "I heard the full story about what happened earlier today." She was smiling slightly.

"What of it?"

"You didn't kill him."

He smiled too now and said, "I keep surprising you, don't I?" She didn't say anything but seemed to acknowledge that he had a point. "I haven't had time to think it through, but Matty would've been under a lot of pressure—we all are—and that's why he made the wrong decision on this. I'm guessing it's also why he hesitated before pulling the trigger, which is what gave me the edge. But we've got some history, Matty Hellström and me, and he's a decent guy. He's separated, I think, but he has a wife and two small kids. It'd take a lot more than what happened today for me to kill him."

She sat staring at him for a good few seconds, then seemed to snap out of it and reached down for her coffee.

Finally, after putting the cup back down, she said, "Well, I still think you did the right thing, and it would have been easy for anyone, even someone without your history, to do . . . the wrong thing in that situation."

He stared back at her, directly into her eyes, and he could tell she found it unsettling in some way.

"I'm not a bad person."

"I know that now and, yes, I'm surprised by that because . . . Well, you've done some really bad things, horrible things."

"I know."

When she realized he wasn't going to say anything more, she said, "How do you live with that?"

He shook his head.

"Truth is I just do. I get paid, I do the job I'm paid to do. I've killed some people, I've handed people over to be killed, or tortured, or imprisoned, but the targets are never exactly innocents themselves."

Even as he said it, though, he thought of Ramon Martinez, torn away from his family—Dan had been well paid for tracking him down, but he wasn't certain he'd been paid enough to justify it, and he couldn't help but think of the boy, wondering who would take him to school each morning now.

With what seemed an uncanny change of subject, as if she'd been reading his thoughts, Inger sounded curious as she said, "Have you never been tempted to settle down, have children?"

He looked back at her. It had been the one thing in his life he'd found hardest to talk about, even with his closest friends, and yet for some reason he wanted to tell her, and it seemed the easiest and most natural thing in the world to do so. He wasn't sure why he felt so comfortable around her, why he felt able to share thoughts he'd hardly dared acknowledge himself, but he did all the same.

He shrugged and said, "Actually, I did, kind of. I had a son nine years ago." He could see her astonishment, and knew it was the one thing that wouldn't have shown up in her research. "We weren't a couple. It was just a fling really, a bit of fun . . ."

"Why am I not surprised?"

"Don't get me wrong, it wasn't a one-night stand or anything like that. What I mean is we both knew we probably wouldn't stay together. We didn't even live together. And then Emilia fell pregnant and we had a son. Luca."

She looked mesmerized by the revelation, and said, "You don't see him anymore?"

He hesitated, certain he should have made it clearer, sooner. Her face fell in response, as once again she seemed to preempt what he was going to say.

"He died." He nodded to himself, conscious of how rarely he'd said those words aloud, how rarely he'd even acknowledged them. His son had died, and a bit of Dan had died with him, leaving him not quite whole. "He died. I was away on a job, off the grid, just a couple of weeks, and he got meningitis." She gasped a little in shock and sorrow. "Killed him within twenty-four hours. When I left he was thriving, you know, eighteen months old, healthy, strong. He'd just started calling me Papa, and then I came back and he was gone, like he'd never been there. Something I always say, you can't disappear completely, but Luca did. He vanished, like he'd never been there at all."

She put her hand on his and said, "Dan, I'm sorry, I . . ."

"Wish you hadn't asked?"

"No, I'm glad I asked, and I'm glad you told me."

"So you haven't changed your mind about coming with me?"

She looked nonplussed and said, "Not at all. Why would I? And in fact I know it might sound strange, but it makes me hope more than ever that we'll find the person who killed Sabine Merel and, if we can bring him to justice, even better."

Dan nodded, liking her sentiment, though he wasn't sure of the connection she'd made. Perhaps it was only that so many of the bad things in life were beyond their control, that it was all the more important to take on the things that could be tackled.

For every random death—Luca's, Redford's, the other children on that bus—there were those that should not have happened, that demanded justice, and Sabine Merel's murder was among them.

Chapter Twenty-one

They arrived in Limoges late the following afternoon. Dan had managed to call the Merels from a payphone in Gare Montparnasse so they were at least expecting them. The man he'd spoken to had been surprised at first, but had accepted Dan's request without any questions. Maybe, after all these years, they were just happy that anyone was showing an interest, no matter who they were.

They booked into the Candide, a grand-looking hotel near the center which had seen better days but still had a dash of old-world charm. And then they immediately took a cab the short distance to the Merels' house. Dan noticed Inger looking a little nervous now that they were here and about to do this.

He'd never been to Limoges itself, but it reminded him of plenty of other French cities. It had that mixture of old and new piling on top of each other, vying for precedence, a jumble that should have looked anonymous and yet still managed somehow to look entirely French.

The Merels also lived close to the center, in a house set inside its own little oasis behind high, off-white walls. They rang the bell and were buzzed in, the door opening onto a beautiful lawned garden that stretched around the house. And the house itself looked like it belonged in the countryside rather than the middle of the city, a big place with wooden shutters on the windows.

The front door opened before they reached it and a man came out to meet them. For some reason, Dan had been expecting an old man, and he guessed Merel was sixty or thereabouts, but he looked young and fit. His clothes were casual enough, cords and a pale-blue sweater, but again, there was something more youthful and fashionable about the look of them, as if he were someone who worked for a glossy magazine or in the media.

He smiled uncertainly and said, "Mr. Hendricks?" Dan had dropped the idea of using an alias, and doubted Inger could even remember that he'd briefly been David Porter.

"That's right, thanks for agreeing to meet us, Monsieur Merel. This is Inger Bengtsson—she works for the Swedish government."

Merel had been about to say something else, but the mention of Inger's name and her employment threw him briefly.

After a moment, he recovered, greeted Inger first, shook Dan's hand and said, "Please, call me Sebastien. And do come in."

He took them inside, the hallway and the rooms off it reinforcing what the outside had already suggested, that these people had money. He showed them into a large sitting room then, a baby grand filling one corner, the top adorned with family photos.

"Please, do sit down. A little drink; some wine, or cognac?"

"Thank you, whatever you're having."

Inger nodded, still looking a little nervous, and said, "Yes, anything."

He smiled, and glanced over at the array of photos before saying, "I'll be back in a moment. And my wife also—she's just talking on the telephone."

He left. Dan could hear his wife now, talking in another room, a low hum, conversational rather than conspiratorial. They were probably surprised by the visit, but he doubted they'd see it as suspicious or something to alert the police about, not after all this time.

Inger was sitting like a girl outside the principal's office, but Dan stood and walked over to the piano. There were a lot of people there, suggesting that the Merels had maybe three or even four surviving children, and a whole clutch of grandchildren, a mixture of dark and fair but nothing in between, all of them remarkably attractive.

But there, right in the middle of the frames on display was the hole in the middle of their world. It was unmistakably her, Sabine, but a different picture to the slightly formal one they'd seen in Redford's office. Here she was smiling, caught off guard at an al fresco dinner, maybe in the garden Dan could see beyond the windows. She was beautiful, but it was more that she was full of life in that picture, full of possibilities and futures—it had to break their hearts every time they looked at it.

Dan didn't have any pictures of Luca in the Paris apartment. There were several in the house in Italy, and he wondered now if that was why he'd all but abandoned that house, because it was linked always in his mind with the unfinished loss of his child.

One picture in particular, of Luca looking over Dan's shoulder, smiling at Emilia and therefore at the camera, had torn at his heart. Framed, it had hung in the hall, but on his last visit he'd taken it down and put it in the drawer, exhausted by the emotional pull of it every time he'd tried to walk past.

He heard a noise and turned to see Sebastien Merel coming back in, carrying a tray with a decanter and four glasses. Clearly, given what Dan and Inger had come to talk about, he'd decided cognac would be better.

He saw that Dan was looking at the photographs, and gave a slight acknowledging smile that seemed to speak of the sorrow still weighing him down, but said, "As you can see, we're blessed, in spite of everything."

He put the tray down on the table and started to pour four hefty measures. He was still doing it when his wife walked in, the same expensive and attentive informality, the same young looks for someone in her sixties, her hair dark. She apologized in French for keeping them, a rapid but welcoming monologue before her husband stopped her and turned to Inger.

"Inger, you don't speak French?"

"No, I'm sorry, I don't."

"I'm so sorry," said Madame Merel. "Inger? I'm Catherine Merel, Sabine's mother."

She turned to Dan and he smiled and said, "I do speak French, so I understood. Delighted to meet you, Madame Merel, and thank you for agreeing to see us."

They all sat down on two sofas that faced each other across a coffee table. Dan sat next to Inger now, and he noticed Sebastien Merel pat his wife on the leg as he sat down next to her, offering reassurance of some kind. It made Dan hope all the more that they'd be able to offer some closure for this couple, limited as it would be.

Dan and Merel both sipped at their drinks, the fire of the cognac a reminder to Dan of his meeting with Patrick, the meeting that had set him on this road. Inger and Catherine Merel nursed their glasses but he noticed neither of them drank.

Before Dan could start, Merel looked at Inger, puzzled, and said, "Inger, I hope you don't mind me asking, but what is the involvement of the Swedish government in this?"

"I don't mind at all. The new evidence concerning your daughter's murder came to light in Sweden, from someone living there."

The couple looked even more baffled by that, but Merel said, "So you're police? You're working with the French police?"

Dan cut in and said, "It's bigger than that, Sebastien. Sabine's murder is part of a complex investigation, the nature of which means it has to be carried out under the radar. It's best that you don't ask too many questions, but rest assured that we'll do everything we can to get to the truth."

Whether it was something in Dan's tone or just the words he'd used, Sebastien Merel nodded eagerly and, to Dan's slight concern, hopefully. He looked at his wife as he said, "Of course, what can we tell you?"

"First, just some basic details. Did Sabine have a boyfriend at the time, or mention that she was seeing anyone? Was she happy with her roommates? Had she seemed nervous at all, or troubled?"

"I think everything was fine, more or less. Only Catherine . . ."

"The last time I spoke to her," said Catherine Merel. "I think it was two days before, I couldn't quite . . . I didn't know what, but I felt something was wrong. I asked her more than once, and finally she laughed and told me I worried too much."

Inger said, "Her roommates also, they thought everything was fine?"

"One can never tell, at a time like this. I thought everyone was lying to us."

Dan said, "Do you have contact details for either of the roommates? I appreciate it's a long time ago, but . . ."

Merel smiled and said, "But of course. Only for one, Sylvie. She always kept in touch. She works for *Vogue* in Paris."

His wife smiled a little, perhaps with the bittersweet reminder of what her daughter's contemporaries were doing now, but then she said to her husband, "And Yousef."

"Of course, Yousef! He was a colleague of Sabine, and is now quite a successful artist, also in Paris. He was in the studio with her that night."

The final words were delivered with delicacy, as if there was something fragile about the statement.

Dan said, "The boy they questioned. The accusations of racism."

"Anyone who knew Yousef at all would know it was ridiculous for him to be questioned."

"Why?"

"Because he's the most gentle person." He turned again to his wife and offered her a smile, something almost apologetic about it, then faced forward and said, "Sabine was punched in the face, I'm sure you have read. One single punch, they think, but it was powerful enough to break her nose, fracture her cheekbone and knock out two teeth." Dan was conscious of Inger taking a drink of her cognac for the first time. "They think he waited until she was fully conscious again. She was face down. He was kneeling on her back, with so much force that he also broke two ribs. Then he strangled her with her own scarf, and even then his violence was beyond belief, crushing her windpipe, rupturing blood vessels in her neck. I repeat, if you knew Yousef, you would know that's impossible for him."

Catherine Merel's face had sunk as she'd listened, the story so familiar and yet still visibly sapping her will and her energy as she sat there.

"Thank you for telling us about it," said Dan. "And we'd really appreciate those details for Sylvie and Yousef, and perhaps if you could call them, tell them we'll visit in the next day or two."

"Of course, if it helps."

"There was one other thing I wanted to ask. Had Sabine ever mentioned any American friends, any American connections at all?"

Catherine Merel looked up again, an urgency about her, and she said, "You think she was killed by an American? Somebody important?"

Inger said, "Why do you say important?"

Her tone was accusatory in response, saying, "It is what you said. It's bigger than the police. And now you ask about Americans. You know something you're not telling us."

Dan quickly cut in and said, "We know lots of things, Madame Merel, but nothing certain. I wouldn't play games with you. I know it means too much."

She nodded, accepting what he was saying, acknowledging the final point, that it meant too much, and she turned to Inger with a brittle smile and said, "I have some photographs, if you would like to see?"

"I'd like that very much," said Inger.

She got up and crossed the room, coming back with a photograph album.

Merel smiled and said, "Dan, please, let's leave the ladies to look at photographs. If you come to the study with me, I'll get you those details, and see if there's anyone else who might be of assistance."

Dan could imagine Inger's response to being cast in that way, the ladies left in the drawing room while the men got on with business, but he was relieved not to have to look at photos himself. He followed Merel into the study and stood there in silence as he made a note of the two names with addresses and phone numbers.

He looked up then and said, "We have a contact for the police too, but I imagine you have that side of things covered?"

"Yes, we do." On the one hand, he was thinking a police contact might have been useful, but it seemed unlikely the kind of person they'd been given as a liaison would be much use to Dan. Merel handed him the piece of paper and he said, "Thanks. I hope we'll be back in time to visit them tomorrow."

"I'll call this evening and let them know." He glanced at the door, then, and said, "It's impossible for you to know how important this is for us, for our whole family. But for my wife, especially, it's become . . . an obsession. The finding of the murderer."

"I understand."

Merel nodded, but as if he hadn't heard.

"I worry sometimes, what will happen to her if the murderer is found, because then there is no barrier left between us and our loss—we have to face it raw."

"I understand that too."

"Yes, I believe you do, Dan. I see in the newspaper, reports of murder, and it's such a simple thing; a man is murdered here, a woman there, covered in a few lines, so easily forgotten. But it's complex too, no? For those of us left, it's a puzzle we'll never solve, no matter what we learn."

"You still want to know."

"Naturally," said Merel. He looked ready to say something else, but only fell back sadly on the same word. "Naturally."

Dan could barely imagine the level of their grief, but he could understand how this unsolved crime, the need to find the person who'd taken her from them, had become something to hang their lives on. And if it went, if the murderer was caught, they would have to face all over again the stark early morning truth that it solved nothing, that Sabine was still lost for ever.

Even knowing that, though, as he stood there in Merel's study, vaguely aware of Catherine Merel and Inger talking in the other room, Dan wanted nothing more than to provide this decent and dignified couple with those answers. If it secured his own future into the bargain, all well and good, but if it didn't, at least he'd have done one irrefutably good thing in his life, and finished the work that a better man than him had started.

Chapter Twenty-two

They took a cab back to the hotel, the streets busy with the buzz of early evening. Inger seemed subdued, but he wasn't sure what to say and his own energy levels had taken a knock, so they sat in silence. They went to their adjoining rooms with some vague idea of having dinner downstairs. Dan slipped the piece of paper with the contact details into his bag, then heard a door open and turned to see Inger standing there with a surprised look on her face.

"I'm sorry, I didn't realize—I thought it was just . . ." There was a connecting door between the two rooms, something Dan hadn't noticed himself until now. She laughed a little, but she still looked down, and a bit of him wondered if the mistake of opening that door had been intentional, if she just wanted some company.

"Are you okay?"

She nodded but without conviction, and then she said, "I think it's just, I never lost anybody, you know. Well, a friend at school when I was fourteen who died from some rare kind of cancer, but no family members, nothing like you've known, or them. It was just difficult being there. They were lovely people, weren't they?"

"Yeah, I liked them, but it was tough. Must have been tough looking through the photographs."

She lowered her head, as if unable to sum up how difficult it had been; pictures of Sabine from across the short span of her life, each with a happy association, but all equally possessed of a terrible sadness, a sepia tint visible only to those who knew.

"It made me think of you too, the way you lost your son."

Fleetingly, he regretted telling her about Luca, because he was certain he didn't deserve her sympathy, but at the same time, he couldn't deny that it felt right in some way that he'd finally shared it with someone, and that the someone was her.

Even so, he said, "What happened to Luca is . . . What I mean to say is, you can't compare my loss with theirs. Even I can't begin to imagine what they've been through."

She nodded, and the light in the room was so soft that it took him a moment as she stood there to see that she was crying. He stepped closer, unsure of himself, and reached out to put a hand on her shoulder.

She shook her head, saying, "It's stupid of me." But she held onto him all the same. He could feel the heat of her breath against his neck as she said, "She was so full of life. It was unbearable, and her mother so matter of fact and dignified. I knew it would be terrible to go there."

"I know you didn't want to go, I should have . . ."

"No, it's just me. I've been spoiled by life."

Neither of them spoke for a few seconds, but she held him still, and he became increasingly aware of the warmth and softness of her body against his, but more than that, aware of the affection he felt for her and how stealthily it had crept up on him. Without thinking, he kissed her head where it nestled against him and, immediately, he knew he'd made a mistake.

She pulled back, though her arms were still around him, and stared at him with a look he couldn't quite read—accusing, insulted?

"Sorry, I didn't mean . . ."

He fell silent, the air charged between them, and he found himself oddly nervous. He still wasn't sure how to read her or the situation, so he remained motionless and then she kissed him, tentatively at first, but then with more ease and confidence. He felt the first stirrings of adrenaline, his thoughts spinning slightly out of control as she started to pull at his clothes.

Quickly, he worked at her clothes too, and having believed and accepted that she was out of reach, he found himself almost like a teenager again now, a wave of excitement and heightened desire with each revelation; stomach, breasts, thighs. He couldn't get enough of her, and couldn't catch up with the fact that it seemed to be mutual.

A couple of times as they made love he wondered at this change in her, if she was bisexual, if she'd ever had a boyfriend before, because she seemed easy and comfortable and self-assured with him. He said nothing, a selfish part of him not wanting to ruin the moment or break the spell.

It was only as they lay afterwards in his bed that he said, "Er, have you . . . always been a lesbian?"

She laughed loud, doubling up, her leg curling around him. He laughed too, not even sure if they were laughing at the same thing.

She fell onto her back again and said, "I'm not a lesbian."

He felt like punching the air, but he was curious too, and said, "Why did you tell me you were?"

She didn't reply at first so he turned to look at her and she looked embarrassed as she said, "To avoid this happening."

"You could've just told me you had a boyfriend."

She turned to face him now, looking into his eyes as she said, "I don't think you're the sort of person who would see that as an obstacle." He was still trying to think of a response to that when she said, "I was wrong though. Despite everything, I think you're quite honorable, and quite sweet."

"It's been a long time since anyone's called me that."

"Honorable or sweet?" She was teasing him and didn't wait for an answer. "You see, you know your way around a woman's body, but not a woman's mind. It's like, in a way, all these years of adventure and always moving on, a part of you has remained . . ."

"Immature?"

"I was going to stay stunted."

He laughed, but said afterwards, "I don't want to be that person, and I'm trying to find a way of moving on, but, it's not easy."

"Can you ever move on? Isn't that what some of these other guys did, and it still caught up with them?"

She was right about that.

"I guess I'll know soon enough. But wanting it's a start, surely?"

She nodded and leaned in to kiss him, and that amorphous desire for something resembling a normal life seemed even more pressing now, because he realized she wanted it for him too, and that made it feel tangible. She didn't necessarily see herself as part of his future—why would she?—but she cared about what happened to him, a rare enough occurrence in his life that he wanted to hold onto it.

Chapter Twenty-three

They woke early the next morning but lingered on in bed, and before either of them thought to check the time it had turned nine.

Inger jumped up and said, "We need to be quick if we're catching that train."

He smiled, even as she gathered up her clothes and walked through the connecting door into her own room, but then he lay back on the pillow. He still wasn't quite sure what had happened, or what it signified, whether it was a one-off or whether there might be more to it than that.

But that was where his thoughts ran aground, because for all the talk of moving on, he didn't know what the coming months held, and as much as she wanted a better life for him, he couldn't imagine that she'd want to be a part of it.

He could hear that she'd gone into the bathroom, could hear the shower running, and finally he jumped up and went into his own bathroom. He'd been in the shower for a few minutes when he heard a door close, or what sounded like a door closing. He didn't think much of it, though he was vigilant enough that he remained tuned in for further sounds from the room beyond.

He heard nothing more until he turned off the water and stepped out of the shower, but as he started to dry off he heard Inger say, "Dan?"

Her voice was faint, as if she was calling from her own room.

"Yeah, what is it?"

"Could you come out here, please?"

He thought again now of the closing door and the strange tone in her voice. He put the towel around his waist and looked around quickly—there was nothing he could defend himself with if she wasn't alone out there. At a loss he picked up another towel, knowing that anything he threw might give him a moment's edge.

He opened the door and immediately saw her sitting on the end of his bed in her underwear. In spite of knowing something was wrong, for a fleeting moment he was distracted again by her simple beauty, but then his eyes fell to what she was looking at. Between the bathroom door and the door to his room, a guy was lying crumpled on the floor.

Dan dropped to one knee behind him. There was a gun on the floor so he leaned over and slid it out of reach, then looked at the guy. He was average height but stocky, wearing what looked like a ski jacket. His hair was dark and cropped close, and Dan could see a little blood at the base of his skull and a larger area that looked misshapen.

He was unconscious at the very least. Dan pressed his fingers into the warmth of the guy's neck, held them there for a few seconds, then turned him on his side and checked his pockets, finding nothing.

He stood again and turned, looking at her. He also saw now that one of the heavy metal bedside lamps was on the floor next to the bed.

He pointed and said, "You hit him with that?"

She turned, in shock, and looked at the lamp on the floor as if reminding herself, then nodded. He walked over and crouched in front of her, taking her hands in his.

"Dan, he had a gun. He was going to go into your bathroom, and . . ." She seemed vague, but was hit by a wave of clarity then and said, "Is he dead?"

"Yeah, he's dead. Must have been a lucky hit."

"Lucky?"

"Yeah, lucky. You might have hurt him but not killed him. You might have hurt him but just made him angry."

She nodded, accepting the point, recovering her composure by the second, and she sounded almost her usual self as she said, "I know I had to do it. He might've killed you, or both of us. But . . . I never killed anyone before."

He nodded, still holding onto her hands, and said, "It's not an easy thing, I won't pretend it is. But you did do the right thing. And you must have known this day might come when you joined the Security Service."

"The *Swedish* Security Service," she said, and managed a weak smile.

"Point taken."

She looked over at the body and said, "Do you know him? I hope to God he's not CIA."

Dan looked behind too, though he couldn't see his face clearly from here. "I don't recognize him. I'm pretty certain he isn't CIA. He looks wrong."

He didn't say it, but he also guessed Bill Brabham was reluctant to use his own people now that Dan and Charlie had hit back and he'd taken casualties. So he was using freelancers where he could but, of course, thanks to Bill Brabham himself, a lot of the better freelancers were now dead.

"But how did he know you were here?"

"Beats me. Either there's a leak in your office or in Patrick White's. I don't have an office."

"It must be Patrick's, so we have to tell him. He was expecting you to be on your own, I think, so that suggests he was following you, not me."

She was right, and she was thinking straight which was good.

"You're probably right, but we won't tell Patrick. We just keep moving for now. Chances are, Brabham will have someone in Paris anyway, so we need to be vigilant."

"And the body?"

The body.

"Okay, there's a stairwell at the end of the corridor, a fire escape, looks like it's never used. I'll dump the body there. You need to get dressed."

For a second she looked confused and he feared she was going to object, suggest they had to wait for the police or call it in to her head office.

But she snapped out of it again and said, "Do you need help moving it?"

"I don't think so. Maybe only as a lookout."

She nodded, and they both stood and she walked back into her room. Dan took the lamp into the bathroom, wiped it, making sure there was no obvious damage. He checked the floor around the body then, but they'd once more touched lucky—the wound hadn't bled as much as it might have done, as if the surface of the skin hadn't fully broken. There was no blood on the carpet.

He finished getting dressed, got everything together, then waited for Inger. She came through a couple of minutes later, fully dressed. She offered a strained smile—she was dealing with it pretty well, though he knew from his own experience that she would never quite shake this off, that it was part of her now.

He tested the guy's weight, but he was too big to do anything other than drag him.

"Okay, take a walk in the corridor, check that there's no noise from any of the other rooms, no one about, no cleaners. Once you're confident it's clear, tap on this door as you walk past and then keep an eye on the main stairwell."

She nodded and left.

Dan turned the guy onto his front and waited. Inger tapped on the door as she walked past, so he opened it, held it with his foot and hoisted the guy up by his arms, dragging him out into the corridor and in one swift movement to the end and the fire exit.

He was moving through the door even before Inger had reached the main stairs. He hesitated then, making sure there was no one about, that the lower floors of this stairwell weren't being used for service. It was silent though, and noticeably colder than the rest of the hotel, which he guessed was a promising sign in itself.

It was an open stairwell, with a gap in the middle over which he could see all the way to a dark concrete floor at the bottom. He turned the body and lifted it up now, so the middle of his back was resting on the metal rail, a position that would have been painful if he'd still been alive.

And then he tipped him and looked over himself to watch the descent. The body didn't fall straight and the head hit the rail on a lower floor with a glancing but visceral blow, before finally landing in an oddly shaped heap at the bottom. That would do, enough to sow confusion for a while, and perhaps indefinitely.

Dan walked back along the corridor, past his room until he was able to catch Inger's eye. She came back with him and once inside they both got their bags together in silence.

Only as they were about to leave the room did he stop her and say, "I'm sorry, I should have said earlier, but thank you." She looked confused, and he said, "You probably saved my life, and you definitely covered my back."

"I didn't see it quite like that."

"Well, you should, because this'll stay with you, but you can at least be certain that you did the right thing, for the right reason. That's a luxury most of us don't have."

She smiled a little, grateful, for his intentions if nothing else. He wanted to kiss her, but thought she'd consider it inappropriate in some way, so he held back. Maybe it was for the best anyway. She had just killed a man and Dan wanted to kiss her, and in those two facts, ironically, lay the difference that would probably always remain between them.

Chapter Twenty-four

They both slept on and off during the journey to Paris, making up for how little sleep they'd had the night before. Inger was in low spirits too, understandably given what she'd been through. She looked as if she wanted to talk about what had happened that morning but, rightly or wrongly, Dan got the feeling she didn't want to talk about it with him. With some small amount of guilt, he was grateful for that.

As they traveled from Gare Montparnasse in the cab he said, "We'll book into the Hotel Vergoncey if they've got rooms. It's a nice place—I've used it before."

She agreed blankly, but a moment later she said, "Why did you need a hotel in Paris before now—you have an apartment, don't you?"

"I've only owned the apartment for eighteen months. Actually, I lived in the Vergoncey for about six weeks when I was searching for the right place."

She made no obvious response to that, but turned to him as if preoccupied and said, "We'll need two rooms."

"Of course," he said and, ridiculously, felt stung all the same.

"I really enjoyed last night. I like . . . I like you, Dan. But it's too quick to . . . and it's not because of what happened this morning."

He shook his head, and put a reassuring hand on her thigh, immediately feeling queasy with the memory of Sebastien Merel comforting his wife in the same way.

"I understand, and you're right. Don't try to explain." He waited a beat and added, "Connecting rooms?"

"If they have them. After all, you need my protection."

He smiled, because she was joking about it, which was a first step.

They checked in—there were no connecting rooms available, so they were placed directly across the corridor from each other—and then Dan made a call to the cell phone of Sabine's old college friend Sylvie. She was working at home and gave them the address of her apartment in the 17th arrondissement.

They hadn't really talked about the plan from here on in, but as they rode in the cab to Sylvie's place, Inger said, "Who else do we see today?"

"After Sylvie, we visit Yousef."

"You've called him?"

"No, I'll ask Sylvie if I can call from there. Then I have to try to meet with another contact Patrick gave me, but I'll go alone to that."

She looked at him, immediately suspicious, and said, "Why alone?"

"You can come if you like, but I think he's more likely to talk openly with me. He's DGSE and he's meeting me off the record."

She still looked on the verge of objecting, but accepted it grudgingly and said, "And then?"

"I'm hoping we turn up something among those three people, because there's no one else on the list." The cab pulled over and he said, "We're here."

As they got out and looked at the building, Inger said, "It's a nice place. A nice neighborhood."

"Yeah, it's pretty good. Actually, my apartment's a couple of blocks in that direction."

"Oh." She sounded surprised, which made him wonder what kind of neighborhood she'd imagined him living in. "Maybe we could . . ." She stopped herself before the thought had even fully formed, probably realizing that it was impossible to visit Dan's apartment. Even so, he liked that she seemed curious about it.

"Exactly. Brabham wouldn't expect me to show up there in a million years, but I imagine he'll still have someone watching it. You'd be disappointed anyway—it's quite minimalist."

They were buzzed up, and met at the door by Sylvie, a stylish woman in her mid-thirties, not pretty exactly but striking, with a bone structure that seemed to hint at a childhood spent in a country château and a lifelong love of horses.

She smiled and said, "Sebastien called me about you. Nice to meet you. So you know I'm Sylvie, and I presume you must be Inger." She kissed her on both cheeks. "And Dan."

"Thanks for seeing us."

She waved away the thanks and walked on ahead of them into the apartment. They might have been in the same neighborhood, but that was where the resemblance stopped between Dan's place and Sylvie's.

The apartment they were in was vast and expensively furnished, a mixture of antique furniture and modern art. There were a couple of children's toys lying about here and there, and a picture book open on a rug in the large sitting room. He thought Sylvie would pick it up, but she appeared not even to notice it. Dan couldn't hear children, or any other noise in the apartment.

"Might I get you something to drink?"

Dan was almost tempted to say yes, just to see if she went for it herself or rang a bell, but he said, "No, thank you, and we won't keep you very long at all."

"If you're here to talk about Sabine you can take as much of my time as you wish." She walked across to a table against the wall at the side of the room and said, "This is one of hers."

They both walked over and looked at the abstract bronze sitting on the table, abstract but somehow a completely feminine form, curved and fecund. Inger reached out and stroked the belly of it.

"It's beautiful."

Sylvie smiled sadly and said, "She was so talented. Women, especially, can never resist touching it. Such a lovely piece." She gestured across the room then. "Please, let's sit down."

She sat on the edge of her chair with a remarkably straight posture, and looked expectant, as if to say she was completely at their disposal.

Dan cut straight to it and said, "Catherine Merel, when I asked her if Sabine's roommates had noticed anything, she seemed a little confused, as if perhaps she thought you didn't tell her everything at the time . . ."

He thought she might object but instead, she said, "We told the police. It was never made public, so we saw no need to upset Sabine's parents."

Inger sat up herself, as if mimicking Sylvie's posture, and said, "So something did happen?"

"Yes. She said some guy tried to rape her at a party, about a week before, perhaps ten days. She managed to fight him off, but I think it shook her quite badly. And then he kept pestering her, telling her he was sorry, she'd misunderstood, that it hadn't been what she thought. She had wanted only to forget it, but in the end she told him if he didn't leave her alone she would go to the police and report it."

"She didn't?"

She looked skeptical as she said, "A woman going to the police two weeks after a party to say someone tried to rape her but failed?

Sabine wasn't stupid, she said it only to get him to leave her alone, but I think he believed it. She said he became quite threatening."

Inger looked grave as she said, "You said you told the police, but nothing came of it?"

"We had no name, there was no record of suspicious calls. There was nothing to go on. And the entire case—it was as if it just vanished in the following months. Nothing. As if Sabine never existed."

Dan started, "Were you ever tempted to—"

Sylvie put a finger up, silencing him, and she smiled, saying, "There is one more thing that happened. I've never told anyone else, but I knew this was a clear indication not to get involved." Both Dan and Inger stared at her, waiting, intrigued. "We left the apartment later that summer. Neither of us were happy there after what had happened to Sabine, and something hadn't quite felt right afterwards. You probably think me foolish if I talk of a sixth sense, but we both had the same feeling. And then, when we were packing up to leave, we found two . . . electronic bugs, one behind a picture, one behind a bedside cabinet. We didn't know what they were, of course, but I took them to a friend at the university and he knew right away. A coincidence? Possibly. But I'm confident, we both were, that somebody had bugged our apartment, and I think what they wanted to discover was if we knew the identity of the man who tried to rape Sabine."

It was quite a leap, but Dan could understand how they'd made it, and knowing what he knew, he guessed they'd probably been right.

Inger said, "Did you show the bugs to the police?"

Sylvie looked a little wistful as she said, "We were twenty. Innocents, really, but we knew enough, had seen enough scary Hollywood films, to know that it was best we forget all about it. We wouldn't help Sabine, or find her killer, only bring more trouble for ourselves. So, no, we didn't go to the police again. You think we were wrong?"

Inger didn't answer, but it seemed Sylvie was waiting for a response, so Dan said, "No, I think you did the right thing. I'm guessing you never heard any more after you left the apartment?"

"Nothing. But if the bugs were for the reason I think, they would have known by then that we knew nothing, the man at the party, it was a mystery to us. And afterwards, I almost forgot about it."

Almost, thought Dan, *but not quite.*

"Thank you, Sylvie, you've been more help than you could know."

She shrugged noncommittally and said, "You're going to Yousef?"

"Yes. In fact, do you mind if I call him from here?"

She stood and said, "I'll call him for you, tell him you're on the way."

As she reached for the phone she pointed at a sweeping canvas opposite, abstract oranges and browns and sandy yellows. "That's one of his. He's very successful now."

They both got up and looked at the canvas as she spoke animatedly in the background, a light-hearted catching up before the more serious business of telling Yousef about the visitors.

She ended the call and joined them in front of the picture and Dan said, "For some reason I thought he was a sculptor, maybe just because he was in the studio with her that night."

"You're right, he did start out with mainly sculpture, but then he moved into painting and became a great success." She smiled, pleased with herself as she said, "I paid very little for this, back when we were all still poor, and now it's perhaps the most valuable piece in my collection."

Dan smiled, thinking of Sylvie, probably never poor the way most people saw it, supporting her artist friends, staying true to them through the years. And Sabine might have remained part of that circle, had the events of fourteen years ago not reduced her role to that of a tactile bronze, a talking point for memories.

She walked them toward the door, pointing out other paintings, ceramic pieces, another bronze, but then Dan thought of something else and said, "Did Sabine ever mention anything about the man who tried to rape her, how old he was or his nationality?"

"Never. I've always assumed he was American, because of the party, but I don't know for a fact."

Inger beat Dan to it, saying, "Why, where was the party?"

Dan had assumed until this point, and maybe so had Inger, that this had been some drunken student party, but Sylvie said, "It was some dreadful thing, celebrating cultural ties, lots of young and promising artists invited. I'm not sure why Sabine was invited, perhaps she was suggested by her tutor, but it was the kind of thing that seemed to happen back then—there were so many parties. And yes, so it could have been a Frenchman, because there were hundreds of people there, but the party was at the residence of the US Ambassador."

She shrugged, as if excusing herself for making what might have been a fanciful leap. And she probably didn't understand the expression on Inger's face, and on Dan's, or even begin to appreciate that neither of them thought she was being anywhere near fanciful enough.

Chapter Twenty-five

They managed to hail a cab right away, but as Dan held the door and let Inger in first, he looked along the street and noticed a car with a couple of guys in it. He knew right away that they were company men, though he couldn't take a long enough look to see if he recognized them.

Inger had shuffled along the seat and he climbed in next to her, but sat at a slight angle, as if eager to talk to her. He only had a peripheral view as a result, but he could see the car pulling into the traffic behind them.

Before he could say anything, Inger said, "How old is Bill Brabham?"

It was obvious she'd been preoccupied with the thought since hearing about the location of the party.

"I think he's sixty now. So he would have been around forty-five or forty-six at the time, height of his powers, supremely confident." By way of clarification, he added, "I don't know the guy at all, but boy do I know the type, and yes, to answer your question, it's entirely feasible someone like that might assume a friendly young sculptor at a party was genuinely interested in him."

She took in what he was saying, sighed heavily and said, "We need proof."

He didn't respond directly, but said, "By the way, we're being followed, two of Brabham's guys."

"But . . ."

"My fault. We were careless. They knew we were in Limoges, probably had a good idea we'd be coming back into Montparnasse. With the resources this guy has available to him, we would have been easy enough to track."

"But they're only following us?"

"For now. Obviously, I don't have a very high opinion of Bill Brabham, but I guess he's still smart enough to know his superiors wouldn't appreciate his guys shooting me in a busy Paris street in the middle of the day, and they'd appreciate it even less if a member of the Swedish Security Service got hit in the crossfire."

"So I saved you again?"

He laughed and said, "You could say that. If I'm reading him right, his guys will keep track of us, but if he's still got some freelancers in reserve, he'll use them for the hit."

She seemed genuinely shocked by his relaxed tone and said, "Aren't you worried?"

"Not really. You know, I'm not James Bond. I let a guy sneak up on me this morning, I let Brabham track me from Sweden to Limoges to here. But I've been doing pretty risky stuff for a long time and I *am* still here. I'm not infallible, but nor are they."

She looked reassured, and leaned over and kissed him quickly, and said, "They can report that."

Yousef's studio was an old factory of some sort, dark soot-stained bricks on the outside, but light and white and modern inside. He wasn't alone in there either. There was a woman behind a desk fielding calls, a couple of young women and a guy working on frames and priming canvases.

Yousef was also in his mid-thirties, but he had a shock of white hair, his eyebrows alone showing how dark it had once been. He greeted them warmly and looked immediately fixated by Inger, a look that simultaneously pleased Dan and made him uncomfortable.

Yousef asked the woman behind the desk for some coffees and then showed them down to an area at the far end of the room where mismatched sofas and easy chairs formed a small lounge area. He pointed out the works in progress and explained things about the building as they walked, as if he was used to being visited by journalists.

"I'm glad you came," he said, as they all finally sat down. "It's been too long that I spoke to Sylvie, a year at least, but we'll have dinner next week."

Inger said, "She showed us your painting—it was really beautiful."

He seemed to thank her, though without words and hardly any facial movement, and said, "You're from Sweden?"

She nodded, on the edge of being uneasy under his gaze. If he'd always been like this, Dan could begin to understand why the police had talked to him. He had to hand it to him, though, he had taste, because Inger was ridiculously beautiful, a quality Dan couldn't even quite narrow down—he just felt good being with her, looking at her, and he could understand Yousef feeling the same way.

"Yousef, do you mind if we ask you a couple of things about Sabine?"

He turned to Dan and said, "Coffee." The woman had arrived and put the tray down, the next minute or two taken up with arranging the drinks. They settled again and Yousef picked up as if there'd been no pause, saying, "Of course not, but I know very little, certainly much less than the police thought I knew at the time."

Even after all these years, it clearly still rankled with him, and understandably so.

"You were in the studio with her that night?"

He smiled, to himself, as if the question had taken him back to some golden age in his youth, and said, "Those two weeks before, nearly every night, just Sabine and me, we were always the last to leave. We had so much to do, but it was fun because we both liked to be there together. Crazy. Maybe I wouldn't have remembered those two weeks if she'd lived, but now, I think about them so often."

Inger said, "Was there a relationship between you, or just friendship?"

"She was so beautiful, just like you, but a different kind of beauty."

Inger looked embarrassed or uncomfortable, but Yousef didn't seem to notice.

"Yes, beautiful, but it was never like that between us. I had a lot of girlfriends then, and I think Sabine was popular with the boys, but with each other, we were more like brother and sister. It was fun."

"Did she seem okay the night she died?"

"Hmm, maybe, maybe not. She was okay, but she had a couple of messages on her cell, and it made her mad. She didn't tell me what they were about. I guessed it was guy trouble. And I couldn't be sure—the police, they kept asking me again and again, 'this man you *claim* you saw', like I'm lying—no, I couldn't be sure, but when she left I thought I saw a man waiting for her along the street, and . . ." He stopped, this thought playing out across his face, and as if concluding some internal argument, he said, "It was dark, and I couldn't have known. How could I?"

"What did you see?"

"Who knows if I saw what I thought, or if I imagined it. The man was along the street, he stepped out and waited for her as she approached. And I thought she hesitated when she saw him, almost as if she might turn back. But she didn't and I went back to my work without thinking. I was perhaps the last person to see her alive." But then he corrected himself, forlorn as he said, "Second last."

Dan could see how that one tiny detail, the moment's hesitation he'd witnessed in Sabine's footsteps, so easily discounted at the time, would have preyed on his mind in the years since. What if he'd followed her out, called to her? What if?

"You didn't see him clearly," said Inger.

"A shadow, nothing more."

Pressing him, she said, "You mean a silhouette?"

"Yes, of course."

"But from a silhouette you can see, sometimes, how a man is dressed, how big he is, even how old sometimes."

"The police asked me this too." He laughed as if at some private joke. "I think he was older than us, only because . . . All I could see was that he wore a long coat, a heavy coat, like you wear over a suit, so he looked like a banker or finance worker or something like that. But it's guessing, no?"

"It's better than nothing," said Inger, which seemed to please him.

And when they stood to leave a short while later, he seemed oddly energized, and pointed at them, saying, "You're gonna get this guy, I know it."

Inger looked about to speak, but Dan replied first, and said, "We will, and he'll pay for it."

They left and walked a hundred yards or so before seeing a cab. That suited Dan anyway, because it gave him a chance to study the street. The same car was parked a little way up, but there was no one else, which suggested they were biding their time.

In the cab, Inger said, "Do you think we'll be safe in the hotel?"

"For now, and after the guy came for me in Limoges, he knows I'll be ready for that, so I think he'll try something else. Probably when I'm out on the street." He thought of Mike Naismith in Baltimore and said, "Probably need to take care crossing the road."

"And what time do you meet your contact this evening?"

It was the one meeting that had been set down for him, Patrick's DGSE contact dictating the time and the location.

"Nine. I have a few hours yet."

She didn't respond and he turned to find that she was staring at him intently, a look in her eyes that made it perfectly clear how she wanted to spend those few hours, a directness he found refreshing, and almost instantly arousing. He smiled in response, and willed the taxi to move faster, willed the traffic to clear, willed himself some place only with her.

Chapter Twenty-six

There was no time for talking afterwards, as much as he just wanted to lie there in bed with her, as much as he had a thousand questions and things he wanted to know about her. He was falling for her, ridiculously, because he doubted she was being so foolish—she probably saw him as an enjoyable fling, but hardly boyfriend material, and definitely nothing more than that. And he felt even more ridiculous for hoping he might be wrong.

He was dressed again and ready to leave when he glanced back at her, lying in the bed, the sight of her scrambling his thoughts. He walked back, kissed her again.

"How long will you be?"

He shrugged, shook his head, making clear he didn't know, but that the answer should have been obvious—he wanted to be back as quickly as possible. He kissed her again and left, down the service stairs, through the kitchen where no one seemed to pay any attention, out into a side street and quickly into the city.

The bar was in Rue Delambre in Montparnasse, a little too far to walk, but he walked all the same, cutting quickly along streets, keeping an eye all the time on the cars moving around him, on the people.

He was as certain as he could be that he'd reached the bar without being followed, but he didn't hesitate for long out on the street once he was there. It was a small place, a bar to one side with white-jacketed barmen, a couple of alcoves at the back, maybe a dozen customers in all, though it was still early. He'd never been there before.

Immediately, he saw a guy of about Patrick's age raise his hand from the back of the room. Dan nodded in response and walked towards him. He was rougher around the edges than Patrick White, his hair with a slightly wild salt-and-pepper look to it, a jacket but with an open shirt, the look of an aging film star. He also looked like he'd been able to handle himself when he was younger, and probably still could.

"Dan Hendricks?"

"Georges Florian?"

He smiled, shaking his hand, and said, "Please, join me." There was a bottle of red wine on the table, one glass already full. He filled a second glass as Dan sat down and they drank.

"Patrick speaks very highly of you," said Florian. He narrowed his eyes then, calculating, and said, "Did you take Habibi?"

It seemed everyone wanted to know if he'd taken Habibi.

Dan smiled and said, "He disappeared from Paris. I assumed your people had taken him."

"I knew it," said Florian, ignoring the tongue-in-cheek denial. He shook his head, pleased with himself, as if he'd just solved a long-standing mystery. Then he grew somber and said, "I know you were a friend of Benoit Claudel. I didn't know he was dead until Patrick told me."

"You knew him?"

"I met him a few times. We didn't serve together—he was quite a bit younger than me—but I had a drink with him once or twice. He was a good man."

Dan nodded. He'd been a good man who'd tried to settle down and move on, and that had probably made him an easier target and helped seal his fate.

"The man who killed him is dead." Florian looked grudgingly satisfied with that. "But I'm after the man who ordered his death."

"The same man who also wants you dead? Bill Brabham?" Dan nodded. "So, according to Patrick, you want to talk with me about Jack Redford, and the events of fourteen years ago."

"That's correct. What can you tell me, Georges?"

"Nothing at all. You and I never met." He smiled, took a long sip of his wine. "It seems there's a foreign bank with a building across the street from the entrance to the alley where Sabine Merel was killed. It has twenty-four-hour security, and it has cameras. On the night in question, the security guard on duty was a man named Gaston Bergeron. He saw nothing at the time, but early the next morning, just before his shift ended, the body was found. Normally, they reused the tapes unless there was something of note. Well, as I said, Gaston had seen nothing unusual, but because of the body being discovered, he put the night's tapes in the security locker and loaded new ones. He might never have checked them but, two days later, two people from the US Embassy came to the bank and asked for the security tapes from that night. They were told the tapes were reused and so there was nothing to see. Of course, Gaston became suspicious. Why would the Americans want the tapes? So that night he went through them and, we think, he saw the man walking with Sabine Merel into the alley where she died. He thought of going to the police, naturally, but the involvement of the Americans worried him. He knew his nephew's father-in-law, Jean Sainval, was in quite a powerful position at the DGSE, so he mailed the tape to him."

"That name's familiar, Jean Sainval. Maybe from when I was starting out."

"Of course, you were in SIS for a time. Yes, you probably heard about his death, but we jump ahead. Sainval watched the tape and put a call through to a friend at the Interior Ministry, who agreed to come over the following day. But it seems someone was listening. Sainval was killed in a traffic accident that night."

"And the tape?"

Florian gave him a roguish smile and said, "So this is the crux! Did the great Jack Redford infiltrate La piscine and steal the tape, with just one day's notice?" He nodded, impressed even by the memory of it. "The tape disappeared, and it took several days before we were positive that Redford had been in the building. But the body in the Seine—that was nothing to do with us."

"It wasn't Redford anyway."

"We know that now. We didn't for fourteen years."

"So whether or not he saw the tape himself, he knew what was on it, and knew that Brabham would come after him for that knowledge."

"Or maybe he handed it over and they tried to kill him. Who knows why he ran? Maybe he just felt it was time, that he'd . . . ridden his luck too long."

"The security guard, Gaston . . .?"

"Bergeron. Gaston Bergeron."

"Did any of your colleagues speak to him?"

"I think so, but he couldn't tell anything, or didn't want to—he knew Jean Sainval was dead, and had his suspicions about how."

Dan drank and Florian topped up both glasses.

"So, we can have all the suspicions we like about who killed Sabine Merel and why Jack Redford went on the run, but there's no proof, no witness . . ."

"Apart from Gaston Bergeron."

"Who didn't know anything."

"Who didn't *say* anything. I don't know even if he's still alive—he would be quite old by now, but sometimes old men talk more than young ones."

"Do you know how I could get in touch with him, if he is still alive?"

"Let me see." He got up, taking his phone out as he walked over and leaned on the far end of the bar.

He spoke briefly into the phone and then put it on the bar and chatted amiably with the two barmen, laughing and joking about something. Maybe he was a regular here or just the kind of raffish charmer who could drop into any drinking hole around the world and make new friends.

Even from there, Dan saw the phone light up a few minutes later. Florian answered, then gestured to the barman who hastily furnished him with a pen and a piece of paper.

When Florian came back he was smiling, and as he handed over the piece of paper, he said, "Still alive. He retired back to the village he came from, in Burgundy, not far from Auxerre."

"Thanks, I'll head out there tomorrow."

"And if he can't help, or won't?"

Dan thought it through quickly, realizing they were running out of leads, but knowing he could only count on one outcome.

"As long as Brabham's still in circulation I've got the dot on me. If I can help Patrick to rein him in, great, if not . . . I won't go down easy."

"I like your style. But the reason I ask is, it might also be an idea to speak to Eliot Carter, if you haven't already."

"Eliot Carter? I've never heard of him. Who is he?"

Florian responded with a look of mixed disappointment and superiority, and said, "An American, living here in Paris, in Le Marais. He was CIA a long time ago, but his special skill was forgeries, documents, passports. He did a lot of work for Redford, but they were good friends too."

Dan checked his watch, conscious that his own time had a limit set to it, and said, "You think I could see him now, tonight?"

Florian smiled, took his phone out and put in a call. He kept his seat this time, which made Dan wonder why he'd wanted to shield the other call from him. A brief exchange followed and he ended the call.

"He's expecting you."

"Good, thanks. What the address?"

"It's on the back of the piece of paper I gave to you. Almost like the old days, no?" He looked lost in thought for a moment, the appearance of someone remembering his own past, then seemed to come back to himself, and said, "Is Habibi dead or hidden away in Guantanamo?"

"He's dead. His heart gave out under interrogation. Romania."

Florian shrugged and said, "Just curious. He wasn't a French citizen. It's only that he was in Paris when he disappeared."

"A lot of people seem to disappear in Paris."

"That's true. And, Dan, if this doesn't work out, you should make yourself one of them."

He knew Florian was right, and he'd spent his whole life disappearing, but it felt desperate now, as if the stakes were much higher. And it wasn't even the fantasy of there being a possible relationship with Inger to consider—if anything, it was because he knew it *was* a fantasy that he now so urgently wanted to change his life.

Chapter Twenty-seven

He jumped in a cab not far from the bar and traveled the short distance to Eliot Carter's apartment, conscious of having left Inger alone too long already, not knowing how safe she would be. He was buzzed up but had to ring the bell when he got to the third floor. He could hear some sort of North African music playing inside.

The door was opened by a young and skinny Arabic guy in a tight T-shirt that looked three sizes too small, and low-slung white jeans, a stretch of midriff visible between the two. His features looked incredibly delicate and feminine, and then Dan realized it was because they'd been subtly highlighted with makeup and eyeliner.

At first he thought he'd got the wrong apartment, but after looking him up and down the young guy smiled and said, "Are you Eliot's friend?"

Dan guessed the answer was yes so he nodded and was shown in. Eliot was lounging in a Moroccan-themed sitting room, as if modeling his expat existence on the life of Paul Bowles, and when he spoke he had the same slightly arch, over-fussy American accent.

"How do you do, Mr. Hendricks? Do excuse me not getting up. Georges tells me you want to talk about Jack."

"I do. I won't keep you very long." Carter looked ready to dismiss the suggestion, but Dan added quickly, "I'm afraid the same people who were after Jack all those years ago are after me now."

Carter responded to the seriousness of that statement by sitting up and plumping the cushions behind him. He looked to the door but the young guy had left them alone.

"Not even time for a drink?"

"I'm sorry, I don't."

He produced a tired little laugh and said, "Jack was always the same, rushing off here or there, but, oh, he was such a decent man. A terrible shame the way it happened." Dan's heart sank as he took on board that Carter didn't know about the most recent developments, that he probably still assumed Redford had died years before. "You want to know about the last job, of course."

"Yes, did he tell you about it?"

"In passing. He needed some paper and needed it quickly." With a flourish, he said, "I obliged, of course."

"Did he tell you what the job was?"

"Well, naturally, given what he was asking of me, I knew it was DGSE headquarters—La piscine, they call it. I remember complimenting him on how audacious it was. But that's about all I can tell, other than what I knew of him . . . what I mean is, what I knew of him instinctively. You see, he wasn't quite himself, if I might put it like that. He was preoccupied."

"Worried about the job?"

"Possibly. I believe he never had any fear in his life, but I suppose it's conceivable he knew something wasn't quite right about the job. Of course, it's also entirely feasible that this is just me using hindsight to create a completely false impression. As I said, jobs never troubled him like that, and there *were* other things."

Dan waited for him to continue, but Carter simply stared at him, eyebrows raised, inviting Dan to play his part.

Dan obliged, saying, "What do you mean by that, what other things?"

"He'd had a letter a little while before, someone he knew from Beirut—the previous year he'd spent six months there, relaxing, having fun. Whether the letter was a billet-doux or something else entirely, he wouldn't say, but he did tell me he'd received it and that it was weighing on his mind in some way. You see, what I'm saying, Mr. Hendricks, is that the air of preoccupation might have been nothing to do with the job, it might have been the letter. Nobody sends letters anymore, do they? Such a shame."

"You said he didn't discuss its contents, but thinking back to Beirut, do you have any idea what it might have been?"

"I wasn't in Beirut. Hassan!" He looked towards the door, and when the young guy appeared he smiled and said, "Would you bring my Rolodex and some paper and a pen? Thank you." He turned back to Dan and said, "I'll give you the address and number of Tom Crossley in Geneva. He was in Beirut, but they were old friends, in some army unit together. He may well have some idea."

"Thanks. I have some other stuff to deal with first, but I'll give him a visit."

Carter looked thrilled and said, "And I do hope you'll visit us again, for longer next time. Are you in Paris often?"

"Not as often as I'd like, but I'll keep you to that invite."

As for Tom Crossley, and finding out what had happened in Beirut, Dan knew it was hardly relevant. Finding out the secrets of Jacques Fillon had been geared to two specific ends, helping Patrick to rein in Brabham and, at the same time, getting Brabham off Dan's back. The final pieces of the mystery would hardly make any difference to either of those.

Yet he wanted to know. He wanted to know exactly what had been on that tape, not just for his own security, but for the knowledge of it, for Sabine Merel, for her friends and family. And he wanted to know exactly why Jack Redford had run and become Jacques Fillon.

He'd visit this guy Tom Crossley once this was all done, if he was still in the position to visit anyone, because Redford's story mattered to him now. It mattered most of all, perhaps, because it could so easily have been Dan's story, and in some ways might still become it yet.

Chapter Twenty-eight

He had the cab drop him a few blocks from the Vergoncey and approached with a mixture of casual pace and complete vigilance, wanting to know exactly how much sand had slipped through the glass in the time he'd been away.

He saw the same two company men in their parked car, about a hundred yards this side of the hotel. But he noticed someone in a leather jacket squatting down and talking to them on the passenger side. He wasn't CIA, and if they'd brought in the freelancers that could mean they were planning to take Dan down tonight.

He turned and went back the other way, so that he came to the hotel along the side street where there was a small, rarely used entrance that was locked after a certain time at night. And just as he turned into the doorway, he noticed another guy standing up on the corner ahead, but looking in the other direction. He was casually dressed, but wrong somehow, wrong for that street, in the way he was standing, in everything about him.

It suggested they were escalating the situation, putting all their available assets in place, and that meant Dan and Inger had to move out of here now. With that thought, he picked up his speed and turned before reaching the main lobby, climbing the stairs rather than waiting for an elevator.

The corridor on their floor was empty, a deceptive calm, but he stopped for a moment between their rooms, listening, taking in the quality of the stillness. He knocked on her door then. There was no reply, but there was no movement, either. He checked his watch and knocked louder, thinking she might be asleep or in the bath.

He checked his watch again, took out his gun, and attached the silencer, an emptiness creeping into his stomach. He was tempted to knock one more time, but he knew there would be no answer now and didn't want to think through the possible reasons for that silence.

Instead, he opened his own door, his gun at the ready, though the room was apparently empty, even emptier than he'd left it. He hadn't got around to unpacking his case and had simply left it near the door, but it had gone now.

He stepped inside, covering the angles, checking the bathroom, even the closet, and all the time he was trying to imagine a benign scenario that might explain the disappearance of both Inger and his case.

It was only once he was satisfied the room was empty that he spotted the sheet of notepaper left on the desk. He walked over and glanced down at it without picking it up, a couple of lines scrawled across the page.

Get out of the hotel! Switch on your phone!!

She hadn't signed it, but despite the alarm of the message he couldn't help but smile, relieved—she'd left of her own accord. He could even allow himself some bemusement now, that she was actually a step ahead of him.

He walked over to the window as he switched on his phone. The two guys were out of the car and a couple more were standing talking to them. The guy who'd been crouching down near the car earlier had gone, so by Dan's reckoning, that meant there were at least six here.

The phone buzzed in his hand and he looked down at the screen—three missed calls from Inger. He returned one of them and held the phone to his ear.

She answered instantly, saying, "Where are you?"

The men standing down by the car had a businesslike air about them, he thought, as if they were gearing up for something rather than just idling or awaiting orders.

"You left a note," he said.

"Dan, you have to leave. I'll tell you more later, but you have to move now."

Her voice was calm, but there was an urgency about it that set him on edge.

"Okay, I'll call back."

"No, wait! Do you have a pen?"

"Sure." He walked over to the desk, grabbed the notebook and pencil and scribbled down the number she reeled off to him. "Thanks. I'll call you soon."

"Dan . . ."

She hesitated, perhaps torn between what she wanted to say and her need to keep a professional veneer.

"Twenty minutes, max. I'll call you back."

He ended the call and turned off the phone as he walked back to the window, then searched the street below, his heart kicking up a gear as he realized they'd gone—the car was still there, but the guys who'd been standing there a minute before had moved on.

He acted quickly now, slipping out of the room, walking fast along the corridor and down the stairs. He hadn't gone far, though, when he heard an American accent heading in the opposite direction, talking quietly, but clearly audible in the thick-carpeted hush.

"Just heading onto second. Hold position . . ."

Dan backtracked, skipping back up the stairs and along the corridor, in through the door to the service stairs. He hurtled down them, taking each short flight in a couple of steps, and paused only briefly at the bottom to catch his breath, to listen to the hotel around him.

Six—there were at least six of them, a few to cover the exits, a few to trawl the hotel. On the other hand, it was a big place, so maybe that would work against them, stretching them thin.

He stepped out through the door and turned into the corridor that led to the side entrance. But he'd only covered half the distance when he noticed there was a car parked there now, and even as he was wondering if it was one of theirs, a guy strolled into view, chatting on the phone, perhaps the guy who'd been standing on the corner a little earlier.

Dan turned on his heel, heading back the other way, knowing he couldn't follow this corridor all the way to the main lobby. Yes, it was a big hotel and there were plenty of places to hide, but he was already getting hemmed in and he cursed himself now, for being sloppy, for spending too much time talking with Florian and Carter.

He dropped into another service corridor and headed for the clatter of the kitchens. It was busy in there, busy enough that he had to dodge a few bodies on the way through. A couple of the chefs and other staff threw glances in his direction, noting his presence without seeming inclined to challenge it.

He pushed out through the double doors on the other side, out into the narrow alley at the back of the hotel, lined with food bins and discarded produce boxes. He turned towards the street but instantly saw someone up ahead.

Dan recognized him right away; the guy in the leather jacket who'd been crouching down talking to the guys in the car. He walked directly towards him and the guy stood still and looked at

Dan, as if waiting for him to come into the light, a look of general hostility in his eyes.

The guy seemed to realize who he was then, a moment of adrenalin and panic, a lunge towards his gun. Dan shot him in the face and picked up his pace, walking swiftly out onto the street and away.

He kept walking for a couple of hundred yards, then found a payphone and called the number she'd given him. It was only as he stood there that he realized he was out of breath, his heart kicking along at a canter.

When she answered, he said, "It's me."

"You're out of the hotel?"

"I'm out of the hotel."

He thought he heard a faint sigh of relief and couldn't help but smile gratefully in response.

"Come to Hotel Bernet, Room 422."

"Okay, I'll see you soon." He was about to hang up when his thoughts began to catch up with everything that had just happened, the missing suitcase, Inger's disappearance, her warning. "Are you alone there?"

"No, I'm with a colleague." She paused and added, "He's fine. He's probably the reason we're still alive."

Dan ended the call and looked back along the street, thinking through his exit from the Vergoncey, wondering how much of an edge Inger's unseen colleague had given him. He knew it wouldn't stop now, either, that the threat would remain at this pitch from here on in. Dan's only real hope was to get to Brabham before his men finished the job.

Chapter Twenty-nine

The Hotel Bernet was a couple of blocks off the Champs-Élysées, nice but anonymous, in a busy street. He walked straight through the lobby and up to the room he'd been given. He stopped and listened then, the sound of Inger and a man talking in Swedish, the tone and volume of a normal conversation.

He knocked and the talking stopped abruptly and he could hear some hurried movement before Inger came and opened the door.

She said something even as she opened it and stepped aside, and Dan saw the guy behind her putting away his gun in response. Dan looked at Inger, smiling, and she gave a relieved laugh back before closing the door.

He looked at the guy now, mousy hair, a close-cut beard, youthful and sporty-looking.

Inger said, "Dan, this is Ville. Dan Hendricks."

They shook hands, and Ville said, "Good to meet you."

"Likewise." He noticed his suitcase standing near the bed. "So what's happening?"

Ville looked at Inger, uncertain, and she nodded and said, "Confusion is what's happening. Our people heard that Brabham has made you his priority target and they were coming for you tonight. The order was to pull me out of there."

She smiled at Ville and he smiled too, and said, "Inger and I go back a long way, so I know she gets what she wants. This is the confusion she talks about. It seems you and her moved on before I could get there. It's the only way for Inger to stay part of this."

Dan nodded and said, "I have to move tomorrow anyway, out of Paris. I've got a lead." He was distracted even as he spoke, looking at Inger. "Maybe it's better if you do take a . . ."

She shook her head, a barely perceptible movement, but letting him know that she was part of this, that she would remain part of it, no matter what Brabham was planning.

In the pause that followed, Ville said, "You got out with no problem?"

Dan looked at him and said, "They were moving in. Another five minutes and I might have been in trouble. But no, I got out okay, thanks. Killed one guy in the alley behind the hotel, not CIA, a freelancer."

"Oh, sure. I see." Ville looked shocked, perhaps by the fact that Dan's version of a trouble-free exit including killing someone. "Well, anyway, you should be okay for a while."

Dan looked at the room, but Inger said, "Not here. I've booked us into a business hotel. It's better that way, so Ville doesn't know where we are. We go there now."

Dan shook Ville's hand again and said, "I appreciate everything you've done for us. I don't suppose your channels picked up anything else that might be useful, anything on Brabham?"

Ville smiled, saying, "I hate to break the bad news, but I think you're already becoming the number-one expert on Bill Brabham."

Dan nodded, taking it as a joke, hoping it was a joke, and hoping even more that Bergeron would give him something decent the next day.

They left Ville in the room and traveled a little way out to the business hotel she'd booked. In the car they hardly spoke but she held his hand the whole time and seemed to express more in the clutch of her fingers around his than if they'd talked.

When they did talk, it wasn't about Brabham, and it wasn't until they were lying in bed together, much later, that she said, "Where do we go tomorrow? You said you had a lead?"

He almost didn't want to think about the next day, or that day as it now was, not many hours ahead of them. How long, he wondered, would they be able to just hole up here and keep the world at bay? The simple answer was never long enough.

"There was a security tape from a bank, which by chance covered the entrance to the alley where Sabine was killed. The security guard was related to someone at DGSE headquarters, so he sent the tape to him—"

"So it's true! Jack Redford got into the DGSE?"

"Not only that. The guy who received the tape had set up a meeting with a colleague from the Interior Ministry the next day, but the guy died in a car wreck that night."

"And Redford disappeared. But without the tape?"

"I'm guessing so. What we saw in the shelter suggests Redford was trying to reconstruct the case after the fact. With the tape he wouldn't have needed to do that."

She nodded impatiently, as if annoyed with herself for not seeing that, and said, "So, presumably, he handed over the tape, maybe they tried to kill him or he got nervous, and he ran."

Dan nodded, thinking back over what he'd heard the night before, and said, "Someone I spoke to said he'd received a letter from an old friend in Beirut, that it had unsettled him, so maybe that played a part in him disappearing. There's someone else I can see about that, but it's hardly the main issue right now." He waited a beat, and said, "The tape may be gone, but as far as we know, there is someone still alive who saw it—the security guard. He lives near Auxerre, about an hour and a half's drive from Paris. That's where we're headed tomorrow."

"But why is he still alive?"

Dan shrugged and said, "Who knows? Maybe Brabham got complacent, maybe he reasoned a dead security guard would arouse more suspicion than a security guard who might make claims but wouldn't be able to back them up. Maybe the guard is crazy. Maybe Brabham saw the tape and realized it proved nothing. Whatever it is, we'll find out tomorrow."

"Auxerre," she said, as if just for the pleasure of saying the word.

"Near Auxerre," he said, correcting her.

"We'll need a car."

"I have a car, here in Paris. They might not even know about it, but even if they do, we'll probably be just as under the radar in my car as we would with a rental."

She looked at him as if he'd said something extraordinary.

"You have a car, here in Paris?" He nodded. "What kind?"

"It's a Mercedes. An SUV. I haven't driven it in ages—be nice to get behind the wheel again." She looked at him, a lightly mocking smile on her lips. "What?"

"It's something I've thought several times, that you're quite a lot like Jack Redford. And now I find out you also have an SUV that you hardly ever drive. Another similarity."

"Yeah? Maybe I should go the whole hog and move to Sweden." Already, this soon, it was only half a joke, and he studied her face carefully to gauge her expression—she was trying to play equally cool, but he couldn't help but think he detected a certain interest, even happiness in her eyes. "I could rent a place to begin with, not up in the north like Jack, but maybe some nice neighborhood in Stockholm. What's your neighborhood like?"

Looking like someone determined not to be teased, she was offhand as she said, "You know it. We met for coffee there."

So he was right, the café had been near where she lived, and he thought back to it now, imagined being in that neighborhood, getting to know her properly, seeing if there really could be anything more than this between them.

"It was a nice area, what I remember. So maybe I could just sell the place I've got here, buy something outright there."

She was dismissive as she said, "Perhaps you're used to gullible women, but I'm not one of them."

And he wanted to tell her, that as ridiculous as this sounded, he was firing up with adrenalin and possibility at the thought of it.

Instead, he said, "Unless I get Brabham off my back I wouldn't want to be within a thousand miles of you."

"And if you did?"

He kissed her, and said, "I'm not stupid or crazy. I know we've only been together a few days, and even then, in pretty wild circumstances." He paused, smiled. "That's why I'd rent a place of my own, to see how it would be. To live like people do. And I wouldn't if you didn't want me to. But right now, I couldn't think of anything I'd rather do than move to Stockholm."

She nodded and said quietly, "I would like that."

"Really?"

She could see how genuine the doubt and surprise in his voice was, and she laughed and rolled on top of him, holding his face with both hands as she said, "Yes, really."

And that was how easy it would be, he thought, how easy it would be to find a life with someone like her, someone to be with, to be part of. It was how easy it would be, if Brabham was removed from the picture. That was where the dream fell into shadow at the edges—Brabham, and there'd be no guaranteed future of any kind for Dan until that shadow was dealt with.

Chapter Thirty

They took a cab the next morning, but once again cautious, they had it drop them a block short of the underground garage where he kept his car to make sure there was no one keeping the place under surveillance. It looked clear, and despite the sense of being slowly encircled, Dan knew that for Brabham it would feel the opposite, that his prey was almost impossible to pin down.

They headed down and Dan picked up the spare keys from the office. He took a torch from the glove compartment and looked under the car, then stood again once he was satisfied.

"Looking for a tracker?"

"Or a bomb," he said, and she laughed a little, unsure whether he was joking or not—he wasn't.

For the first half hour he checked his mirrors constantly, but as they moved haltingly out of Paris, and then with more speed into the French countryside, he relaxed a little. They weren't being followed. That didn't mean they still weren't being tracked, but it was something.

The days were falling away towards winter, but with the sun shining on it the country looked as if it was basking in one last summer flush, still ripe and full green. A couple of times as they drove, Inger made a comment about it being beautiful, about the view or the sunlight.

She did the same when they were on the back roads and a village came into view on a small rise in front of them, speaking in Swedish before saying, "Such a pretty village."

"I guess that's why Gaston Bergeron moved back there."

"That's it?"

"That's it."

But Bergeron's place was even more idyllic, an old millhouse sitting on its own in the middle of the woods, the stream that ran past it lit up by the sun falling through the trees.

As they got out of the car, Inger breathed in deeply, closing her eyes briefly before saying, "Isn't this the most beautiful place you've ever seen?"

"It's beautiful, no doubting that, but what is it with everyone hiding out in the woods?"

She smiled, but before she could say anything, a door opened with a bang and a spaniel came sprinting over to them, sniffing around them as if searching for drugs.

Someone called out in French, "What do you want?"

The question wasn't friendly, and when Dan looked toward the door of the house he saw a surprisingly fit-looking guy casually leveling a shotgun at them. Bergeron had retired, and Dan guessed he was around seventy, but he was tall and broad-shouldered, a thickness around the waist, but no real paunch.

They stayed by the car, and Dan called out, "Monsieur Bergeron, I'm Dan Hendricks and this is Inger Bengtsson. We're here to ask you about Sabine Merel, the girl who was murdered in Paris fourteen—"

"You don't have to tell me who she is. Who sent you?"

This could prove tougher than he'd anticipated, but he said, "No one sent us. I spoke to someone last night, someone from the DGSE. He knew Jean Sainval, and he gave us your address."

"Jean Sainval is dead. I don't talk to anyone."

He looked ready to turn away, but Inger stepped out from the partial cover of the car door now and said, "Monsieur Bergeron, do you speak English?"

He nodded as he looked at her, though he didn't seem swayed as he said, "Where are you from, Sweden?"

"Yes, I am," she said, her voice full of warmth, as if impressed that he'd got it in one. She walked closer as the dog trotted back to its owner. "Monsieur Bergeron, the man who stole the tape from the DGSE had to hide afterwards because the Americans wanted to kill him. He went to Sweden, and for fourteen years he tried to prove what he'd seen on that tape. He died without finding it. My friend here is also trying to prove it, and the same Americans want to kill him. The same Americans who killed Jean Sainval. We want to stop them, Monsieur Bergeron, but we also want justice for Sabine Merel. We were with her parents two days ago, and we promised them we would do everything we could. In two weeks Sabine would have been thirty-three."

He nodded, thinking about that for a moment before he said, "Did they have other children?"

"Yes, they did."

"Still . . ." He scratched the top of the dog's head before looking back up at Inger as he said, "You should come inside." He turned and walked into the house. Inger and Dan glanced at each other, and as he closed the doors on the car, she walked on ahead.

For some reason, Dan had imagined Bergeron living on his own out here, but as he stepped into the house it seemed tidier and decorated with more care than he associated with an elderly man living in isolation.

But as Dan joined them in the kitchen, Bergeron said, "I'm sorry, I can give you coffee, but that's all. My wife is visiting our daughter in Toronto."

"Coffee is fine, thank you."

He gestured for them to sit down at the heavy table and then talked to them as he got the coffee, saying, "I've thought about it many times, of course, but they left me alone, and it was easier that way. My own daughter wasn't much older than Sabine Merel. She lives in Canada now, as I said. Our son lives in the village here. If you have children of your own, you always think, what if it had been them. So yes, I thought of it often, and I felt bad many times for never doing more, but I had my own family to worry about too."

He brought the coffee over to the table and as he sat, Dan said, "Why did you go to Jean Sainval instead of the police?"

"Actually, it was luck. I kept the tapes for that night because I was still on duty when the police arrived across the street, but I didn't look at them, I just put them in the locker in case the police asked to see them. The next day I was unwell, but when I returned the day after that, I heard that two Americans had been, and that made me suspicious. I looked at the tapes that night, saw clearly the man with Sabine Merel, and I . . . I added everything together. He was from the American Embassy, he had to be, that was why they wanted the tapes. So I thought it was safer to send to Jean. It turned out safer for me, not for him."

"The police spoke to you afterwards?"

He laughed at the understatement, saying, "Not just the police, everyone, with the Americans there sometimes. I always told them the same thing, almost what I just told you, but I told them as soon as I heard the Americans had asked for the tape I didn't even look because I knew it had to be dangerous—I just sent it to Jean."

Inger said, "And they believed you?"

Bergeron shrugged, as if his continuing presence in the world was proof in itself, then said, "I haven't talked about it since. A journalist came once, ten years after the murder, and I told him to get off my land or I would shoot him."

Dan smiled, not doubting it for a minute, picturing the journalist jumping back into his car, but then he said, "Why didn't you do the same to us?"

"I nearly did," he said with a laugh that was as much in his eyes as on his mouth, a mischievous quality about him. He looked more contemplative then and said, "Luck again, your luck this time. I've thought about her many times over the years, and wondered if I had done the wrong thing, for the right reasons perhaps, but still wrong. And maybe because my wife is away, a man gets to think, and this last week I've been thinking very much about Sabine Merel. I never met her, saw only that little film and the pictures in the press, but I can't help thinking . . . I am responsible."

"There was nothing you could have done."

"To save her, no. But to find justice, for her, for her family, that was the responsibility given to me, placed into my hands, the thing I've been thinking about so much this week. Then you turn up here. It's like fate."

To Dan's surprise, Inger said, "Monsieur Bergeron, I told you people have tried to kill Dan, and they're still chasing us. If you think talking to us will put you in any danger at all, we should leave right now."

Bergeron smiled warmly at her, but said, "What is it that you want to know?"

"We want to know what you saw on that tape, but again . . ."

He put his hand up to stop her and said, "I don't want to talk to you about what I saw. How would it help you, anyway? To this day, I don't know who the man was, and now I'm old and . . . No, I don't want to tell you about it, but the time has come." He stood up. "What I would like is to *show you* the tape."

Dan stood immediately and said, "You made a copy?" It should have been one of the first questions, and maybe he'd been asked it at the time, but he seemed so straightforward, so guileless, that Dan could understand why the police and everyone else had believed him and left him alone all these years.

Inger stood as well, as Bergeron said, "I never even told my wife. How could I?" And Dan understood that too—how could he ever tell his wife that he had a tape in his possession that could easily get them both killed?

Chapter Thirty-one

He took them up one flight of stairs, along a landing and then up another flight, to a room on the top floor that had been turned into an office or study. It seemed to be littered with all kinds of household accounts, but also a computer and shelves laden with books, a lot of them on country pursuits, but a fair number on genealogy too. This was clearly Bergeron's den.

He turned the computer on, then reached up without looking and pulled a couple of books from a shelf. He reached blindly into the space and pulled out a disk before putting the books back.

"It was a video cassette, but I converted it, not so difficult as you would think." He handed the disk to Inger and said, "It's yours now."

"You have another copy?"

"On here," he said, pointing at the computer which had already booted up. "And a copy of the disk with my . . . with my lawyer, in a box." He sat down in front of the computer, and went through a few folders before clicking on a file. As soon as it opened though, he paused it, and said, "There is another file with three hours of the camera, but this just shows thirty minutes. It's the key."

They nodded and he pressed Play again and tilted the screen upwards so that both of them could see it without crouching down.

There was no sound, and it was a static view, covering the entrance to the bank, but also obliquely, a portion of the other side of the street, including what Dan imagined was the entrance to the alley. For a full minute the shot was completely empty, the timer in the corner steadily clicking away. They kept their eyes fixed on the screen, even Bergeron who knew what was coming, and then two people emerged across the street, moving with an urgent disunity from left to right across the frame.

The woman was Sabine Merel, immediately familiar as she turned to face the man, and unwittingly the camera, and appeared to shout something. He heard Inger catch her breath at the sight of that face, and imagined her immediately remembering the photographs she'd looked at with Sabine's mother.

Sabine walked on then, as if the shouted comment had settled it, picking up her pace and moving ahead of the man, moving towards the entrance to the alley. She was certainly angry, perhaps afraid, but Dan doubted she could have had any idea that she was walking with such determination towards her own death.

She was almost at the alley entrance, a few seconds from being past it, when the man picked up his pace and ran to catch up with her. She turned, that same confused mix of anger and fear, one supplanting the other as he grabbed her arm and the two of them disappeared into the dark mouth of the alley.

There was only one problem, and as they looked at the picture, once more motionless and empty, Dan said, "We didn't see his face."

"Patience," said Bergeron, and used the mouse to move along the bar. "This is nearly twenty minutes later."

He pressed Play again. For a moment, there was nothing, then a slight shift in the density of the shadows and the man emerged back into view and walked quickly out of the alley and out of shot. They'd hardly registered him, but Bergeron paused it again, wound it back and pressed Play, and this time as the man emerged, he froze the image so that the gaunt face was there, clearly visible even from the other side of the street.

Inger said, "But . . ." And offered nothing more.

"Oh my God," said Dan. He wasn't sure if Inger had worked it out for herself, and the shock of it was still scrambling his own thoughts. "It's not Brabham, it's his son, Harry. Jesus!"

Bergeron span his chair around to look at Dan and said, "You know him?"

Dan shook his head, remembering now that Charlie had known him a little, that he'd talked about him being a decent kid. And this was why Redford had focused on the whole family, because Brabham was the danger, but it was his son who'd committed the murder.

"I don't know him, but his name is Harry Brabham, and he's now a United States congressman."

Bergeron looked to Inger, as if wanting confirmation, and she nodded, but Dan could see she was lost in her own thoughts. This was a much bigger story than they'd ever imagined, but as if the knowledge of it hadn't been dangerous enough, the existence of this recording made it even more so.

"What will you do?"

Dan didn't respond directly, but he knew they needed safeguards now, that one disk wasn't enough, and he said, "Would you be able to email that file to me?" Bergeron shrugged. Dan leaned over and wrote down the email address on a piece of paper sitting on the desk.

Bergeron turned back and spent a minute sending the email and for the whole time it took him, Inger and Dan simply watched him in silence, both of them still too shocked to think much beyond the present moment.

Bergeron said, "It's done."

Dan looked at the screen, checking the details, and said, "Thanks. And now, Monsieur Bergeron, I think it's important that we leave you alone."

He stood up and said, "It changes things, this tape?"

"It changes a lot of things. They don't know we have it, they don't know you have it, but it's still not good for us to stay here too long." He pointed at the screen, even though the image was no longer there. "That man's father is a very powerful person in the CIA, and he wants me dead. They're looking for me now, so the sooner we get away from here the better it is for all of us."

Inger held up the disk too, saying, "And the sooner we get this to the right person the sooner Dan can walk a little safer."

Bergeron smiled at her, and said, "Then I wish you good luck. And I'm happy. For fourteen years I was afraid to do the right thing, but now it's done."

Dan nodded, understanding why he'd concealed it all that time, an instinctive sense of needing to protect his family. That was undoubtedly what had driven Bill Brabham too, and he almost respected him for that, but the way he'd gone about it probably went some way toward explaining the actions of the son—it was what Jack Redford had been trying to prove all this time; that the Brabhams were a family who believed themselves untouchable.

Chapter Thirty-two

They drove away in silence and they were passing back through the village before Inger said, "How dangerous is this?"

"They don't know we have it." He shook his head in amazement, and said, "Jesus, thanks to Bergeron, no one even knows it exists. But I think it tells us why Brabham's coming after me the way he is, and why he sent someone after Patrick White. This means a hell of a lot more to him than shutting down former CIA contractors."

"So we have to get this disk to Patrick. It's the only way."

Dan nodded, and said, "I haven't spoken to him in days. Do you know where he is?"

She held up her hand, her fingers crossed, and said, "He was in London, but he told me he was coming to Paris, I think either today or tomorrow."

"Good."

He'd taken a left and only realized after a few hundred yards that he'd made the wrong turning. They were on a long narrow lane, overgrown woods forming a hedge on one side, open flat fields stretching out on the other to more woods and another village in the distance. He was just thinking about turning when he noticed a motorbike appear in his rearview, a trails bike with the rider sitting high in the saddle.

He kept driving now, but said, "Could be nothing, but we might have someone following us. Guy on a motorbike."

"But how?"

Dan shook his head, trying to think. He looked in the rearview again—he was certain of it, some quality about the guy that suggested he didn't just happen to be on the same road as them. Then he thought of the car itself, knowing that he hadn't been as thorough as he should have been.

"There must be a tracker on the car."

She threw a quick glance over her shoulder and said, "If there's one guy, there'll be more, surely?"

"I guess so." The guy was gaining on them now, and fast. Within seconds he was close up behind them, looming in the rearview, reaching into his jacket. "Brace yourself."

Dan hit the brakes hard as the guy pulled the gun clear, the rider's concentration just a shade enough off for it to catch him unprepared.

Bike and rider hit the back of the SUV with a multiple thump and clatter as if they'd been caught in a rockslide. The back window cracked but held. Dan drove forward, saw the guy on the floor behind them then, with the bike further back. He reversed fast until they hit the guy again, the bump throwing them out of their seats a little, then a gentler, somehow queasier bump as he once more drove forward and stopped.

Inger said something under her breath in Swedish. He looked at her, but then back in the mirror. The guy was lying motionless, but a black car had appeared in the distance behind them.

As if sensing it, Inger turned and said, "CIA?"

"I'm not sure it matters now, especially out here." He could hear another motorbike somewhere, then saw it approaching from the distant village to the far right. The lane they were on curved around to the right up ahead, but he could also see a turning into the woods.

He drove on until they reached the turn. The road through the woods was straight for as far as they could see, and he was pretty certain there was another car, just visible, at the very far end of it.

He turned to the left, into the woods, and Inger looked behind again and said, "Don't you think this is what they want? They have us surrounded."

He didn't answer, but said, "There's a rucksack in the back. Put everything you need in it, including the disk. Then open my bag—you'll find another rucksack inside—it's already got everything I need."

The final comment seemed to throw her, perhaps leaving her wondering if he lived constantly in readiness for flight, but she put the question on hold and clambered into the back seat. He carried on slowly along the track. The car ahead was approaching but at a crawl, and both the car and the bike had appeared in the sunlit opening from the woods behind them. Five guys in total, by his reckoning.

"Okay, I'm done."

She was about to climb back into the front when he said, "No, don't bother." He stopped the car now, turned off the engine. "I loved this car."

He turned to face her, and she said, "So this is your plan, to make a run through the woods? To where?"

"My plan is to get into the woods, kill five guys if I can, then make a run for it."

"If we kill all five we could come back for the car."

"The tracking device isn't on us, so it must be in the car, and we haven't got time to find it. We'll make our way into Auxerre somehow, take the train back up to Paris."

She thought about it for a second, then said, "Okay, it's a plan. I still don't know that it's a good plan. But let's do it."

In the rearview he could see that the two guys had got out of the car behind them, and even from here he could see one had a rifle, so he said, "We'll head for the right, along that path. Let's go."

Inger jumped out of the door on the right-hand side, Dan out of the driver side on the left. He knew if they took a shot they'd go for him first, so that would give her enough cover to get off the track and into the woods. But he was quick, and if there was a shot in the time it took him to catch up with her, he didn't hear it.

They ran hard, a good fifty yards into the woods, before cutting off on another path, heading towards the car that had been parked ahead of them, roughly parallel to the track. They stopped then and dropped down into a squat, shielded from view by the undergrowth which was thick and almost impenetrable in places.

Dan couldn't hear anything at first, as both of them fought to slow their breathing. But then, as the silence took hold they began to pick up voices, one ahead of them through the trees, the other more distant and off to the left. He got the feeling they were talking to each other on the phone.

They were still listening when a shot went off, cracking through the branches off to their left. A couple of birds took flight in response.

Whispering, Dan said, "Just shooting for the hell of it, seeing if he can flush us out." He put his rucksack on the floor, attached the silencer to his gun and said, "You stay here, look out for people approaching from the left. I'll be back in a minute."

She looked ready to object, but he was already on his way, moving fast and low through the undergrowth, going out of his way to stay on the straggling natural paths that cut through it, ending up circling behind the two guys who'd originally been ahead of them.

He stood behind the partial cover of a tree then and looked out. He could see the parked car, facing away from him, one guy standing closer to Dan's hiding place, smoking and kicking his heels. The other guy, the one on the phone, was in front of the car.

He didn't recognize either of them. The one at the back was solidly built, the one on the phone more sinewy, but he could imagine both of them working the door of a nightclub. They were both dark-haired, the bigger one almost a skinhead, a white scar visible through the hair on his skull. The guy on the phone was speaking in a Slavic language of some sort, and that matched their looks too.

There were too many trees between him and them to be sure of hitting them both from here. He looked at the undergrowth, following the nearest rough path to where it hit the track, but it was a good twenty yards beyond the car, not a great place to emerge.

He could always walk through the undergrowth, and it looked mostly like bracken, but if he hit a patch of briars he'd be in big trouble. Briefly, both guys had turned so that they had their backs to him, so Dan moved one tree closer, then a second. It did seem to be bracken alone, and he was close enough now that he might even have been willing to take a chance at shooting them from there.

Then the phone call came to an abrupt end and Dan heard the motorbike kick into life again in the distance. It had taken them long enough, but they'd decided on their next move. The big guy stubbed out his cigarette on the floor and walked towards his partner.

Dan slid out from behind the tree and moved towards them, easing through the bracken. And he was almost on them when he heard a violent rustling in front of him and an explosion of movement and feathers as a game bird of some sort burst out of the bracken and flew up into the branches above.

Both guys turned, the big guy going for his gun, the other only momentarily hampered by still having his phone in his hand. Dan fired, hitting the big guy in the chest. He fell back against the car and Dan fired at the other, hitting his shoulder. He dropped his phone, but scurried behind the front of the car.

The big guy was wheezing, trying to get control of his gun arm again. Dan shot him in the head, then threw himself into the bracken so that he was lying on the floor near the edge of the path. He could see the smaller guy now, crouching behind the front of the car. Dan fired twice, under the car, both hitting him—he crumpled onto the dirt floor.

Then a round from the sniper rifle hit the windshield with explosive force, shattering it. A second round came a moment or two later, hitting one of the front tires. The guy was pretty good, there was no doubting that, hitting the car at that distance, with Dan's own SUV in between.

So that had ruled out the possibility of taking their car, and Dan also didn't wait now to check that the smaller guy was dead—he was pretty bashed up at the least. Dan scrambled back to his feet and ran back towards Inger, conscious all the time of the motorbike, the sound of which he couldn't quite pin down to a specific direction.

He saw her lowering her gun again as he emerged along the path, and he nodded, liking the fact that she was taking no chances.

He dropped down next to her and said, "I took out the two who were over there, one dead, the other dead or badly hurt. The guy with the sniper rifle's pretty good though."

"He was shooting at the car?"

"Yeah, took out the windshield and one of the front tires."

The motorbike revved and produced some weird kind of Doppler shift as if it was suddenly coming towards them, and they both looked into the woods.

Inger pointed at the path on which Dan had just returned, and said, "We can either stay and try to get the other three, or we can take that path until we're out of the forest."

"I think if we follow that path it would put us on the right side of the woods to get into Auxerre."

Again, the motorbike noise shifted, as if he was sweeping through the woods trying to flush them out.

Dan looked in that direction and said, "We could take them, I'm sure we could, but we don't know how long it would take, or how many more people they've got nearby."

"So we go?"

He nodded, but didn't move, and said, "Only trouble is, as long as we're here in the trees, the sniper's got a tough job, and the bike doesn't have much of an advantage. We get out of these woods, we're in open country."

She seemed to be weighing it up too, but they both looked into the trees again as the sound of the motorbike clearly changed direction and grew more distant. On the back of it, they could just hear a car starting up too, the sound of it reversing, turning, driving away.

Inger said, "What are they doing? They want to lure us back to your car maybe."

"Maybe, and the fact he didn't shoot my car up suggests there is a tracker hidden on it somewhere. Or maybe they've worked out our options and they're circling around."

"It doesn't matter. We go, now, and when we get to the edge of the forest, we decide the best strategy."

He smiled, at the seriousness of her face, the clarity in her eyes, her skin glowing in the partial sunlight, and he felt suffused with a strange contentment. The woods were peaceful around them now, and he wanted to tell her, that whatever happened from here on in, he was probably happier in this moment, being with her, than he had been for many years.

He knew though, that he would not find the words, or that he'd make it sound wrong, and so he only leaned in and kissed her lightly, and said, "Let's go."

They didn't run, but walked a fast steady pace, making little enough noise that they could hear the woods around them, the sounds of birds, a distant tractor somewhere. Once Dan thought he heard the motorbike again, but it came to nothing.

They could see ahead of them when the woods were coming to an end, the brightness blurring the lines of the trees. They slowed a little more, approaching the road beyond with an increased level of vigilance.

Before breaching the undergrowth that bordered the road, they both crouched down, embedding themselves within it. Dan took the binoculars from his rucksack and scanned the open country in front of them.

He could see a road cutting across the flat fields to a village beyond, and if he had his bearings right, Auxerre was a little way beyond that. To get to the town, they had to cross at least some open country, and there was precious little cover once they were out there.

Then he noticed a stand of trees halfway between them and the village, though slightly off to the right, and just visible from their position was the front of a black car that was parked behind it. He couldn't be certain it was the same car, but he was as certain as he needed to be about what it was doing there. Briefly, he wondered if he'd been wrong to abandon the car. It hardly mattered, but it undoubtedly looked now like they needed a new plan.

Chapter Thirty-three

Dan lowered the binoculars and said, "The trees over there, the car's parked behind it. Not sure if it's the same one, but I doubt they're birdwatchers."

She didn't look but said, "Then we should move back a little."

They edged backwards slowly, deeper into the undergrowth, though Dan doubted the guy would be bothered to search the tree line—he knew Dan and Inger would have to break cover sooner or later.

As they crouched there, neither of them readily suggesting a next move, he heard the motorbike again, approaching from the right along the narrow road in front of them. He didn't seem to be doing any great speed, which suggested he was scanning into the trees as he rode.

Dan looked back at the path they'd walked along and said, "Can you ride a motorbike?"

"No, can you?"

"Not since I was about fifteen, but I can." There wasn't time to discuss it. He said, "Stay here. With any luck, the motorbike will hit the deck right in front of you. Pull it into the undergrowth and back onto that path if you can."

He jumped up, ran about ten paces off to the right, crouched again. The bike was approaching, the revs a menacing purr at that speed. Dan held still as the guy passed immediately in front of him. It was a risk, because the guys in the car were probably watching the biker, but it had to be worth taking.

The biker was past now and Dan jumped up, stepped out and fired off a couple of shots in quick succession, one into the bigger target of his back, then one higher. The guy immediately fell sideways, the bike revving and sliding out from under him.

Dan didn't see any more, diving back into the undergrowth, scurrying away, and even then he only just made it, a shot cracking into the branches close by. He didn't wait for more but ran back towards Inger.

She'd pulled the bike through the undergrowth and was pushing it now onto the narrow path they'd used. She already had her rucksack on and he could see his over the handlebar.

He grabbed it, taking hold of the bike at the same time. Another shot clattered through the air, splintering into a tree a few feet away.

"Start running down the path. I'll catch up."

She glanced at him, wanting to be sure that he would follow, then set off along the path. He dropped his gun into the rucksack, threw it over his shoulder and jumped on the bike. It only took a second, coming back to him now, but just before he kick-started it again he heard the car engine start up somewhere behind him.

She'd got a fair distance along the path, but stopped when she heard him approaching. She jumped on the back, sliding her arms around his waist, and even now, even in the middle of fleeing, her touch ran through him, mingling with the blood rush of the chase.

He rode fast, letting his instinct guide him, knowing all the time that they'd be circling back around the woods at speed themselves. They reached a firebreak and he turned right, opening it up even more, slowing as they reached the barrier onto the road where he'd parked earlier.

He edged around the barrier, glanced up, saw his own SUV still parked to the right, but didn't hang around, making headlong for the road at the edge of the woods.

At the junction, he stopped briefly, looking at the road as it curved away and made for the distant village. He turned instead and headed back the way they'd first come, the dead rider and crashed bike still on the pale road surface ahead of them.

He was about to ride around him, but hesitated, glancing back into the trees, seeing now that the undergrowth here wasn't as impenetrable as he'd first thought when they'd driven past it.

He stopped the bike and said, "Let's get off here."

She jumped off and he climbed off too, and they pushed the bike in among the trees. Once it was far enough from the road to be invisible, they edged back toward the tree line. The car was approaching at speed from the road that curved round to the distant village, a trail of white dust rising up behind it.

He pointed and Inger looked puzzled and said, "Is it a different car? It's coming from the wrong direction."

"No, the woods are an irregular shape. He knows the road through the woods is blocked by his friend's car, my SUV, so he's had to come all the way around. He's in a hurry too. People make mistakes when they're in a rush."

He took his gun from the rucksack, and she took out her gun too, though he hoped she wouldn't have to use it. He heard the car slow a little as it took the bend, then speed up again. It was already faintly visible now, a darkness rippling through the trees to their left.

He hit the brakes again as he reached their hiding place. There was no ditch between the road and the open field, but the ground was uneven enough that he needed to take it easy going around the fallen biker.

Dan ran a couple of paces into the open. The driver hit the brakes harder at the sight of him, the car swerving slightly. Dan aimed directly at the driver's chest through the windshield and fired, three bullets in quick succession. He had to jump back then, the car veering wildly and plowing into the fallen bike.

With an odd sense of dislocation, Dan recognized the guy in the passenger seat, a Ukrainian he'd met a couple of times but whose name he didn't remember. The guy had his gun in his hand, trying to work against the chaotic momentum of the car to lower the window, take a shot.

The window was only a little way down, when it shattered with an explosive burst of noise—Inger, who'd emerged from the trees next to him and taken a shot at the passenger. He was hit, but still lifted his gun arm and pointed it, even as the car ran off the road into the open field, denying the guy a firing angle.

Dan ran after the car, the noise of Inger's shot still raw in his ears. It came to a halt after twenty yards and the passenger door flew open, the guy falling out of the car like a stuntman. His face was covered in blood, but he was still trying to get a shot off—Dan had to admire him for that.

Dan fired once, hitting him in the top of the head with a force that jerked his neck back before his face crashed into the dirt. Dan readied himself to fire again, but there was no need.

Quickly, he checked the driver—he knew him too, again by sight rather than by name, a Bulgarian, a sniper with a reputation, which explained a lot. He jogged back to Inger, slapping the side of his head at the same time.

When he reached her, he said, "Do you have a birthday coming up?"

She looked baffled and said, "Why?"

"I'll buy you a silencer." She laughed and he said, "Come on, joking aside, that shot would have been heard all over. We'll get the bike and get out of here."

"Did you know them?"

"Yeah, I recognized them. One was a Ukrainian, one Bulgarian. I didn't know them really, just to look at."

"Hopefully they're the last."

"I doubt it, and Brabham hasn't even—"

"No, I mean, once we get the disk to Patrick."

"Oh, I see."

And yet even now, he wasn't convinced that it would ever be that easy.

The disk would give Patrick White and the ODNI the ability to bring Bill Brabham to heel, possibly even wind up his entire operation, but Dan was fully aware that his own long-term safety wouldn't necessarily be a part of that. He hoped it would, but hope on its own was worth nothing to him.

Chapter Thirty-four

They rode the bike to Auxerre and left it on a side street before walking towards the station. Once they got there and checked on the trains, Dan put in a call to Patrick White.

When Patrick answered, something about the quality of his voice made Dan say, "It's Dan. Where are you?"

"I'm in DC."

"Did I wake you?"

Patrick sounded bemused as he said, "I wish it were so. I'm in the back of a car on the way to a breakfast meeting. If I sound groggy, blame the report I'm reading. But anyway, good to hear your voice, Dan."

"Yeah, well, there are seven dead guys and counting who tried to stop me making this call, but here we are, and we need you in Paris."

"Bill's guys, or freelancers?"

"Freelancers. Eastern European, I think."

He didn't respond, but Dan knew he'd be relieved to hear that.

He was more businesslike as he said, "I'm sorry I couldn't get out of this trip home, but I'll be there day after tomorrow at the latest, sooner if I can." He paused before he said, "How much have you managed to find out?"

"A lot, enough for you to do what you need to do, and hopefully enough for you to keep your side of the bargain, get them to leave me and Charlie alone. I mean, Jesus, they're squeamish about the things we did for them, but they've been using some low-life gangsters this week."

There was another pause, a second or two only, but in some way, Dan knew it was ominous, an emptiness creeping into his stomach.

He was expecting bad news, but still wasn't sure he quite heard right when Patrick said, "Dan, Charlie's dead. His body was found yesterday. He was in Croatia. I don't know how they tracked him down."

Dan immediately thought of Tito, the doctor in Innsbruck. Dan had never trusted him and he was pretty certain now that Tito must have played some part in selling Charlie down the river.

But he felt sick at the thought that Charlie had gone to Croatia, no doubt looking for Darija and the memory of another summer. He'd been overtaken by dreams of settling down and this was the price he'd paid.

Dan felt hollowed out by the news. He'd lost other friends in the last few weeks, but in Charlie's death he'd lost one of the great certainties in his life. He'd always been there when he'd needed him, right up until the end, taking a bullet that had been meant for Dan. They'd all been there for each other at different times, but now Charlie was gone too, and Dan was on his own.

"Was it Brabham?"

"His people, yes. Maybe freelancers, although I know a lot of those resources were tied up with you."

"How was he killed?"

He needed to know. He wasn't sure why, but it mattered.

"Shot."

"But how? Execution style, in a gun battle, sniper? How?"

"Dan, does it really matter? Charlie was a good guy, he got shot."

Patrick was keeping something back, Dan knew it, and now he said, "Patrick, tell me how it happened. You know I'll find out and I won't be pleased if you're holding back on me."

There was another silence, but Dan didn't fill it, and a little while later, Patrick sighed and said, "He had multiple gunshot and knife wounds. It looks like they tortured him."

"To get information on me?"

"Maybe. Or if it was Brabham's own team it might have been . . . retaliation, for Jack Carlton and Rob Foster."

And at last, something filled the hollowness. Dan had liked Jack Carlton, just as Jack had liked Benoit Claudel, and maybe none of them had been possessed of enough humanity, but they'd lived by the same informal rules, had respected each other in some way. The anger he felt now wasn't just for the death of Charlie Hamsun, for the loss of him, but for the manner of it.

For the first time in the last two weeks, Dan could see the way forward with total clarity. He knew exactly what he had to do now. He'd been thinking about his own future, and that was tied up in this, but he had to act now for Charlie and Benoit, for Mike Naismith and Karl Wittmann and the others.

Yes, they'd all done bad things, but they'd been good men, and they'd acted for the agency and the government that had killed them. Jack Redford, too, had been targeted by the people he'd served. And Dan didn't feel he was in much of a position to take a moral stand, but he was the only one left, so he knew it was up to him, and that he *would* take this back to them.

"Dan . . .?"

"Patrick, when you get to Paris, get in touch with the Swedish Embassy—that's where Inger will be, and she'll give you the proof of what I'm about to tell you. Fourteen years ago, Harry Brabham— that's Congressman Harry Brabham—murdered Sabine Merel in Paris. His father oversaw a crime against the French Government, including the murder of Jean Sainval of the DGSE, and has done everything in his power ever since to keep this hidden. But that's what happened. Jack Redford knew about it, which is why Brabham knew exactly who Jacques Fillon was."

"*Harry* Brabham?" The surprise was evident in his voice, backing up what Dan had suspected before, that Patrick had expected the evidence to point to the father. "You said you have proof?"

"We do, and if anyone happens to be listening to this and thinking of intercepting Inger Bengtsson, don't bother because we've got more than one copy. We have the security tape, Patrick, the tape that Brabham ordered Jack Redford to steal from the DGSE."

There was another brief silence, and then Patrick said, "I'll be there tomorrow night, I'll contact you and Inger as soon as I arrive."

"Contact Inger at the Swedish Embassy. I won't be in Paris—I have something else to do."

"Yes, I can contact Inger," he said, failing to mask his unease. "But, Dan, I hope your other plans have nothing to do with what I've just told you."

"I have some personal business to deal with, that's all. But let's catch up soon, Patrick—I'm sure we'll have a lot to talk about."

He ended the call, offering Patrick no more time to argue against things that were already decided.

And when Dan turned to Inger, she looked full of the same misgivings and said, "Why would I be at the Swedish Embassy? And you're not going to be there, why?"

"The Swedish Embassy is safe, safer than anywhere else you could arrange to meet him. And no, I won't be there. Like I said, I have some stuff to do."

"But . . ."

"They killed my friend Charlie. Not just killed, they tortured him."

"Oh my God." She put a hand on his arm. "I'm so sorry, Dan."

He nodded, but pointed then and said, "Here's the train."

She tried to say something, but stopped herself. He could appreciate that too, because what was there to say? So they waited as the train glided along the platform and they boarded in silence.

It wasn't until they were on their way that she said, "When will you leave? We can stay together tonight?"

He thought of how easy it would be to say yes, how much he wanted to be with her tonight. But for the time being, at least, he knew his own internal momentum was too strong, that he had to move, had to see this through to what he saw as its logical conclusion.

"I won't be staying in Paris tonight. I'll be moving on right away."

"Then I'll come." When he only smiled, she said, "We made a pretty good team, didn't we?"

He nodded.

"I don't want you with me." She looked stung and he said, "Not like that. The opposite. I don't want you involved in the things I have to do now."

"So maybe you don't have to do them. You could . . ."

"Go and live in the forest?" She smiled in response, but there was a sadness about her that was unbearable. "It's not just about me, it's about everything, Charlie and the others, the stuff we did, it's about Sabine Merel . . ."

"But we have the tape."

He didn't need to spell it out, though, that having the tape and seeing it broadcast were two different things. Certainly, Patrick would use it as leverage, to ensure the withdrawal of funding, the reassignment of key personnel, any number of things that would fall short of what Dan and Inger wanted, what the Merels and Bergeron wanted, what Jack Redford had wanted.

Inger seemed to acknowledge that fact, and in the end, said only, "I'm just afraid you don't know what you're walking into, even with your background."

"I have a pretty good idea." He nearly added that it was nothing he couldn't handle, but Inger didn't look as though she'd be reassured so easily, and in the present circumstances, he felt it might be tempting fate anyway.

Chapter Thirty-five

He traveled in the cab with Inger, leaving her at the Swedish Embassy.

One last time, she said, "I can't change your mind?"

"I promise this is the last time ever, but no, you can't."

"So when will I see you?"

"In Stockholm. I'll be there. Soon."

She shook her head, as if in response to a lame joke, but sounded desperately concerned as she said, "Please be careful."

"I'll be in Stockholm. You haven't seen the last of me."

She leaned across and kissed him, and he held her until the obvious impatience of the cab driver parted them. He watched as she walked into the embassy, and turned only when the driver asked where he wanted to go. Dan gave him the address of his apartment in the 17th and sat back in the seat.

He was fired up enough now that he was almost hoping to encounter more of Brabham's guys in the area around the apartment, but there was no one that he could see, and he wondered if that was because they'd all been called away. A handful had followed them down to Auxerre, all dead, another he'd killed at the Vergoncey. Another team had gone to Croatia to take care of Charlie.

His thoughts snagged once again on Charlie's death, and he forced his mind in a different direction, trying to work out what those various logistics told him about Brabham's team, the numbers and resources at his disposal. He was guessing from past experience that he probably had a dozen working for him directly, most of them in the field.

Of course, there was always an endless supply of freelancers, but the quality was variable, and that had already shown in the people Dan and Inger had come up against. Nor would Brabham want freelance people hanging around his office in Berlin. It left him confident that he could do this, that maybe he could even come out of it alive.

As he stepped inside and closed the door, he could tell the apartment was empty. Anybody would have known it was empty, and as he walked through the sparsely furnished rooms he thought of how another person might have filled this space with life.

He thought of Sylvie's apartment nearby, stamped with her personality, and he wondered if he even had it within him to live like that, to live. Foolishly, his thoughts made a run for Stockholm, to some imagined domesticity with Inger, and he was embarrassed by how alluring he found it, a woman he hardly knew and who hardly knew him.

He also knew he couldn't afford to be distracted. Whatever promise the future held, he had business to finish with his old life first, and he needed to focus on that above all else.

He threw some clothes into a bag, then went into the secure room and put together another bag. He checked the trains then, and headed back out, knowing he couldn't rely on Patrick to get him through airport security this time.

He took a late-afternoon train to Cologne and picked up the night train there, grabbing a few hours' sleep but arriving in Berlin just before five in the morning. There was a boutique hotel just along the street from the address he had for Brabham's office so he'd arranged an early check-in.

It was still dark when he arrived, and bitterly cold, but he could tell why Brabham had chosen this location. It was a quiet, anonymous street in Charlottenburg, a mixture of offices and residential, the odd store or bar, a cobbled road surface. No one would ever suspect it.

In fact, the neighborhood was so ordinary that the hotel, small and incredibly stylish, looked as if it had been transplanted from somewhere else. The room he was given faced outwards, but the view was obscured by the trees that lined both sides of the street and had not yet shed all their leaves.

So he went back out and took a stroll until he was standing opposite the building. It was a nondescript-looking place, probably built in the 1950s, a pharmacy at street level and a door to the left for the lobby that served the two floors above.

There was no one about at this hour so he took a closer look, a keypad on the door, a plaque for name plates, but none on there—maybe Brabham had both floors. He turned and looked at the building facing. It was older, or looked older, an ornate *fin-de-siècle* quality with little balustrades outside each of the windows on the upper floors. He could also see that it was empty, with mail lying on the floor just inside the lobby door.

He went back to the hotel and picked up one of his bags. He worked the door of the empty building, then made his way to the top floor and set himself up in one of the rooms, clearly a former office, with phone and modem points dotting the floor. He lowered the blinds too, enough to give him cover should one of Brabham's people choose to look out of the window.

And then he settled in for the wait. They were looking for him, had been searching for him for weeks, and he knew, because he knew the mindset of these people, that it would never occur to them that he was right here, right now.

They'd have increased their security levels, but they still wouldn't expect him to actually show up here. And for all their knowledge of his history, they wouldn't understand that it wasn't in his character to play the part they imagined for him. Whether they knew it or not, whether they were ready for it or not, they were the targets now.

Chapter Thirty-six

The first to arrive came just before eight. It was light but the street still had a sickly pallor, as if a real sunrise wasn't guaranteed for the day ahead. The guy looked in his late twenties, suit and over-coat, carrying a coffee and some sort of breakfast food in a bag. He moved the bag into the same hand as the coffee and nonchalantly hit the numbers on the keypad.

Dan was looking through his binoculars and scribbled the number down as it went in. He waited a few minutes then, and watched as the lights flickered into life behind the top floor win-dows, though the blinds prevented him seeing anything beyond.

The next two arrived about twenty minutes later, one in office clothes, the other dressed like someone who worked at some Inter-net start-up in Seattle. He couldn't see the keypad clearly as the formally dressed one punched in, but the pattern looked the same for the numbers he'd written down.

Within minutes, a man and woman came along, both in office clothes, and he realized now that this whole office was on the young side. He guessed they were all in their late twenties or early thirties. The last to arrive was a guy in a heavy sweater and padded jacket, a scarf wrapped around his neck, a lanyard hanging outside the jacket—so they probably needed to swipe the card to get through the inner door.

Even from Dan's position, he could see this guy was struggling with a heavy cold. He sneezed two or three times in quick succession before finally managing to key in the number. He was slow doing it and once again, Dan got a pretty good view and was certain he'd got it right now.

No one else arrived before nine o'clock and Dan relaxed a little, doubting there'd be much to see for the next few hours. He also knew this wasn't the full outfit. These were backroom people, though he'd show them no more mercy for that.

The first movement came at lunchtime. The man and woman who'd arrived together went out, strolling along the street and coming back after half an hour with what looked like a lunch order.

He was average build and height, with the kind of boy-next-door good looks that had almost run their distance—he was beginning to look doughy, his hair receding. She was attractive, dark hair pulled back, possibly Hispanic, and she was clearly the more observant of the two, glancing around, even taking in the building where Dan was hiding, though never reaching up to his floor.

Not long after lunch, he saw a black BMW pull into the street. It stopped outside the building as if the driver was searching for a place to park, then reversed, and turned into a narrow gateway that led behind the buildings on that side.

There obviously wasn't a back entrance because, a few minutes later, the two guys strolled from the same turning and down to the building. Dan recognized them right away, the two guys who'd been parked outside the Vergoncey.

One was fair and, once again, late twenties. The other was a little darker, and closer to Dan's age, though he didn't know him. Both of them had a restrained swagger, a misplaced confidence that set them apart from all the other people who'd headed into that office.

Dan watched for a while, but after an hour he guessed they weren't coming back out. Would they usually spend the day in the office, he wondered, or had they been sent there for additional protection? Brabham would know by now that there had been a death at the Vergoncey and a bloodbath in the countryside near Auxerre, and he'd possibly also heard that Dan was no longer in Paris, so perhaps this was just a precaution, and a half-hearted one at that.

Dan kept watching through the afternoon, and then with the street once again in darkness, he watched them leave one by one. For the most part, they left in the same order that they'd arrived, except that the two guys in the car left at the same time as the woman, doing their best to impress her as they walked the short distance along the street together.

Only one guy was left, and when Dan saw the lights go out, he made his way downstairs. The guy was sneezing even as he came out of the door, and if anything, looked worse than he had that morning. Briefly, he looked at the lit window of the pharmacy, but he checked his watch and changed his mind, heading off along the street.

Dan trailed after him, picking up his pace only when he saw that the guy was about to jump on a tram. Dan boarded further down, bought a ticket from the machine, watched casually. The guy was so out of it with his cold, though, that Dan probably could have been standing right next to him and he wouldn't have noticed.

They didn't stay on many more stops, and when they got off, the guy made a couple of turns, into quiet streets of apartment blocks. There was hardly anyone about. Dan checked his watch—just after six, but becoming fiercely cold. He followed him into a small apartment block, not old but already looking dated.

The guy looked at the stairs, and on a better day he'd have probably used them, but with a resigned look he headed to the elevator and pressed the button. Only as he stepped inside did he become aware that there was someone behind him.

He jumped a little, but didn't suspect anything, and nodded, even looked ready to ask which floor Dan wanted. It only took him a second to work out that he didn't recognize Dan from the building but from the office, and by that time Dan already had the gun on him.

Neither of them said anything. The elevator stopped, doors sliding open with a judder.

"I'm just a tech guy."

Dan waved the gun a little and he stepped out and walked along the short corridor to a blank-looking door. He reached into his pocket for a key, and was shaking visibly as he opened the door. Dan stepped in behind him and closed the door.

They walked through into a small sitting room that looked as if a handful of students lived there, empty cartons all over the place, a games console, DVDs and magazines on every surface.

"Take off the lanyard and drop it on the table there." The guy did as he was told. "You live here alone?"

The guy nodded vigorously and said, "I really am just a tech guy, it's all I do, I mean . . . I'll tell you anything, all you need to know."

Dan could tell he was being straight with him—it was too bad.

"All I really need from you is twenty-four hours of silence."

He shot him in the chest, the guy managing an unconvincing, "No, please," before it hit him and his legs crumpled and he fell backwards into a chair. He moved convulsively for a few seconds, and then grew still, his eyes fixed on the TV as if he'd been paused in the moment of seeing something baffling.

Dan picked up the lanyard, looking at the card, which was blank except for its magnetic strip—deniability. He reached inside the guy's jacket, then the pockets of his jeans where he found his phone and his wallet. His name was Adam and he was twenty-seven. He looked north of thirty, but that might just have been the cold.

Dan looked through his messages, then through his sent messages, finding one to someone called Josh which said, "Feeling really unwell, not sure if I'll make it in today."

It had been sent early that morning. And it really was too bad, thought Dan, because making it in had cost him his life.

Chapter Thirty-seven

Dan went back and had dinner at the hotel, then slept for a while and went out again later when the street was quiet. He could see the lights were out in the office building so he punched in the code and stepped inside.

There were no cameras in the lobby. There was an elevator, but he wouldn't want to use that the next day. Around the corner behind it he found the stairs and walked up to the top floor.

Stairs and elevator opened into another small lobby with only one solid-looking door. It was a combined swipe and keypad. He doubted they used the same code for both doors, and didn't want to risk trying it in case the system recorded failed entry attempts.

Instead he went back across the road and returned with his bag. He installed a small camera cut into the side of one of the polystyrene ceiling panels and checked it on the monitor, recording himself as if he were keying in.

Happy, he took the bag back across the road and then went to his hotel. He set his alarm for seven, though he didn't sleep much and was up beforehand. He grabbed some breakfast and made his way along the street.

At eight, he sent a message to Josh on Adam's phone, saying, "Worse this morning. Staying in bed for the day."

Minutes later he got a message from Josh, saying, "Take it easy, buddy."

Dan watched the rest of them arrive, just as he had the day before. The only difference this time was that the two guys in the car arrived before nine. It suggested he'd been right, that they'd been sent to beef up security.

As each one went in he looked again through the binoculars, making sure the code didn't change from day to day. He checked, too, that the camera was working, and just from a cursory glance he already had a rough idea of the key code for the inner door. Once he was satisfied all of them were in, he went back over the tapes, firstly confirming the code, then looking at the other one to see what he could see of the office.

There seemed to be a small reception area just inside the door, easy chairs, so most of the desks had to be to the right and around the corner from it. That would help him with cover if he needed it. The key, though, would be getting the two guys from the Vergoncey first. He had no doubt the others would all be able to defend themselves, but not at the same pitch.

At twelve he started to get himself ready, and at half past the hour he sat in front of the monitor looking at the view through the camera that looked directly at the door of the office.

It was fifteen minutes before the door opened and the same two people, the woman and the guy, came out to go and get the lunch order—maybe they were the most junior, or more likely, they just enjoyed the opportunity of getting out for half an hour. Either way, it would earn them a stay of execution.

As they came out, but before the door had closed, something was said behind them, and the woman laughed as if at some corny joke and turned to say something back. There was the two-man security detail, lounging on the easy chairs right inside the door.

Dan moved to the window and watched as the man and woman came out of the building and walked along the street. He wondered if they were a couple. He doubted it, somehow. When the other guys had been showing her attention the previous evening, her companion hadn't seemed unhappy or possessive.

He waited fifteen minutes, not wanting to wait longer in case they were served quicker today or went somewhere closer. Then he crossed the street, keyed in and climbed the stairs, seeing no one, almost certainly being seen by no one.

He keyed in the other number for the top door, swiped Adam's card and pushed the door open. He hit the older guy first, a shot straight to the head even as he was smiling and no doubt ready to make some comment to the woman about lunch.

The fair-haired guy tried to jump up and go for his gun at the same time, his reflexes pretty good, but Dan hit him in the chest, knocking him back into the easy chair, and fired again at his head before moving around the corner.

One of the suited guys was just sitting at a computer and staring across the room, as if wondering what the commotion was. The other was scrabbling in a drawer, probably for a gun that should have been on him. Dan hit him first, then the static one.

But that was where he ran into difficulties. Because he couldn't see the other casually dressed guy. There was a door to a bathroom, but there was also a desk in the far corner that was surrounded by dividers like a cubicle.

Dan stepped back to the cover of the corner, checking behind him to make sure of what he already knew, that he was surrounded only by bodies. He waited a beat then and said, "If you come out now, I won't hurt you. If you make me come over there, I will."

"I wouldn't do that. I'm armed!"

He was in the cubicle.

"Wrong answer. If you're armed, I'll kill you."

He heard him mutter to himself, "Oh God, oh God." He was panicking, and Dan guessed from the informal dress that this was the other tech guy, probably the Josh who'd exchanged messages with Adam.

Dan had come in here intent on killing all of them, but it was amazing how quickly that need for vengeance had dissipated, or at least become discerning. He'd still take down the other part of the team, wherever they were, probably at Brabham's house, because those were the people who'd done for his friends and tried to do for him. But there was nothing to be gained from killing this guy.

He spoke now, desperately weighing his options as he said, "If I come out . . ."

"Throw the gun out first. If you come out with a gun, I'll shoot."

"How do I know you won't shoot me anyway?"

"If I wanted to shoot you, do you think that cubicle or a gun or anything else would stop me?"

There was silence, and Dan was beginning to get impatient, thinking of the returning lunch party, but then a gun slid across the floor from behind the cubicle.

"Okay, I'm coming out. Please, don't shoot me." He stood with his hands raised. He had longish hair and the beginnings of a beard, a young face beneath it all, like some grad student who'd considered becoming a folk singer but had fallen into this by mistake. "Seriously, I'm just a tech guy."

"Are you Josh?" He nodded. "Yeah, it was me who sent the message from Adam's phone. Adam's dead."

"Oh God."

Dan took the cuffs and threw them to him.

Josh caught them and Dan said, "Come out from behind the cubicle and put them on, hands in front." When he hesitated, his expression pleading for more assurances, he added, "You're still alive. No reason you can't stay that way, as long as you don't try anything stupid."

"I won't, I promise."

He stepped out, desperately trying to avoid anything that might resemble a sudden movement, and put on the cuffs.

"Okay, move over here and sit on the edge of this desk where I can see you."

Josh did as he was told and Dan was pretty sure he wouldn't try anything, but he still kept an eye on him as he moved the two bodies from the easy chairs, dragging them and dropping them behind one of the desks. A lot of blood was visible on one of the chairs, from the head wound, so he took an overcoat that was hanging up and threw it over the chair, the result casual enough that it was unlikely to arouse suspicions.

He walked back to Josh then and said, "They should be back any minute. I'll be straight with you, I'd intended to kill all of you today, for what you've done to me and my friends." Josh tried to respond, no doubt to argue his innocence, but Dan put a finger up and silenced him. He pointed at the two bodies he'd just moved and said, "Those two I would've killed anyway, but I don't want to turn this into something bigger than it needs to be. You understand?"

"I think so." He didn't, but it probably didn't matter, either.

"What I'm saying is your two colleagues who went to get the lunch, I don't want to hurt them, but if you speak or try to attract their attention in any way, I'll have no choice but to kill all three of you."

"You . . . you always have a choice." Dan raised his eyebrows, his expression alone asking Josh if he really wanted to debate this issue. "I won't say a word."

"Good. Is the rest of the team at Brabham's place?"

He nodded and said, "We're only the logistical side here, we . . . we just . . ." Something about Dan's expression cut him short.

They sat in silence for a few seconds. Josh still looked eager to say something else, and opened his mouth but stopped himself when they heard the elevator mechanism spring into life.

Dan pointed and said, "Move onto that desk there." Josh moved quickly and Dan walked to the far side of the entrance door from where he was able to cover all the angles.

He could hear them chatting and laughing as they stepped out of the elevator, then the activity beyond the door before the lock freed itself and they pushed it open.

As they stepped inside, she was laughing at something and he was saying, "Seriously, that's exactly what happened."

They were in and the door had closed behind them before they turned and saw Josh sitting on the desk, though they couldn't see any bodies yet. They both froze, trying to make sense of it. It probably would have come to them after a moment or two but he didn't give them time.

"Either of you move and I'll kill you."

They hadn't been moving anyway, but there was a different quality to their stillness now.

The woman said, "Josh?"

"Everyone else is dead, but he's not gonna kill us if you do what he says."

The guy said, "Mr. Hendricks, Dan . . ."

"Move forward, slowly, put the lunch down on the desk in front of you, and then turn around with your hands visible. Josh is telling the truth, but I'll kill you if you try anything."

They stepped forward, though he could see the guy turn his head a fraction, as if trying to tell her something. She either didn't see him or was better at concealing it, and she put the bags on the desk in front of her. He did the same, clumsily, and one of them fell to the side of the desk.

He made a dramatic effort to save it, but Dan could see exactly what he was doing. The world shifted down into slow motion and Dan was furious with the guy, wondering why he had to do this, why he had to put Dan in this position again.

The guy righted himself, turning, and Dan had to at least credit him with a clean draw from his holster, but it wouldn't be enough. Before the guy's eyes had even locked on their target, Dan had fired, hitting him in the side of the head.

The woman let out a small scream but had her hands up. The guy crumpled, still midway through his heroic turn, and fell, his head crashing against the side of a different desk. He landed with his arm underneath him, looking uncomfortable even in death.

Dan noticed Josh shaking his head, and it seemed his consternation was aimed less at what Dan had done than at his colleague's unnecessary heroics. The woman still had her hands up, but she was breathing deep and rapid, a febrile quality about her.

"Do you have a gun?"

"It's in my purse, next to my desk."

"Okay, turn around, slowly."

She turned, and despite the shaky breathing, she looked resolute and met his gaze directly.

Dan said, "There was no need for that to happen."

"He went for his gun. I can vouch for you on that."

She was trying to appease him, which he didn't like somehow, and he said, "I don't need you to vouch for me on anything." He felt he'd been peevish then. She was scared, that was all, and understandably so. "What's your name?"

"Callie Frost."

"Oh." She looked questioningly, and he said, "No, I imagined you being Hispanic or . . ."

"Spanish. My mom is Spanish."

He nodded, then said, "Take a seat, Callie, the chair over where Josh is sitting." She crossed the room and sat down, and Dan pulled another chair over, gesturing for Josh to move from the desk. Once they were both sitting, Dan rested his weight on the edge of the desk opposite them and said, "What's your role in this team, Callie? Josh is a tech guy. What do you do?"

"It varies. I've been running the external assets."

He smiled and said, "Do you see the irony in that? You've been hiring external assets, most of whom haven't been very good, to help kill some of the external assets who served this agency for years, one of whom has just taken apart your office."

"We've only used them this last week, since you and Patrick White got active. Bill got nervous, but it isn't easy finding reliable people at short notice."

"Which is why Patrick White was so good, because he built up his roster over years." She didn't respond, and he wondered what line they'd been sold on the nature of Patrick's service. "How many people are left on your list?"

She shook her head, but then, as if she saw a threat in his expression, she complied and said, "About a dozen for now. Targets are prioritized and continually reassessed. When they reach level one they go on the list. You're currently the top target."

Dan smiled at that, though he wasn't sure if he'd earned that status because of what he'd been doing these recent weeks, or because a lot of far better, and therefore more dangerous, people had already been eliminated.

He looked at Josh and said, "You hear that description? What does that sound like to you?" He didn't wait for an answer, but turned back to her and said, "To me, Callie, it sounds like a death squad. Makes me wonder if Brabham ever ran a station in South America back in the seventies."

She'd regained her composure again now and said, "Do you really think you're in any position to take the high ground, Mr. Hendricks?"

Josh looked panicked by her response, as if he thought the situation might still be more volatile than it seemed.

"With you, no, I'm not. With Bill Brabham, yes, because the lowest of the low is on higher ground than Bill Brabham." She looked skeptical, but he said, "You don't have to take my word for that—you'll see the proof soon enough."

She looked ready to respond, but jumped a little when a phone on the desk behind her started to ring and vibrate about the surface.

"It's Eric's phone." Dan gestured for her to pick it up and she looked at the screen and said, "It's Bill."

"Speak of the Devil. Answer it. But put it on speaker."

"What I do tell him?"

"The truth. That I'm here, that I've killed everyone, that I'm threatening to kill you."

She nodded but looked confused, and answered the call, saying, "Hi, Bill, it's Callie."

"Hello, Callie. Is Eric away from his desk?"

"No, Bill, there's been . . . an incident."

There was an awkward and lengthy pause, and Dan could imagine Brabham signaling to someone else at his end.

Finally he said, "What kind of incident, Callie?"

"Dan Hendricks, he's here right now. He's killed everyone except me and Josh." Dan waved the gun at her and she added, "And he's threatening to kill us, Bill." There was another pause, and in the end Callie said, "Bill?"

"Callie, is Hendricks listening in right now?"

She looked to Dan for guidance on how to respond and when he gave her a relaxed nod, she said, "Yeah, he's here."

"We'll take care of it."

It took her a moment to realize Brabham had ended the call. She looked at the phone, and Josh looked at her.

It was Josh who said, "What now?"

"We're leaving, but we'll be able to see exactly who comes to save you. Okay, Josh, stand up, put your hands out in front, then come over here."

Josh followed him and Dan loaded up his arms with the lunch order. It would help conceal the fact that he was cuffed, but it was more than that—he suspected neither of them felt like eating right now, but it would be a long afternoon.

"Callie, stand up, put your phone on the desk."

"I didn't have it with me. It's in my purse."

"Okay, come over here, reach into Josh's pocket, take his phone and put it on the desk." She did as he said. "Good, now let's go, Josh you'll be in front. Callie, we'll walk together."

"Where are we going?"

"I know you're a smart woman, observant . . ."

She looked annoyed with herself for not seeing it before, and said, "You're in the building across the street."

She had an air of defeat around her now, as if they'd come up against an unmatchable adversary, and he didn't want to tell her the more startling truth, that complacency had done for them, that they'd believed themselves secure without ever properly thinking it through.

Dan had developed a reputation over the years, for tracking people down, for snatching people off the street, making them disappear. What he'd learned himself was that it didn't take superhuman levels of skill or expertise, it just took being better than the opposition, and the opposition normally wasn't that good. He wasn't special, just above average and, so far, that had been enough.

Chapter Thirty-eight

They'd been in Dan's lookout for nearly forty minutes, not talking at all, just looking across the street. A couple of times a car had come along outside and Callie had craned her neck and looked down before leaning back again in resignation. Josh had been resigned from the outset, and was leaning against the wall, with no apparent interest in what was happening with his colleagues or his office.

They'd been silent for so long that Callie jumped slightly at the sound of Dan's voice as he said, "Brabham lives out at Zehlendorf, right?"

"Yeah, he does."

"You been out there?"

She nodded and said, "It's a big old villa on the shore of the Wannsee."

"That's great, but how long would you say, to drive from there to here?"

"I don't know. I guess, a half hour, forty minutes, depending on traffic."

"They're not coming," said Josh, sounding like someone in a trance.

She knew it, but didn't want to acknowledge what it meant, and said, "They assumed they'd be too late to save us. They're probably concentrating their resources on securing Bill's place. It's what I would have done."

"No, it isn't. I've known you about an hour, Callie, and I can tell you right now you would not have hung two people out to dry like that." She was still in denial, so he said, "And answer me one other thing. He asked you if I was listening in, but he didn't ask to speak to me, he didn't ask what I wanted. Why do you think that was?"

"Okay, I wouldn't have left two people like that, but I can understand why he did it. And I won't decide until I have all the facts."

He nodded, and stared at her for a second, before saying, "The guy you went with to get the lunch, was he your boyfriend?" She looked up at him, accusing, as if asking what business it was of his. He thought of Inger, telling him how he didn't understand women, not really, and he had to hand it to her on that. "I don't mean to pry. I just mean . . . I'm sorry I had to kill him."

She relented a little and after a pause, she said, "Roommates. We shared an apartment, that was all. He was a good guy."

"What about the team Brabham has out at the house?"

"The alpha team."

Incredulous, Dan said, "The *alpha* team?"

"Bill's idea of a joke."

"How many are there?"

"Nine. No, four."

"That's quite a difference—nine, four—which is it?"

"There were nine. Jack Carlton was team leader, but he was hit, so was Rob Foster. Then Alex Robinson took over but he had to fly home yesterday—he needs an operation on his leg. You killed two in the office. That leaves four."

"The guy who needs the operation, Alex Robinson?"

She nodded and said, "He got hit, shooting it out at Charlie Hamsun's place."

"When they were ambushed?" She nodded again, but looked less certain because of his tone. "It was just me and Charlie at Charlie Hamsun's place, but it's important you know this in case you're ever unlucky enough to be in the field with this Robinson guy—he ran. He ran as soon as Jack got into trouble, didn't even fire a bullet. Charlie hit him with a sniper round as he high-tailed it into the woods."

Josh came out of his trance again, sounding angry and irritated as he said, "I knew that story was bullshit!"

"So, this alpha team, it was them who went after Charlie in Croatia?"

"Of course. After what had happened with Jack and Rob, four of them went."

"Good, and what I need to know is whether all four were involved in torturing him, or just some of them, and I want names."

She looked as if he was asking for the impossible, and said, "We don't know who did what, we just know the mission was a success. And it was just the other day. With you running wild in France, we've been fighting to keep our heads above water."

"I don't buy it. These guys like to tell war stories. You heard all about how Jack Carlton and Rob Foster died. You've had two guys loafing around your office since yesterday, the rest of the team holed up at Brabham's place. You're telling me you still have no idea? That no one talked about how they killed the guy who killed Jack Carlton."

She didn't answer, but Josh was suddenly paying a lot more attention and he looked at her and said, "For God's sake, Callie, just tell him." He waited only a moment, and when she didn't fill the pause, he turned to Dan and said, "Alex Robinson was shouting his mouth off about how he cut the big bastard up and shot him six times before killing him."

Callie still didn't speak, but he could see from her expression that it was true. It was a frustrating truth at that, because it meant the guy he most wanted to harm was safely out of reach in America. He wouldn't stay out of reach forever, though.

"Thanks for telling me, Josh. And, Callie, I said you needed to watch your back if ever you worked with Robinson, but you don't need to worry about that. In fact, you can just pass on a message to him—when you see him, let him know that whatever happens, whatever job he takes, the day will come when I track him down and make him pay for every one of those wounds he inflicted on my friend."

Again, she didn't respond but seemed to be turning something over in her mind, and a minute or so passed before she said, "Has it never occurred to you, Dan, that you've picked the wrong side? You assume Patrick White is a force for good here, that Bill Brabham is the bad guy. I might not agree with the way we're going after assets that worked in good faith, but White was a maverick who left this agency in jeopardy. Now he's jumped ship and is trying to take revenge on people like Bill."

"You think Patrick White was a maverick? Callie, you wouldn't believe some of the things Western intelligence agencies were doing ten years ago. There was stuff going on that even the people at WikiLeaks wouldn't have believed. The thing is, though, you believe in it all because you believe in Bill Brabham." He walked over to get one of the laptops and put it on the floor midway between her and Josh. "I'll tell you something else—the only side I ever picked until now is my own. I've had a selfish life, but for the first time ever in these last few weeks, I have come down on one side, because I've learned what kind of person Bill Brabham is, and now I'll show you too."

It took him a minute to set it up using the phone and the laptop, and as much as he knew what he was doing, he felt oddly uncomfortable with Josh watching him, as if the tech guy was about to tell him he was doing something wrong.

Once the footage from the security tape started playing, he turned it back to face them.

"This footage was taken outside a bank in Paris fourteen years ago. In a minute you'll see two people walk into view, a man and a nineteen-year-old student named Sabine Merel. That name mean anything to you?" They both shook their heads while keeping their eyes on the screen. "How strange that Bill would never mention that."

Dan wasn't looking at the screen, but he could see from their expressions that the couple had appeared. Callie in particular looked slightly sick, as if she sensed already what would happen. Dan could tell too, when Brabham and Sabine had disappeared into the alley.

"The man you just saw tried to rape that student at a party a week or so before this, a party at the US Ambassador's residence. She made the mistake of threatening to tell the police, and she didn't even mean it, she just wanted him to back off and leave her alone. What he's doing now while you look at that blank screen is punching her in the face, knocking out her teeth, kneeling so violently on her back that it breaks her ribs, and then waiting for her to regain consciousness before strangling her with her own scarf. Then he'll rob her and pull her clothes off to make it look like . . . something else." He turned the screen to face him again, and said casually, "I'll fast forward because all of that takes him about twenty minutes. I'll go to the point where he comes out of the alley." He found the right point and put it on pause, just as Gaston Bergeron had done for them. He turned the screen back to them then.

"Fuck." Callie covered her mouth, her eyes darting about as if not wanting to actually look at the screen. Josh didn't seem to recognize the guy, but then Callie dropped her hand, her voice little more than a whisper as she said, "It's Harry Brabham."

Finally, Josh did a double take, looking at Dan as he said, "The congressman?"

"The very same. And let me tell you, Bill Brabham has gone to extraordinary lengths to keep this secret, including the murder of a leading French intelligence official."

Josh looked at Callie and pointed at the screen, saying, "Do you know this guy?"

"I met him, once." She looked ready to say something else, but didn't, and Dan suspected she was less than surprised to discover the guy had a dark side.

"While we're at it, Callie. You said you handled the external assets. Did you order Matty Hellström to kill someone in Stockholm last week?"

She looked surprised and said, "Mattias Hellström? No. He's on the list—we have a rule against using anyone on the list."

"There's a surprise. So Bill Brabham, or someone he trusts more than you, contracted Matty and promised him he'd be back in the fold if he did the job, a promise they obviously had no intention of keeping. The target was Patrick White, who was in Stockholm to meet me. And you'd think it might be risky to order the death of a senior official at the ODNI but, of course, Bill was being driven by fear." He tapped the top of the laptop screen. "Because he had a feeling we were onto this."

Once more, she appeared to take in what he said, but was thinking it through, working out how plausible it all was and what it meant, and when she spoke again, she said, "If you have this tape, I presume Patrick White and the ODNI also now have it, and he'll use that to shut down Bill Brabham's operation. But that still leaves a big question."

"Which is?"

"Why are you doing this? Why did you kill all those people before, why are you . . . whatever it is you're planning to do next. If this tape is genuine, you didn't need to kill anybody."

She was right, there was no doubting that. If he was convinced that this tape would be enough to close down both Brabham and his program, there was no need to kill anyone because the dot wouldn't be on him anymore. He'd been around long enough to know it didn't always work like that, but he'd be lying to himself if he suggested that was his main motivation.

"What I'm planning to do tonight is go out to Zehlendorf, kill *the A Team*, and . . . well, I haven't decided about Brabham yet. Maybe I'd rather hurt him some other way. As for my motivation, it's mixed—you'll find that's often the case with freelancers. But I'd say the biggest part of it's revenge, for what they did to my friends, Charlie most of all, and for what they want to do to me."

"Revenge is empty, Mr. Hendricks, you must know that."

He nodded and smiled at her, and it summed up how far removed they were from each other, that Callie thought a stock truth like that would be enough to give him second thoughts.

Chapter Thirty-nine

He didn't say any more about his plans for a while after that. Instead, he released Josh from the cuffs and encouraged them to eat. Callie was reluctant at first, perhaps because the lunch order reminded her too much of what had happened, and the death of the guy who'd walked with her every day to get it, who'd shared her apartment.

In the end, she did eat, and a little while later she looked at Dan and said, "You should eat something too."

He took a ham baguette, and noticed Callie glance at it with an unavoidable recognition, knowing whose order it was that Dan was eating. Afterwards, he escorted them both to the bathroom on that floor, letting one in at a time, keeping the gun on the other.

Then they went and sat again. Dan kept his eye on the building across the street, though no one ever turned up, and even Callie had now given up on looking out.

It was beginning to get dark when Josh said, "Mr. Hendricks . . . "

"You can call me Dan if you prefer."

"Okay, thanks." Callie looked at Josh in annoyance, as if to ask what he was thanking him for. "It's just, I wondered, if you're going out to Bill's place. Are you . . . are you planning on taking us with you?"

"He can't do that, Josh. We'd give him away or get in the way." She stared directly at Dan, that same challenging and resolute stare he'd first seen up in the office. "He's gonna kill us. It's the only thing he can do."

Dan shook his head, bemused, and said, "You've spent too much time with the wrong kind of people. I said I wouldn't kill you, and unless you give me a reason, I won't." He looked at Josh who, conversely, was desperate to believe in him. "I have another set of cuffs. It won't be comfortable but I'll cuff you to the railings out on the top of the landing there." He'd checked them while they were each in the bathroom, the ornate metalwork was sturdy enough and fixed well into the stone floor. "I'll write a note and put it in my jacket, in case things don't work out, telling them that the two of you are here."

It was obvious that Callie still couldn't make up her mind about Dan or this whole situation, but his final comment seemed to throw her more than anything else he'd said. It struck Dan as the most natural thing in the world, that he should make sure they weren't left to starve to death in an empty building if he got killed, but she looked touched by the gesture.

"Dan, you still don't have to do this."

He smiled at her and said, "But I'm going to. And now I need to ask you both some questions." Her face darkened again, as if she suspected she'd been lured into a trap. "Where will they be, these four guys?"

"There's a lodge, but he might only have . . ."

"Josh, shut your mouth!"

Josh looked at her, defiant, as if to remind her that she wasn't his senior officer or, even if she had been, she wasn't anymore, and he was deliberate as he said again, "There's a lodge, but he might only have one guy in there if he's down to four. Maybe two, and one of them will walk the grounds every now and then. The other two will be in the house—they hang around the kitchen most of the time, but maybe not tonight."

"Good. Is his wife there, other family, staff?"

"Staff won't be there in the evening. And his wife's away. They've just had a new grandson . . ."

Callie added, to no one in particular, "Harry's second, born two weeks ago."

At first he thought she was challenging him, but he guessed she was aware of the irony, that Harry Brabham was building a happy family for himself.

"How long till they wait for backup from the Berlin station?"

Callie answered, saying, "He probably called it in as soon as I spoke to him on the phone."

She was trying to put him off going, but Josh laughed and said, "I doubt it. It would be the last resort. And I'm talking the absolute last resort. We don't officially exist, or at least, not here in Berlin. Bill sent someone home in the summer because he went out for a drink with someone from the embassy. He'll barricade the place, but he won't call for backup, not unless he's the last man standing."

"What kind of surveillance does he have in place?"

"Motion sensors on the perimeter, cameras with night vision. There's nothing you can do about the motion sensors but they've been erratic ever since he moved in there, so they ignore them a lot of the time—maybe not tonight, though. The cameras . . ." Josh weighed something up, then nodded to himself and said, "If it would help, I can show you how to knock them out for ten minutes—there's a flaw in the way the computer runs them."

Even as he was still speaking, Callie had looked at him with consternation, and she said now, "Josh, what are you doing? If you help him in any way, you're breaking the law, you're probably committing treason."

"You think?" She didn't respond, and he pointed at the laptop and said, "You think he faked that tape?" Again, she didn't answer. "Exactly. You wanna report me, Callie, you go ahead, but I know I'm doing the right thing. Because we've been helping them sweep people like Dan here under the carpet, but you know what, who's to say in five years they won't be trying to sweep us under it?"

"There are things here that need to be answered, but if you help him, I will report you."

Josh stared at her for a few seconds, then turned to Dan and said, "You could probably breach it without this, but I can set it up on one of your laptops there. Basically, if someone with an authorized code—someone like me—reports a malfunction on the surveillance system, the thing does a full check on itself, and after ten minutes it'll confirm that there's no malfunction. But here's the thing—mother of all fuck-ups—the system shuts down all its elements and brings them back online one by one to check them, but it brings the cameras on last. So for nearly ten minutes, no cameras."

"You can set it up so that I can hit it just before I go in there?"

"Of course. You just hit the Enter key when you're ready to go."

"Good. Set it up."

Josh pulled the laptop over in front of him. Dan thought of telling him to restrict his activities to what they'd just discussed, not to try contacting anyone else, but he could tell Josh was on side now. Callie wasn't, and it was for all the right reasons, but she was still wrong. She was staring at Josh with utter disbelief.

She could tell Dan was staring at her in turn, but she showed no acknowledgement and said only to Josh, "Aiding and abetting in the murder of four CIA officers. As well as treason, I really hope you're calling this right, Josh, because you'll spend the rest of your life in prison if you're not."

Dan said, "Even if he ends up on the wrong side, I guess for Josh to face the consequences, someone would have to report what he's done here. That's not me."

Josh looked up from what he was doing and met Callie's eyes, asking her the question.

"No, I'm not making promises like that. Not until I know all the facts."

Dan saw that as promising for some reason, a sign that she was wavering, but Josh looked blasé now and said, "I'll take my chances. I know I'm doing the right thing." He looked up at Dan, "I'll be straight, I don't know that you're doing the right thing, but I know I am. I always had an idea Brabham was rotten."

Dan smiled in acknowledgement. Callie shook her head, as if unsure how any of it had come to this.

"Okay, this is ready to go. Hit the Enter key and within thirty seconds the cameras will be down and out for nearly ten minutes."

"Good, thanks. You said one of the guys walks the grounds. About how often?"

"On a normal night, every hour, maybe. Tonight, I'd guess every half hour."

Dan looked to the window. It was dark outside now.

"I'm heading off now. I'll have to cuff you, like I said, so you better both have a bathroom break." They stood, and he looked at Callie, seeing more than ever, in the way she carried herself, that she could be dangerous if she had a mind to be. "Callie, despite everything, I like you, I like that you've held your ground, even though I think you're wrong. Now you might be thinking this is your last opportunity to stop me, so I'll warn you again—if you try anything, I'll kill you. You have to believe me on that."

Her eyes were fierce as she said, "Why wouldn't I believe you? It's the only thing you've said for which I've got incontrovertible evidence."

He showed them to the bathroom, then cuffed them to the railings at the top of the stairs. He put his bag together again, being careful to lay the primed laptop on top of everything else.

He stopped on the stairs before heading down, and looked at them, nodding another acknowledgement to Josh. Then he said to Callie, "There is one other thing I said that you know to be true." She raised her eyebrows, giving him nothing. "I said I wouldn't kill you if I didn't have to."

And with that he walked down the stairs and out into the cold Berlin night.

Chapter Forty

He took the black BMW and headed out of the city. It had been overcast and cold since he'd arrived in Berlin, the atmosphere itself possessed of a hollow metallic quality. Now as he drove, the first flakes of snow were falling on the still air. It was early in the year for it, and hard to believe that just a few days before, in Auxerre, it had felt like an Indian summer. Even Sweden had been warmer than this.

Brabham's place was on a quiet and narrow residential street, tree-lined, the road bordered all the way along with a mixture of hedges, fences and walls. The houses on one side were big, mansions and villas, but on the other side, the shore of the lake, they were more like miniature estates with gabled and tiered manor houses, all of them no doubt described with false modesty by their owners as villas.

He parked up before reaching Brabham's place. There were other cars parked on the side of the street, so there was nothing conspicuous about him stopping there, and with the dark and the snow settling, he doubted anyone would pay much attention to a figure walking purposefully.

He kept to the far side of the road, and walked right past and kept going. The property was bordered by a fence of metal railings, about six feet high, with a neatly trimmed hedge immediately behind it that was slightly higher. At the entrance, the fence curved inward to the gates, forming a semi-circle, the gates themselves set into stone pillars. And beyond one of the gateposts was the small security lodge, built in the same stone.

Dan noticed cameras on the fence there, but pointed downwards to see anyone waiting to gain access. He could see a light on in the lodge too, though couldn't see through the window from this angle. The main house, a big old pre-war mansion, was probably another fifty yards back from the lodge, partially obscured by trees and shrubs, no lights visible bar for an ornate porch light next to the main door.

Once he was a decent distance beyond the property, and onto the next which seemed to be separated by a much higher and broader hedgerow, he turned and walked back again to the car. He kept his head down, and not just for effect because the snow was falling harder now, forming a mantle that was already taking the edge off the darkness—that would make it harder to get in unseen.

He noticed that the border on the side nearest the car was a similarly high and thick hedge. He guessed there had to be something else there too, given that the hedge couldn't extend all the way down to the lake shore. That was probably what they feared most, someone coming in from the neighboring properties or someone coming in off the lake. They probably wouldn't be expecting him to come in the front.

When he reached the car he noticed that one of the guys he'd killed had left an overcoat in the back seat, and he reached in to grab it, thinking it would make a nice decoy, bundled up and thrown over to set off the motion sensors. But then he spotted a football down on the floor behind the driver seat. He could imagine those two guys throwing the ball to each other in idle moments, dreaming of their quarterback days in high school.

He left the coat but put the ball on the passenger seat, then climbed in and checked that he was ready, that he had enough ammunition, that the laptop was primed and ready to go. He drove on then, until he was alongside the property, and pulled up right next to the fence.

He hit Enter on the laptop, watched as it started the process Josh had promised. He got out of the car and couldn't help but smile as he kicked the ball at a thirty-degree angle, roughly over the roof of the lodge, towards the far boundary where he was certain he heard it smack into the hedge and bounce down onto the lawn. That would do it.

He was about to move when he heard a door open somewhere ahead of him, and then a voice, clear on the snowy air. "Okay, okay, I'll check, but I guarantee it's a fault."

The door closed, but a second later it opened again, and a different voice called out, "Teddy?" When he got no reply he said to himself, but still audible, "Jesus, what a mess." And once more the door closed.

Dan guessed the second guy had called out to let Teddy know the cameras had also gone down. Whatever the case, he'd struck lucky with the ball. He ran up the front of the car now, onto the roof and then over the fence and hedge, landing on the snow-covered lawn. He recovered, turned and sprinted toward the lodge, but stopped short.

The door was heavy duty, and he could see from here that it had a keypad. He'd probably have to wait for Teddy to come back, but that solution raised problems of its own. If Teddy came back soon he'd see Dan's footprints in the snow. If he didn't, if he decided to walk the boundary, Dan could be left sitting there for more than the ten minutes he had before the cameras came back online.

The only thing Dan had in his favor was that he knew another motion sensor had gone off, registering his arrival over the fence.

Even if the guy in the lodge didn't pay much credence to it, he'd want Teddy to check it out.

Dan moved around the side of the lodge, looking across the disturbingly light gardens, illuminated by the snow. Teddy was nowhere to be seen. There was a window on the side of the lodge, giving a view over the house. Dan crouched and crept under it, then turned and walked back full height, tapping lightly on the glass as he passed.

He heard the guy inside the lodge say something, and even before Dan had got back around he heard the door open again, and the same voice saying, "I thought you were gonna check the south-east corner before you come back in?"

Dan turned the corner and shot the guy standing there in the chest. He fell backward into the open door, then into the lodge. The door started to close again, but one of the guy's feet was trapped in the gap and held it.

Dan jumped forward, pulled the door open and dragged the guy inside. He moaned slightly as Dan manhandled him out of the way. Dan stared, curious, because he'd hit him neatly—maybe the bullet had taken an unlucky deflection off the bone and missed his heart. He shot him again, then took in the room before him.

There was a bank of monitors, all blank at the moment, a couple of computer screens, one apparently keeping track of the motion sensors, another probably for more general use. The blinds were pulled over enough that no one would be able to see in from outside.

There were another couple of rooms off the main one and he checked them out quickly—a toilet and a room that looked unused but had a bunk in it. He moved a chair into the middle of the main room, facing the door, and sat down to wait on Teddy's return.

But he was still sitting there when the monitors all kicked into life again, the screens flickering before producing otherworldly views of the house and its surrounds. He turned and looked at them, spotting Teddy immediately.

Dan got his bearings and saw that Teddy had decided to do a circuit after all. He'd been down and walked along the lake shore, and was now heading back up the eastern boundary. Dan kept watching; as he turned, as he headed back toward the lodge, as he spotted something and crouched down.

He should have covered his tracks—it hadn't been snowing long enough to erase them. Dan heard a distant tinny voice, and realized it was an earpiece on the dead guy. He reached over, grabbed it, listened in.

"Something definitely came over . . ." Dan glanced at the monitors, could almost see him follow the tracks with his eyes and see where they led to. When he spoke again, it was low and cautious, "Rick?" He cursed lightly under his breath when there was no response, and drew his gun. Nothing more came through the earpiece, but even in the fuzzy light of the cameras, Dan could see he was talking to someone else.

Dan looked back down at the guy who'd apparently been called Rick. He'd tried to call Teddy before he was out of earshot—it hadn't occurred to Dan that he then would have spoken to him over the wires, telling him the cameras were down, to check that corner. That was why Teddy had taken the full tour.

At the moment, Teddy was still standing exactly where he'd been inspecting the snow, as if waiting for backup, though Dan couldn't see anyone emerging from the house. Then he understood exactly what Teddy was waiting for, because the monitors died again, shut down by someone in the house.

He couldn't stay here. He hit the lights, then eased the door open and stepped out into his old tracks. He moved along the wall of the lodge, where the snow had not yet gathered, and into the shelter of the hedge, where he dropped to the floor which was cold but had once again been sheltered from the snow.

Dan lay still on his side, his back pushed under the hedge, listening. He could hear cars in the distance, but almost nothing else. Nearby, he could even hear the soft patter of the snow making contact. There was nothing from the house, and nothing to see either, because it was all but out of sight from where he lay.

He seemed to have been lying there for minutes when he became aware of other sounds, as indistinct as the snowfall, but definitely there. Teddy was edging toward the lodge, keeping his own movements slow and careful so that he could listen out for Dan in turn.

He couldn't see him though, even against the snow, even when the sound had become distinct enough to suggest he wasn't many yards away. Dan tipped his head, and realized now why he hadn't seen him. Teddy had come up with the same idea, and was edging carefully along the hedge, using its shadow for cover.

From the lodge it would have camouflaged him, but from where Dan lay, he could see his shadow clearly, rippling along the front of the hedge. He'd have been able to get a better shot by rolling out into the open, but he didn't want to risk the movement, so he just brought his arm around in one swift movement and fired.

Teddy groaned with the impact, and let off a volley of shots, one of them hitting the door of the lodge. He fell then, slumping, easily visible now as a black mass upon the white lawn. Dan fired into his crumpled body again and jumped up.

He ran towards him, taking a head shot as soon as he had a clear visual, though unlike with Rick, it seemed he'd hit lucky with the first two. As he looked down at the messed-up face, a barely audible, insect-like noise sounded in Teddy's earpiece, one of the guys in the house responding to the shots, which even with the silencers had produced a racket.

Dan ignored it. He readied himself to move instead, thinking through how best to approach the house, but the decision was made for him. Because when Teddy didn't respond to the voice in his ear, the owner of that voice answered in his own way by turning on floodlights which tore through the darkness, blinding him, lighting up the gardens like some Christmas theme park. There was no time left for strategy—Dan started running even before he heard the first shot.

Chapter Forty-one

Another couple of shots came in quick succession. It was a sniper rifle of some sort, being fired from high up with a good view over the gardens on that side. Dan dived into the nearest stand of shrubs and trees, and even then, scrabbled to get behind the trunk of one of the trees, knowing the shrubs wouldn't offer much protection.

It was only then that he was absolutely certain he hadn't been hit. But he was still a good sprint across open lawn from the cover of the house. He looked back across the dazzlingly bright snow now, fresh flakes still falling and catching the light, Teddy's body already getting a dusting.

Dan slid down the trunk and onto his belly, then crawled along the back of the stand of shrubs. He wasn't visible, he knew that much, but a shot still fired out and he felt it pull at his back and plough into the snow with an explosive thud. He crawled faster, made the cover of a bigger tree, sat up.

He didn't feel hurt, but gingerly slid his hand behind his back and felt his jacket. The bullet had ripped shreds through it but hadn't touched him. Ironically, it filled him with unease, because it made him feel he was riding his luck.

He also guessed they were using thermal cameras, given that they'd known exactly where to fire. And that meant they knew exactly where he was right now, probably even knew what his next move would be. He had no choice but to make that move, though—all he could do was play it fast.

He pushed himself up into a standing position, glanced out from one side of the tree, and before he'd even heard the shot that followed, he leaned out the other side, fired a shot at the upper windows, then ran, hurtling across the lit lawns, ignoring the cover now but aiming only to tighten the angle and get to the house.

One, two, three shots, but all somewhere behind him. He kept running, found a side door—locked—kicked it in and stepped inside. It was a boot room or pantry, in darkness, perhaps leading to the kitchen that Josh had mentioned as their usual haunt.

He moved on, found an alcove set back, not even sure what it was, and he stepped back into its shadows and waited. He could hear footsteps somewhere above, hurried, and then a voice, though he couldn't make out the words.

Then he heard the same voice again, this time raised, saying, "Bill, he's in the house!"

Dan didn't hear Bill's response, but whatever it was, a door slammed and footsteps hurried across the floor. They stopped again, but Dan picked up the faint creaking of a stair. A few moments later he could sense that there was someone just along the corridor from him, not far away.

The guy had probably seen the forced door, but he was too smart to investigate. Dan could hear the faint sounds of him backing away again, followed by an ominous total silence, and then the alcove he was in filled with light. He guessed the lights could all be controlled centrally and the guy had turned them on.

He let his eyes adjust, then turned and saw a small wooden door behind him, up a step. If he was right, there was a flight of stairs behind that door, once used by the servants of the house. There was a metal latch on it, and carefully, Dan lifted it and eased the door a fraction.

It let out a brief high-pitched creak, so he stopped, but he could see there were definitely stairs beyond. He just had to hope there was still an opening at the top and the house hadn't been remodeled, because as soon as he pulled this door open all the way he'd be giving his position away.

He opened it swiftly, the hinges letting out a horror-film creak, and ran up. The stairs were stacked on both sides with various cleaning supplies and he could see another door at the top, but he'd committed himself now. He hopped up between the bottles and cans and brushes, reached the top, clicked the latch. Nothing.

He could hear the guy running too, along a hallway, up the main stairs. Dan was at a disadvantage because he didn't know the layout of the upper floor, didn't know where this let out, even if he could get it open.

He barged into the door and it yielded, thickly at first, then loosening as something crashed on the other side. He could see a lamp on the floor in front of him, guessing a small table had been placed in front of the door.

And now he could hear the guy reaching the top of the stairs ahead of him along the landing. Dan dropped back down the flight he'd just climbed, onto his belly, and as the guy appeared on the corridor Dan fired off a couple of shots, hitting him in the leg.

The guy managed to return fire, or fired simultaneously, but it hit the door high above where Dan was lying. The guy staggered, fell backwards into the door of one of the rooms. Dan heard him try the handle and mutter something—it was locked.

For a short while there was silence. Dan listened out for signs of Brabham and the other guy. He'd imagined from listening that the room they were in would be behind him, but looking ahead he suspected the stairs rose up in the middle from a central hall like an inner courtyard, the landing forming a square with rooms on all four sides.

The conversation had definitely come from this side of the house, so if Brabham wasn't behind him, the room he was in had to be ahead of him and to the right. There was only one problem; the guy ensconced in the doorway, bleeding, but no less lethal for that.

Dan pushed himself back to his feet, stepped lightly up the remaining stairs and to the edge of the doorway. He waited again.

Then the guy started to speak, saying, "Hendricks, the game's up, we've called for back—"

Dan stepped out, walked directly towards him and fired twice, both to the chest. The guy dropped his gun and slumped against the door with an astonished look on his face. He slid down it then, his legs buckling under him. The thigh wound had been bleeding out badly anyway, probably weakening him, slowing his responses.

Dan waited a second, heard the telltale insectlike scratching coming from the guy's earpiece. He stepped over him and moved to the edge of the big square landing that looked down over the hall.

There wasn't much margin for error here, because if he was wrong about them being on the side to his right, he'd be caught in the open, an easy target from the cover of any other doorway looking out over the stairwell.

He went back, picked up the dead guy's gun, then returned to the corner of the landing and tossed the gun out on to the stairs. It clattered down half a dozen of them before coming to rest.

In the silence that followed, he heard a whisper, nothing more, backing up his hunch. He edged out, to the first door, moving to the side of it before turning the handle and pushing it open.

There was no response. He moved along, repeated the motion, then with the third door. Instantly this time, a shot was fired, so eagerly that it clipped the door even as it opened and ricocheted into the frame. Another followed immediately afterward, whistling out and hitting the wall across the other side.

Dan smiled, and said, "How do you want to play this, Bill?"

"That's up to you, Dan."

The other guy in the room said, "No, with all respect, sir, it isn't."

That put a location on them both in Dan's mental map of the room, but Brabham's voice came back avuncular, aimed at Dan more than the guy in the room, saying, "Relax, Jim, I'm sure Dan doesn't want to kill anyone else this evening."

Once more, Dan took advantage of the split in concentration, moving as Brabham spoke, stepping into the room, firing as soon as he had even the promise of a sight, hitting the guy in the head. In turn, Jim also managed to get off another shot, but only into the floor a yard in front of where he was standing.

Only now, only as he turned and leveled the gun at Brabham, did he get any sense of the room they were in. It was a study, the walls lined with books, a desk at the far end with a view out through the window, which he guessed looked out over the lake.

On this side of the room, there was a leather chesterfield sofa on the wall facing Dan, and a couple of high-backed leather chairs. Brabham was sitting in one of those chairs, but turned to face the door rather than the sofa, as if he'd been choreographing this meeting all along.

Brabham looked at the dead officer on the floor beyond the sofa, and said with a bemused tone, "Well, I got that wrong, didn't I?"

Chapter Forty-two

"Are you going to kill me too? I hadn't thought so, but it seems I'm not much good at reading your intentions."

He looked older than in the pictures Dan had seen. He was carrying a little more weight, his hair greyer, but he looked healthy and relaxed, like a man who was comfortable with where he was in life and what lay ahead.

"Are you armed?"

Brabham responded by opening his jacket for Dan to see. Dan walked over and sat on the chesterfield.

Brabham stood and said, "Can I get you a drink? I usually treat myself to a single malt around this time of evening. You'll join me?"

Dan could see the bottles and glasses on a small table near the desk. He nodded and watched as Brabham walked over and poured two hefty measures. He couldn't see which brand it was. When Brabham came back he put the drinks on the table in front of the sofa, then moved his chair so that he was facing Dan.

He picked up his glass then and said, "Good health." Dan followed suit and they both drank. "What's the aim of all of this, Dan? I ask because, if you thought you were making yourself safe, you've wildly miscalculated. Even if you don't kill me, what you've done here today will just make you an even higher priority."

"That'll be less of a problem if your operation's shut down."

Brabham looked incredulous, as if he were talking to a child, and said, "This operation won't shut down. If I resign they'll just replace me. There are people higher up the food chain who want this, who see a need to draw a line under the past excesses of people like Patrick White. Yes, I'm sure he's painted himself to you as the sheriff, tidying up this town, but it's his mess we've been trying to deal with."

"Interesting way of going about it." Dan put his gun on the sofa next to him and said, "But while we're talking of excesses, you surely know this wasn't just a response to your people coming after us. It's about some of your own excesses, about why you sent someone up to Jack Redford's place." Brabham raised his eyebrows, feigning surprise, doing a good job of it. "You know what I'm talking about, Bill, I'm talking about your son murdering Sabine Merel and you covering it up."

There was a flicker of something behind Brabham's eyes at the mention of Sabine, panic or fear, but then he rallied and laughed, saying, "I don't know what kind of line Patrick White has sold you, but—"

"We have the tape. Patrick has the tape. You thought you got hold of the only copy but there was another."

Brabham didn't respond at first, and in the silence Dan was pretty sure he could hear vehicles approaching outside, too many for it to be just a random car passing.

Brabham smiled weakly and said, "I'm still not doing very well at reading your thoughts, Dan, but I suspect you've miscalculated again if you think Patrick's likely to go public with this tape of yours. He won't. He'll use it as leverage, to undermine me and the agency, to shore up his own position. He'll never make it public because, if he does, he'll lose that leveraging power."

Dan nodded. There was a good chance Brabham was right about all of it.

"You still made a mistake when you tried to kill me, Bill. And you made a bigger mistake when you killed my friends."

Brabham glanced over at the dead guy, and sounded bemused again as he said, "Yes, well, we can all be prone to miscalculations."

He could definitely hear cars outside now, and said, "Did you call for backup?"

"Reluctantly, yes. We put a call in to the Berlin station. I expect that's them now."

Dan felt his phone vibrate and took it out. It was Patrick.

He answered and Patrick said, "Dan, we're outside. What's the situation in there? Is it secure?"

"It's secure. I'm with Bill in his study upstairs. Everyone else is dead."

"Then I'll be up shortly. Try not to shoot me."

Dan ended the call, and in response to Brabham's look of expectancy, he said, "It's Patrick. He's on his way up."

"What a pleasant surprise—I haven't seen him in a few years. In fact, it's been too long."

Dan didn't respond, but sipped at his drink and said, "Is this an Oban?"

A door slammed open somewhere down below, followed by the sound of many footsteps, the suggestion of urgency but not high alert.

Brabham looked pleased and said, "Yes, it is Oban. You know your whisky?"

"I know this one."

"What a shame we couldn't have shared a glass under different circumstances."

"The circumstances wouldn't matter. You'd still be Bill Brabham."

"Touché."

Dan looked to the door as footsteps approached and Patrick White appeared, still in his trademark heavy overcoat, looking none the worse for the amount of travel he must have put in over the last few days. He looked at Dan and shook his head, smiling as if at his own folly rather than Dan's.

"Hello, Bill."

"Hello, Patrick. You're looking well. Your new role obviously agrees with you."

Patrick's smile dropped and he walked into the room, glancing at the dead body before saying, "Aren't you ashamed of yourself, Bill, on so many levels? I don't just mean Paris. I mean going after assets that served this agency, that served our country, and showed no signs of ever becoming a liability." As he talked, Dan noticed someone else appear in the doorway behind him, a guy with dark hair, not much older than Dan, looking more like a movie mob boss than someone from the intelligence community. Neither of the other two could see him from there, and Patrick continued, saying, "You're done, Bill, this is all finished."

Brabham didn't look fazed, and said only, "With all due respect, Patrick, you don't have the authority to make that decision."

"But I do," said the other guy, who stepped into the room now. He'd been looking at the body all the time he'd been in the doorway, but now his gaze found Dan, and looked full of disgust. "How many of my officers have you killed today, Mr. Hendricks?"

"I haven't been keeping count, but I guess around ten."

"You guess?"

"I guess. And you know, there's an easy way to ensure I don't kill any more—just don't have them try to kill me."

Patrick said, "Dan, this is Associate Deputy Director Frank Canale. He flew out with me. And, Frank, whatever the rights and wrongs, Dan was working for the ODNI and his actions were a direct response to attacks made on him, and on me."

Canale looked at him, but didn't answer, his expression alone seeming to suggest he didn't care. He nodded to himself then, looking around the room before he settled on Bill.

"There'll be a full investigation into all of this. We need to look at the decisions made in recent months, and at the actions that followed those decisions. We also need to look at some of the questionable practices that took place in the past, and those responsible for them." He threw a look at Patrick as he said this, before turning back to Brabham. "And we also need to look at people misusing agency resources to cover up past misdemeanors, because that's something that can't be tolerated."

Dan laughed and said, "Misdemeanors?" All three of them stared at him, and he repeated, "*Misdemeanors?* His son tried to rape a student in the US ambassador's residence in Paris."

Brabham sounded outraged and said, "That's ridiculous! You have no proof of that."

"No, we don't, because the one person who could have testified, is dead, murdered by your son."

Brabham had clearly had enough time to think since Dan had mentioned the tape to him, and he said now, "We tried to suppress the tape, I'll own up to that, and it was wrong, but any father would do the same. Because Harry didn't kill that girl. She was alive and well when he left her. It's as simple as that, and you can't prove otherwise, with the tape or without it."

Patrick looked at him and said, "The tape may not prove it categorically, Bill, but I'm sure you wouldn't want it to come out, all the same."

Canale sounded impatient, saying, "Enough. This isn't the time to discuss what we do with the tape."

Patrick smiled, probably taking satisfaction after the comments Canale had aimed at him, and said, "Actually, Frank, *we* won't decide anything. The tape is in the hands of the ODNI."

Giving ground, Canale said, "Very well, then we'll have to come to some arrangement about what's mutually beneficial." Patrick gave a barely visible nod in response, something Dan understood all too well. "Bill, I think it best you come back to Washington with me."

Bill nodded, downed the remainder of his whisky and stood. This was how easily things would be tied up, justice for the Merels and Redford and everyone between slipping through the cracks as they all jostled for influence and power.

Dan shook his head, laughing at the brazenness of it, and played nonchalantly with his phone as he said, "Oh, Frank, by the way, you asked how many of your officers I killed?"

His impatience growing, Canale said, "What of it?"

Knowing that it was riling him, Dan continued to sound distracted, pausing as he concentrated on the phone, saying, "Only, you didn't ask . . . about the ones I didn't kill. See . . . bear with me . . . yeah, I cuffed a couple of them to the railings . . . in a building across from Bill's office. They're unharmed, but . . . ."

Canale looked at Dan's phone and said, "You think you could deal with that after you finish telling me whatever it is you're telling me?"

"I'm almost done." He finished up on the phone, then looked up with a smile. "Done. Yeah, they're okay, unharmed. As for the phone, it's something I set up earlier, because you people are all the same. Maybe the tape doesn't prove he killed her, but even so, that tape, and the whole story, and contact details for the people who can back it up, has just been emailed to around thirty news agencies around the world. The *Washington Post, New York Times,* Reuters, CNN, the BBC, *Le Monde*—*they'll* be interested. You craven cowards, all of you. You'd rather have an attempted rapist and murderer serving in the US Congress than upset the apple cart. Well, shame on you, because it's out there now, so deal with it."

Dan held up his phone and smiled.

Brabham looked rattled for the first time, the color leaching from his face. He reached a hand out to the back of the chair, steadying himself.

He looked at Dan, full of hatred as he said, "You bastard. His wife's just had a baby, for God's sake."

"Two words, Bill—*Sabine Merel.*"

Bill shook his head, as if he hadn't heard or understood. He started to walk without conviction towards the door, but there was a strange quality about his movements, as if he might collapse. And then he went, his leg appearing to buckle, and too late Dan saw it was a feint—within seconds, Brabham had scooped up the dead man's gun and had it leveled now at Dan's face.

Dan didn't have time to react, only to take in the hatred and agitation in Brabham's expression. Patrick and Canale both flinched in response but stopped, seeing the same volatility Dan could see.

Dan had pushed him too far, and with an odd feeling of resignation, he knew this was it. He'd often wondered how he'd feel when he finally faced certain death, and here it was, an almost out-of-body acceptance that the time had come and he could simply stop trying.

Brabham wasn't quite ready to pull the trigger, though, and said again now, "You bastard! He was a good kid and he's a good man, and he doesn't deserve this, people like you . . ."

Canale said, "Bill . . ."

"No! You know the script, Frank—he broke in here, killed a load of people before we took him down. It's what he deserves."

"I'll testify to that not being true," said Patrick.

Without taking his eyes off Dan, he said, "What makes you think you'll testify to anything?" He stepped forward now, as if wanting more certainty. His hand was shaking slightly but the aim was true, the barrel of the gun oddly compelling from Dan's perspective. "You lowlife piece of scum."

Dan braced himself. The shot exploded, the room breaking apart. Patrick fell backwards, almost losing his footing. Brabham's face distorted and crumpled and he seemed to dive sideways to the floor, gun-hand flailing like a last desperate wave.

It took Dan a moment to take in that he hadn't been shot himself, another to make sense of the scene, the blood, the wound to the side of Brabham's head, Canale's own outstretched arm. Dan looked at him, still not entirely certain that this meant he was out of danger.

Maybe Patrick was just as unsure because he spoke first, saying simply, "Frank?"

Canale holstered his gun, looking remarkably calm considering he'd just shot someone in the head at close to point-blank range. And Dan wasn't naïve enough to think he'd done it to save *his* life—there had been some other calculation, perhaps just a realization that Bill had become a liability.

Now Canale said, "It's a different script, that's all—it'll be easier to tidy up this way." His phone started to ring and when he took it out and looked at it, a flash of anger crossed his face. He looked with contempt at Dan and put the phone back in his pocket.

"We'll talk, Patrick." He pointed at Dan, then, and said, "I hope for your sake, Mr. Hendricks, that we never cross paths again."

Dan didn't respond, the last couple of minutes having convinced him that he didn't want to make any more an enemy of Frank Canale than he already had. Besides, he was still too surprised at being alive to throw it away on a quip.

Canale took one more look at Brabham, bloodied and twisted, and strode out of the room, leaving Dan and Patrick with the corpses and a whole load of uncertainty. The only thing Dan really knew for sure was that he'd done what was right. Maybe it wouldn't prove to be the right thing for his own future, but it had been right all the same, and perhaps against the odds, he was still alive, for the time being at least.

Chapter Forty-three

Patrick looked down at Brabham and said, "What have you done, Dan?"

"You were gonna sit on it, weren't you?"

"I was going to use it to rein in Harry Brabham, and to bring an end to all of this." He gestured at the room around them, as if that encompassed Bill Brabham's entire operation. "And yes, with the tape public . . . I don't know, who can say what might happen now."

"You're saying I might not be safe?"

"I've no idea, frankly. I'll try to keep you safe and, chances are, you will be. I'm just saying, releasing that tape makes everything more volatile." He gestured towards Brabham as if to demonstrate that point. "Why did you do it?"

"Two reasons. Firstly, Sabine Merel. She was murdered, Patrick, and her family and friends have a right to know what happened, to have peace of mind, and they deserve justice."

"I wouldn't bank on justice, even now, and if you think this'll give them peace of mind, you're fooling yourself."

"Maybe, but I know I would want to know, if she'd been my daughter."

Patrick seemed to accept that, then said, "You said there were two reasons."

"Yeah, the other's Jack Redford. I don't know what kind of affinity I had with the guy, but he was up there in the middle of nowhere, working towards this, and he couldn't come out of hiding, so he never tracked down the copy. It just felt right to finish his work for him. I didn't know the guy, but I felt I owed him that much."

Patrick took in what he said, not passing comment, and said finally, "Well, whatever else happens, you did the job I asked, so I'm grateful for that, even if the denouement proved a little excessive."

"You gave me their contact details—you must have known I'd come to Berlin at some point."

"Sure, I thought you'd spy on them. I didn't honestly anticipate that you'd come and wipe them out." He laughed a little and Dan laughed too. "So what's next? You're done with this?"

"Not quite. I met a guy called Eliot Carter, and he gave me the details for someone called Tom Crossley. You know either of them?"

"I knew Eliot years ago. Tom Crossley, I'm not familiar with. What's his part in it?"

"They were friends. Carter thinks he might know more about Redford's disappearance. I hope so, anyway. Like I said, the guy got under my skin in some way—don't know why."

"Don't you? Isn't it because you look at him and wonder if you're looking at your own future?"

"Maybe." They fell into a brief silence, the continuing sounds of the team going through the house around them, doing whatever it was they did in this kind of situation. "What about you? What's your next move?"

"I carry on. As long as you're not too hot to handle, I might even have some more work for you if you're interested."

Dan suddenly became aware of how strange it was to be talking in such a measured way, surrounded by the visceral wreckage of all this violence.

He stood and said, "We'll have to see about that, but come on, let's get out of here." They made for the door and out onto the landing, looking down at the people coming and going in the hall below them. "By the way, one of the guys I cuffed over in Charlottenburg, a tech guy called Josh, he could be a real asset to you, and I think he'd willingly jump ship, if you make him an offer."

"I'll bear that in mind—what about the other guy?"

"The other guy would be a real asset too, but I'm less certain about her jumping ship."

"I see." They walked down the stairs, ignored by most of the people moving about, some of them in regular clothes, some of them in combats. "I do wish you hadn't killed quite so many people. I had a feeling you would as soon as I told you about Charlie, but even so . . ."

"Yeah, and ironically, the guy who tortured Charlie wasn't even here—he'd flown home for an operation on his leg."

"The guy Charlie shot in the woods?"

"The same. One Alex Robinson. And I have to warn you, Patrick, whether or not I work for you again, whether or not I want to cross swords with Frank Canale, if I ever encounter Robinson, there'll only be one outcome."

He smiled at Dan and said, "Then let's hope you don't bump into him."

They crossed the hall and out through the front doors, which were wide open. The grounds were still floodlit and the snow was falling heavier now. The various vehicles parked randomly in front of the house were already snow-capped.

Patrick looked around, and for a moment Dan thought he was about to say something about how beautiful it was, but he said, "Damn it, I came with Frank and it looks like he's already gone. I'm not sure how I'll get back."

"I'll drive you back. I stole one of their cars—it's parked out on the street."

"Oh. Well great, I appreciate that." They walked along the drive, beyond the reach of the floodlights and out into the darker street. "The Swedes are very happy, by the way. I think I'll be able to rely on their assistance again in the future, not that I envisage much call for it."

Dan thought of Inger, wanted to call her, wanted to board a plane that night and land in Stockholm, become a new person. It would have to wait a few more days though, at the very least.

"I don't suppose you much envisaged working with them this time."

"How very true." He walked for a few paces, before adding, "One thing I'll say about Jack Redford, he really knew how to disappear."

Dan nodded, again thinking of his own future, and of the day when he might need to do the same. For all he knew, that day was today, and with that thought he walked on with Patrick White, back into the snow and shadows.

Chapter Forty-four

Dan had expected to find Geneva similarly blanketed with snow, but though it was cold, the streets were dry and the sky was clear and blue. He called Tom Crossley first, speaking to a woman who told him he was expected, then headed over there.

It was a modern apartment building, in the middle of the city. The same woman answered the door, a woman who looked Southeast Asian, though he couldn't be sure of the country. She smiled and showed him in to a sitting room where Crossley was playing with a very young child and a wooden train set on the floor.

It sent a wave of sadness through him, but he packed it away again and took in the view through the windows—despite being in the middle of quite a built-up area they had a great view over toward the lake and the mountains beyond. It was a nice place too, spacious, tidy, lots of clean lines.

Crossley glanced up, a guy in his fifties and looking it, his face lined, but also still looking incredibly fit, his arm and chest muscles still neatly defined under his T-shirt, his shaved head giving no indication of whether he was grey or bald. He smiled, and said, "Dan Hendricks?"

"That's me. Thanks for seeing me, Mr. Crossley."

"Tom, and I'm glad you came." He jumped up in one fluid motion and said, "You've met Patty." He looked at her then and said, "We'll go in the study."

"Drinks?"

He looked questioningly at Dan and Dan said, "I'm fine thanks."

"We'll be okay. Thanks, Patty."

Patty nodded, and went and took Tom's place with the child, talking in her own language—Vietnamese, he thought, now that he heard her speak.

As they walked through to the study, a more cluttered space, full of military and travel memorabilia, books and journals, cuttings from papers, Tom said, "So you saw Eliot Carter—who put you on to him?"

"Georges Florian, from DGSE."

Tom gestured to a chair, but stopped short of sitting down himself, saying, "Georges Florian? Was he in the Foreign Legion years ago?"

"That's the guy."

"Jeez. I thought he was dead." He sat down now, and said, "And how's that old queen, Carter? Still shacked up with his Arab boys?"

"Yeah, his apartment was very much a Little Morocco."

Tom laughed and said, "God love him. And let me tell you, in our line of work, that guy is worth his weight in gold."

Dan wondered how much Tom knew about his own career, or if he was just assuming they were in the same kind of business.

"Are you still active, Tom?"

"Not really. But you know how it is." He reached into a drawer and searched around for a few seconds before pulling out an aged-looking envelope.

He held it up then and said, "It's funny, I was only looking at this the day before Eliot called to say you were coming. I was relieved when he told me. See, when he disappeared, Jack sent me this key for a safety deposit box in Paris—the details are in there with it. He said he'd pick it up himself one day or that someone would come for it. Well, I guess you're that someone."

He leaned over and put the envelope on the desk next to Dan.

Dan was about to object, to explain that he had no right to act as Redford's representative, but he didn't. At first he told himself that Patrick would probably make use of whatever was in that box, but he knew the real truth, that he just wanted all the details he could find about Jack Redford and why he'd run.

"Thanks. Do you want it back?" Tom shrugged, shaking his head as if to ask why he'd want it back when he'd only just managed to pass it on. "On the subject of letters, Eliot told me Jack had received a letter not long before he disappeared, someone from Beirut, that it had unsettled him."

Tom looked doubtful and said, "Not a letter, not that I'm aware of, anyway. I sent him an email and I know that upset him. A friend of ours, someone who'd been in Beirut with us, he was killed in a hit and run."

Dan immediately thought of Mike Naismith in Baltimore, and said, "Suspicious?"

"Who can tell? Jack thought it might be. It upset him, I know that much. So chances are that's what Eliot meant when he talked about a letter."

That was disappointing, and apart from the promise of the key to the box, Dan felt he'd slightly wasted Tom Crossley's time by coming here.

Almost as a way of making up for that and giving the brief meeting some substance, he said, "What were you doing in Beirut?"

He smiled broadly and said, "Cutting loose. It just so happened we were all of us free. I had some friends out there and suggested to Jack he should come out for a while. Then a couple more guys got wind of it and showed up. We were there for about six months, I

guess." He got up and moved across the room to an oriental chest
of drawers, searching through them before pulling out a fat brown
envelope. "It was a good time to be in Beirut . . ."

"So this was after the hostage crisis and all that?"

"Long after, years after. Yeah, things were looking up for Beirut back then, talk of it returning to the way it was before the war.
Doesn't look like it'll happen now, but those were good days."

He pulled a bundle of photos out of the envelope and flicked
through them. He pulled one out and handed it to Dan. It was of
three guys standing with arms over each other's shoulders. One was
Tom, his hair cropped but not shaved as it was now, but otherwise
not looking much different. The one in the middle was tall and
blonde, with chiseled features.

The third guy looked smaller, though Dan guessed he was average size and only looked small because of the scale of the two guys
he was with. He looked relaxed, his hair scruffy, his shirt tucked
in on one side but hanging out on the other—the kind of good-
looking traveler who turned up in places like that with a guitar.

As he looked, Tom said, "The guy in the middle is Jonny, the
guy who was killed in the hit and run."

"Jonny? He looks German or . . ."

Tom laughed and said, "Everyone always thought he was German. He was from San Diego, a real surf dude—slightly crazy but a
good guy to be around."

Dan nodded and said, "What about the guy on the right?"

As if it was obvious, Tom said, "That's Jack."

"Really?" Dan looked at it again. "It's not like the pictures I've
seen. Is this how he looked?"

Tom reached out and took the photo back, smiling as he looked
at it, saying, "Yeah, that's him alright. He was a charmer, could
charm the leaves off the trees. Very unassuming guy, but, I don't
know, I guess that was part of his appeal. And I tell you, those

were happy days." He flicked through some more of the photos and handed another one to Dan. "That's kind of a typical night out there, typical dinner."

Dan looked at the picture, which showed half a dozen people sitting at a restaurant table which was laden with plates and wine bottles.

"You're not in this."

"I was probably taking the picture."

Jonny, the blonde guy was there, his face slightly flushed from the heat and probably the drink. Jack Redford was there too, and Dan was reinforcing this new image of him in his mind—this was how he looked. Then he noticed the woman sitting next to him, and felt a strange, almost tectonic dislocation in his thoughts.

He held it closer, staring at her features as he said, "Who's the woman with Jack? That's if she is with Jack?"

"Oh she's with Jack, alright. Maria. Beautiful, huh?" Dan nodded without speaking. "They were inseparable. Met at the end of the first month we were there, just stayed together. I think he seriously contemplated settling down with her."

Dan still couldn't take his eyes off her, because he recognized this woman, and his voice sounded distant even to himself, as he said, "Why didn't he?"

"You know how it is, in our business. Settling down isn't such an easy thing to do."

Dan looked up and said, "You seem to be doing okay."

Tom grinned and said, "Yeah, at my age. Never thought it would happen but, man, I'm blessed."

"Can I keep this photo?"

"Sure. I've got plenty and I hardly look at them anymore. Very few buddies left to sit and reminisce with."

Dan nodded, understanding that, but his own mind was reeling away from him. These past weeks, he'd thought one thing after another about Jack Redford, and yet the man had managed in some way to elude him, just as he'd eluded everyone else, until the bus crash, until now.

When Dan had first gone up to what had then been Jacques Fillon's place, he'd pictured his life as so limited, tinkering with a bike, riding the bus every day, and he'd almost despised him for it. He hadn't understood then, about the hidden shelter, the quest to bring down Brabham, to get justice for a girl he'd never known and had no connection with, Sabine Merel.

But even when he had learned those things, he'd still only understood half of the man. Jack Redford. He'd acted heroically on the day he died, but in truth, the whole of the last twelve years had been an act of heroism, one little act every day when he'd boarded that bus. That was what Dan only really understood for the first time now as he looked at this photograph—even in hiding, Jack Redford had never stopped being a hero.

Epilogue

He spent two days in Stockholm with Inger. She'd suggested at first that he stay at her place, but for some reason, he'd checked into a hotel not far away instead, not wanting to crowd her. He needn't have worried because he spent the whole time in her apartment anyway.

Two days, most of it seemingly spent in bed. When they went out it wasn't far, to the café where he'd met her that day a few weeks before, or to local stores, the streets clear but cold and the day punctuated with snow flurries.

And for all the time he was with her he was dreaming what this life might be like, imagining himself taking an apartment nearby, or forgetting caution and moving in with her right away. That was the kind of life he dreamed about, where being cautious only applied to not taking things too fast in a relationship.

They flew up to Luleå on the third day, and within twenty minutes of take-off, the landscape below them was already snow-covered, as if bedding down for winter. The last time he'd taken this flight, he'd been warned that the north would be a lot colder but had found it remarkably benign—only now, looking down, did he believe that it could be so different.

Inger had talked about arranging a car, but she'd spoken to Per and he'd been insistent, so he was there to meet them at the airport and talked animatedly about the weather for much of the onward drive north. The deep snow visible all around them was apparently unusual even for them at this time of year.

He drove them directly to Siri's house; a big wooden place, bigger than the one Redford had lived in, but closer to the quiet road, with a few other houses within view. Dan looked at those other houses as they pulled up—they all looked blank and lifeless and he wondered if people lived in them all year round, wondered, too, if any of the kids who'd died in the crash had lived there.

Siri's grandparents came out onto the porch even as Per pulled up. They were grey but trim and upright, reminding him in some way of Mr. Eklund, the same rugged healthiness. Like Mr. Eklund, too, they waved as the three of them got out of the car, though they were not many feet away.

They stepped through the gate and as they walked up the path, the man said, "Welcome Mr. Hendricks, Miss Bengtsson. Hello, Per."

Inger spoke back in Swedish, and Dan said, "Thank you for agreeing to see us Mr. Nyström."

Per said quietly, "Doctor Nyström."

Nyström laughed and said, "Yes, I'm still the local doctor, though I should retire soon."

His wife made some dismissive but good-humored response in Swedish to that suggestion, then said, "I hope we'll be able to help with your inquiries."

"I'm hoping we'll be able to help you."

They showed them into a warm and welcoming kitchen where they sat around a heavy table and Mrs. Nyström served them coffee and some sort of home-made cookies. They'd only been sitting a few minutes when Siri walked in.

Dan stood, and then realized the formality of it made her uncomfortable so he sat again and she sat down opposite him.

She looked shyly at Inger, then at Dan, and said, "Hello."

She was in black again, but this time wearing a shapeless black sweater. Her skin was a little clearer than when they'd seen her a few weeks ago, and it reminded him once more that she would undoubtedly be a beautiful woman. Looking at her grandmother, he could see the same bone structure, the same lively eyes.

Dan took out the two letters he'd found in Redford's safe-deposit box, which had disappointed him at first, until he'd actually looked at them, at what they said. One had also proved Eliot Carter right and Tom wrong, though that hardly mattered now.

He smiled then, and said, "Siri, the man who saved you was an American. His name wasn't Jacques Fillon, it was Jack Redford. He did top-secret work, mainly for the US government."

She smiled, the shyness falling away as she said, "So I was right, about him being a spy."

Inger nodded and said, "We didn't know for sure when we met you—we found out later."

Dan continued, saying, "About fourteen years ago, something went wrong, his life was put in danger and he chose a new identity and disappeared. Two years or so later, he turned up here."

Dr. Nyström said, "Is this connected with what we saw on the news, the congressman and the murder in Paris?"

His wife gestured to her husband and Siri, and said, "They both thought the same thing."

"Because of the dates, that's all," said Doctor Nyström.

Siri nodded in agreement with her grandfather. It was interesting to see the dynamic between them, that they'd discussed this and somehow come to the right conclusion.

Dan said, "It is connected. Jack Redford knew the truth, and that knowledge put him in danger. But it was no accident that he came here. You see, he'd received a letter, from a woman he'd known in Beirut."

The sudden shift in the story didn't seem to be lost on the grandparents. With the mention of Beirut, Mrs. Nyström caught her breath, and put her hand over her mouth. Her husband's eyes were fixed on Dan. Siri alone was looking confused, perhaps not knowing enough of the story to piece it together.

"The woman told Jack she'd had his baby. But because of this job that had gone wrong, he knew it wasn't safe to be near her. I'm guessing that, somehow, he discovered two years later that she'd died, cancer, and that was when he did what he did."

He reached into his jacket, and placed the photograph on the table in front of her. He pointed to the man in it.

"That's Jack Redford, and that sitting next to him is your mother, Maria. She was beautiful, and even though I only saw you once, that day out at Jack's house, I recognized her face immediately I saw this picture."

Both of Siri's grandparents had tears moistening their eyes now, though Siri only stared in wonder at the photo, studying it, apparently mesmerized by the long-lost evening captured there, and by the two key people she had never really known. "That was why he moved here, that was why he rode the bus every day, because it was the only way he had of seeing you. And that was why he saved you that day, not because you were the nearest person to him, but because you were the only person to him; you were his daughter, everything he had in the world."

They were silent for a moment, and then Dr. Nyström said, "It's incredible."

Dan nodded agreement and said, "Here are two letters that he left in a safe-deposit box in Paris. One is the letter from Maria telling him about Siri. The other's essentially his last will and testament, though it also explains why he had to disappear. It's addressed to Maria, and he makes clear that everything he has is left to her and the baby."

The enormity of it finally seemed to hit Siri, the fact that she had seen her father every day for years and never known it was him, the fact that he'd saved her, that she had found him only now, when it was too late.

"But he never even spoke to me. We never even said hello."

"Because he couldn't. Because he was Jacques Fillon."

Dan's mind flitted back to Luca. Many times in the early years he'd dreamed that it was a mistake, that Luca wasn't dead but had been taken away and was being raised by a relative. And often after those dreams, he'd imagined how it would be to meet him again, years later, a stranger, the joy and the sorrow of such an impossible meeting. So he understood all too well the exquisite pain Jack Redford must have felt each day, to be so close, and yet as far away as ever.

Siri looked at her grandparents, then turned to Inger with a helpless smile, and said, "I've tried to remember what he was saying to me before the crash, but my music—I could see him speaking, but . . . I've tried many times."

Mrs. Nyström added, "I've told her not to think about it, but now, with this, maybe I'm wrong."

Inger smiled sympathetically and said, "I think you can imagine the things he might have said. There's not much more you can do."

Siri picked up the photograph to look at it more closely.

Mrs. Nyström glanced at her, but then breathed in deeply and was composed as she said, "This is very difficult to take in, but we're so grateful to you, Mr. Hendricks, for finding out, and for coming to tell us."

"It was my pleasure. I never knew Jack Redford, but everything I've found out about him suggests he was a remarkable man."

Inger nodded in agreement, and though she looked conflicted

in some way, he sensed she was thinking of Sabine Merel, and of Redford's endless quest to bring her justice.

They didn't stay for long afterwards, conscious that this family needed time to digest what they'd just learned, to understand what it meant for them, for Siri in particular. And it seemed strange to Dan, as they waved them off from the porch, that he would never see them again, that he would play no other part now in their journey or Jack Redford's.

Per had hardly spoken, but as they drove away he said, "Would you like to visit the churchyard? It's not much further."

Inger looked bemused by the suggestion and said, "Any reason?"

Dan realized now that Per had also just heard the story for the first time, that he was moved by it, astounded, as anyone in that small community would be if they were to hear it in the coming weeks.

"It's just a coincidence, and I thought you would like to see—Jack was actually buried very close to Maria Nyström."

Dan said, "I'd like to see his grave, thanks, Per."

So they drove on and he stopped near the wooden church and Per walked with them into the churchyard. The snow had gathered even more within the churchyard, covering it in a deep blanket, but Per knew it too well, and pointed to Maria's grave, and to the newer plot, just a few yards away diagonally.

Maria's had a stone, but Redford's had only an unmarked wooden across, and as if embarrassed that the community might be seen to have sold his heroism short, he said, "This is just temporary, of course. There will be a stone, with his name, now that we know it.".

Dan nodded and both he and Inger looked down at it.

Per looked on, and perhaps sensing a different dynamic between them this time, he said, "Well, I'll leave you for a moment. I'll wait in the car."

He walked off, his boots crunching softly through the snow.

Inger had been quiet since they'd left the Nyström house, but sensing his gaze, she looked up now and smiled a little, her cheeks flushed red with the cold, her beauty almost overwhelming.

"What are you thinking?"

She shrugged, but said, "I was just wondering, how he could have been here all this time and never even speak to her. He knew her mother had died, yet . . . it just seems selfish, not his final act, obviously, but all these years."

"That's one way of looking at it. I think it's the most selfless behavior I've ever encountered. He thought they'd catch up with him sooner or later, that they'd find him, and he didn't want her involved in that. Imagine the agony of being that close to her, yet never knowing her. He wanted desperately to be with her, in his own way, but he knew with the life he'd lived, there could never be any more than that. I'm just full of admiration for the guy—if you think about it, that bus ride every day must have been the happiest and most difficult thing imaginable."

She continued to stare at him, nodding slightly, taking in what he'd said, but she'd taken even more meaning from it than he'd intended, and after a little while, she said, "You're not moving to Stockholm, are you?"

She wasn't angry, just resigned and sad, understanding the reasons too well.

"Would you want me to, until I know?"

"Will you ever know?"

He let out a sigh, acknowledging the truth of that. He tried to tell himself that he hardly knew her anyway, that they'd spent so little time together, but he was left feeling sick in the heart all the same. She made to say something else, but stopped herself, and then said more casually, "Okay, we should get back to the car."

"Yeah, we should."

He reached out and took her hand in his, but they didn't move, only stood there, their feet static in the deep snow. It was time to get back to the car, and to everything that symbolized, but they stood silently in that quiet corner of a rural churchyard, an anonymous grave before them, and neither of them moved at all.

Acknowledgements

Thanks to Deborah Schneider and all at Gelfman Schneider and ICM. Thanks also to Emilie Marneur, Alan Turkus, Victoria Pepe, and all at Thomas & Mercer.

There are many moments and chance meetings and briefly glanced places that go into the making of any book, and this one was no exception, but it started in a very particular way. Many years ago, I was traveling on a bus in northern Sweden. It was autumn and the sun was low in the sky, blinding the driver. There was a timber truck coming in the opposite direction . . .

Thankfully, the bus did not crash, except in my imagination, and *A Death in Sweden* was the ultimate result. Among the very few passengers on that sunny morning was a girl whose appearance I stole for the Siri who appears in these pages and so, in exchange for that theft, I dedicate this book to her.

About the Author

Kevin Wignall is a British writer, born in Brussels in 1967. He spent many years as an army child in different parts of Europe, and went on to study politics and international relations at Lancaster University. He became a full-time writer after the publication of his first book, *People Die* (2001). His other novels are *Among the Dead* (2002), *Who is Conrad Hirst?* (2007), shortlisted for the Edgar Award and the Barry Award, and *Dark Flag* (2010). His novel *Hunter's Prayer*, originally published as *For the Dogs* in 2004, has been made into a film directed by Jonathan Mostow and starring Sam Worthington and Odeya Rush.